## Praise for the authors of
### *Western Christmas Proposals*

### CARLA KELLY

"Kelly is a master at emotional, uplifting romances."
—*RT Book Reviews* on
*The Wedding Ring Quest*

### KELLY BOYCE

"Boyce captures the spirit of the American West."
—*RT Book Reviews* on
*Salvation in the Sheriff's Kiss*

### CAROL ARENS

"Sensational... Western fans will enjoy Arens' sense of
humor, fast pace and continuous action."
—*RT Book Reviews* on
*Wed to the Texas Outlaw*

D0951774

**Carla Kelly** started writing Regency romances because of her interest in the Napoleonic Wars, and she enjoys writing about warfare at sea and the ordinary people of the British Isles rather than lords and ladies. In her spare time she reads British crime fiction and history—particularly books about the American Indian Wars. Carla lives in Utah and is a former park ranger and double RITA® Award and Spur Award winner. She has five children and four grandchildren.

A lifelong Nova Scotian, **Kelly Boyce** lives near the Atlantic Ocean with her husband—who is likely wondering what he got himself into by marrying a writer—and a golden retriever who is convinced he is the king of the castle. A longtime history buff, Kelly loves writing in a variety of time periods, creating damaged characters and giving them a second chance at life and love.

**Carol Arens** delights in tossing fictional characters into hot water, watching them steam and then giving them a happily-ever-after. When she's not writing, she enjoys spending time with her family, beach camping or lounging about a mountain cabin. At home, she enjoys playing with her grandchildren and gardening. During rare spare moments you will find her snuggled up with a good book. Carol enjoys hearing from readers at carolarens@yahoo.com or on Facebook.

# WESTERN CHRISTMAS PROPOSALS

## CARLA KELLY
## KELLY BOYCE
## CAROL ARENS

HARLEQUIN® HISTORICAL

ISBN-13: 978-0-373-29899-0

Western Christmas Proposals

Copyright © 2016 by Harlequin Books S.A.

The publisher acknowledges the copyright holders of the individual works as follows:

Christmas Dance with the Rancher
Copyright © 2016 by Carla Kelly

Christmas in Salvation Falls
Copyright © 2016 by Kelly Boyce

The Sheriff's Christmas Proposal
Copyright © 2016 by Carol Arens

Recycling programs for this product may not exist in your area.

Printed in U.S.A.

www.Harlequin.com

# CONTENTS

# CHRISTMAS DANCE WITH THE RANCHER

## CARLA KELLY

To my Trask cousins, scattered around the US now, but who grew up in the ranching life near Worden, Montana. I recall some early Christmases in both Montana, and in Cody, Wyoming, where my father was raised. My cousins figured largely in those memories and remain important to me.

Dear Reader,

My years as a writer of Regency-era historical fiction were preceded by earlier times as a writer of Westerns. My first successes came writing about Native Americans, soldiers, stockmen, miners and mountain men and were somehow hardwired into my writer's brain. They remain there even now, except for occasional excursions into writerly territory.

I sometimes have to plead for a chance to write about the American West, but it's always worth it. I've known cowboys and Indians and miners, and I know them to be a fairly taciturn lot, not fans of flowery conversation or anything smacking of insincerity.

Nineteenth-century ranching was a hard life, and Christmas sometimes got short shrift. Ranchers and sheepherders probably understand better than most the kind of desperation that will force a young father and mother to gladly take whatever humble space was offered in a barn. They knew a lot about mangers and hay, and necessity.

I can almost guarantee other Christmas stories you read will be far more flowery and romantic than this one. What you'll find in *Christmas Dance with the Rancher* is courage, doing what the day requires and deep emotion welling up from hearts that, although hardy, are tender.

The best of the holiday season from my part of the West, Idaho.

*Carla Kelly*

# Chapter One

Chastened, subdued and unhappy, Ned Avery woke up to "Cheyenne! Cheyenne! Fifteen minutes" from the porter walking through the rail car and clanking his three chimes.

*I'm not going home without a chore girl*, Ned thought for the umpteenth time.

Why had he left Pete alone with Pa for his recent trip to Cheyenne? Ned had gone over with Pete his plain and simple orders of taking care of Pa for ten days while Ned and his hands pushed the herd through to Cheyenne and onto the railcars for Chicago. Over and over and each time Pete nodded in his kindly way. Bread and tinned meat and fruit were each carefully numbered and arranged on the kitchen table, and still Pete nodded.

*I was a fool to think he'd follow through*, Ned berated himself silently, as the Union Pacific slowed and steamed to a stop at the depot on Fifteenth Street.

Even now, just a day after his return to the ranch from Cheyenne, he could still see the kitchen table with eight days' worth of food gone, but two still as Ned had left them. Sitting in the rail car now, the crisis over, his heart started beating faster at the memory of food uneaten. He had run down the hall through the connecting rooms, calling for Pa, who was still alive for some reason.

Pa's mild indictment, as he deflected any blame from Peter and Ned, had hurt worse than the mess Pa lay in. "Son, I tried to get up and help myself," Pa had told him, his voice softer than a whisper.

The porter opened the door of the car, which pulled Ned

out of his personal condemnation. Silent, he took his carpet-bag from under the seat and waited behind an army officer for his turn to get off the train.

*Who's going to run this ranch if I can't trust Pete when I have to be away?* ran through Ned's mind again. In the end, there was only one solution: they needed a chore girl. Pa railed against being so dependent, but they still needed a chore girl. So he left to go straight back to Cheyenne.

"I don't know where to look," he had whined to Mrs. Higgins, the wife of his nearest neighbor who had agreed to watch Pa and Pete while he made a rapid return to Cheyenne.

"The Lord will provide," Mrs. Higgins had assured him.

He found this platitude not even slightly comforting. After sweet little Pete, as bright a brother as anyone could want, was kicked in the head by an irritated cow, and never grew up much in his mind, Ned hadn't seen any reason to bother Deity.

He knew better than to return a sharp comment to Mrs. Higgins, since she was kind enough to watch Pa and Pete, so he strove for diplomacy. "Mrs. Higgins, if the Lord is busy and not inclined to help, can you think of how He might provide a chore girl?" he asked. "I need a hint."

She gave him a pitying look, as if wondering why a grown man should ask such a question, but at least she didn't turn away. She was going to get her licks in, though.

"Ned Avery, when did you last go to church?"

He thought a moment, hoping for an easy answer, but nothing came to mind beyond Ma's funeral now well over ten years ago when he was twenty.

"My mother's funeral," he said quietly, which at least seemed to deflect the scold he thought he saw in Mrs. Higgins's eyes.

"She was a good woman," Mrs. Higgins said. "The Lord giveth and the Lord taketh away."

This was no time for a theological argument about the Lord's weird choice of people who should quit the earth, so

Ned bit back his own comment. "Where can I find a chore girl?" he repeated.

"Where does the Lord provide the most?" Mrs. Higgins asked, then thankfully answered her own question, because Ned was still coming up short. "Try a church in Cheyenne."

"Just wander up and ask the preacher if he knows of a chore girl?" Ned asked, his patience lurking just this side of exasperation.

"No! Sometimes churches take in unfortunate women who have fallen on hard times."

"So I'll need to count the silverware every night and hope no one tries to take advantage of my chastity?" he teased.

"Try it, Ned," Mrs. Higgins had said, and she did not sound amused. "You are trying my Christian patience."

He tried it, asking the depot master where there might be a church in Cheyenne. Ned just barely remembered Cheyenne before the railroad came through, with Irishmen jabbering and swearing, and Mama trying to cover his ears and Pete's at the same time. Cheyenne's boomtown growth had brought gamblers and fancy ladies and Chinese laundries and cafes, but no church then. The matter hadn't troubled him since, but now, if Mrs. Higgins was right, he needed to find a church.

The depot master knew him. Hell, everyone knew the Averys of Medicine Bow. Dan Avery had been a Mississippi rebel among the earliest of former Confederates who followed the construction of the Union Pacific and stayed. From 1868 up to 1890, they had endured, and now times were better.

"Ned, you might try Third Street. There's a First Methodist Church on the corner." He chuckled. "And you might try the Second Methodist Church on the opposite corner! There was a theological argument, I believe, and some chairs were thrown around."

Uncertain, Ned lingered at the depot. For some reason, he turned his attention to that corner of the lobby where only two nights ago, he had noticed a woman sitting on a trunk, chin in hand. He thought it odd that she wasn't sitting on the bench, which made him suspect she trusted people as little as he did.

She was long gone now, but he remembered her pale skin and her brown eyes, probably nothing special in themselves, except that her eyes were large and the brown so deep.

He also remembered the worried look in them, and how he had just resisted the urge to go over there and ask her if something was wrong, and if he could help. He had even checked back later that evening, but she was gone by then. Whoever was supposed to meet her in Cheyenne must have finally arrived. Ned couldn't help hoping she gave the man— husband, fiancé, whatever—a piece of her mind. Ladies had no business sitting alone in train depots.

Never mind that. "Chore girl, chore girl," he muttered out loud as he went first to the Plainsman to get a room for the night, ate lunch, and then went in search of the First or Second or maybe Third Methodist Church in town. Or maybe it was the Second Methodist Church on Fourth Street?

The First Methodist Church promised some help, if only because a man stood by a signboard, putting up letters to spell next Sunday's sermon. Ned watched for a moment as The Wag turned into The Wages of Sin.

Ned thought about his most recent sin, a pleasant one, really, committed four days ago in Nettie Lewis's parlor house on Third Street. Hopefully the man putting up the sign wouldn't be able to read Ned's misdemeanors on his face.

"Sir, I'm looking for a chore girl," he said, with no preamble. "The stationmaster said you might know some poor unfortunate lady a bit down on her luck and…"

The man pointed across the street to the Second Methodist Church. "He takes in strays."

That was one way to put it. Ned couldn't help conjuring up the image of a bedraggled pup that had wandered onto the Eight Bar many years ago. Mama had let him keep the ragged morsel until it became obvious they were harboring a wolf.

Ned crossed the street to the building with raw, unpainted

wood proclaiming itself the Second Methodist Church. He heard someone singing "Rock of Ages" in a vigorous baritone, and followed the sound.

The singer was a man almost as short as he was round, slapping on paint in rhythm to his hymn. Ned watched in real appreciation until the man noticed him and stopped.

"Did you come to help, sonny?" the man asked.

Ned came closer and saw that the painter was at least a decade older than his own father, but brimming with health and energy that Dan Avery no longer possessed.

"Not quite, sir," Ned told him. "I'm from the Eight Bar near Medicine Bow and I need to hire a chore girl in the worst way. A neighbor lady told me the Lord would provide, so I'm here."

"Reverend Lucius Peabody," the man said. "Racine, Wisconsin, come West to rescue the damned. In the worst way, you say? That's an odd way to phrase your needs in front of a minister of the gospel."

"Oh, no!" Ned began. "I mean I need to find such a person right now to help care for my father, who has heart disease, and look after the house. I'll pay thirty dollars a month, but she has to be respect…"

The minister held up his hand, brush and all, appearing not to notice the paint dripping down his arm. "I don't run an employment agency," he said, "but I might be able to help you. Come closer."

Ned did as he was bid, holding out his own handkerchief when the little man appeared not to possess such a thing. Reverend Peabody took it with a nod and wiped his arms after setting the brush in the tin can.

"Two nights ago, the sheriff brought a little miss here. She'd been waiting for her fiancé from Lusk to pick her up at the depot." The minister had dropped his voice to barely above a whisper.

*I know, I saw her*, Ned thought, filled with chagrin that he had done nothing about his charitable impulse.

"He hasn't showed up yet?" Ned asked.

"Worse than that," Peabody said with a shake of his head. "She said her fiancé was a man from Maine, name of Saul Coffin. Sheriff Miller got a garbled telegram from Lusk's sheriff, something about a shooting that left one man dead or nearly so, and the other in jail." The minister looked skyward, as though expecting a vision. His hand went up to trace imaginary letters, courtesy of Western Union. "Bar fight. Stop. Coffin. Stop. Deader than Abe Lincoln. Stop." He put his hand down. "Miss Peck said her fiancé had a foul temper, but who's to say the coffin was just a coffin, with anybody in it, or the sheriff meant Saul Coffin?"

"If Mr. Coffin never showed up, that's a pretty good indication," Ned began. "What's the law like in Lusk?"

"'Bout like this letter, sketchy, garbled and confused," Peabody replied. "And the sheriff fought for the South. Writing coherent messages has never been his specialty."

He stood there for a long moment, sizing up Ned, who gazed back. "You don't seem like a bad customer," he said finally. "Follow me."

Not sure whether to be offended or amused, Ned followed him around the church to a side already painted, which featured a young woman standing on a wooden box, scrubbing the window.

She was humming to herself and hadn't seen them yet, so Ned hung back just to look at her, the same young woman he had noticed two days ago in the depot.

Her hair was covered in a bandanna, but he already knew it was smooth and dark brown. He couldn't see her entire face yet, but he recognized her trim figure.

"Miss Peck?" the Reverend Peabody called.

Even before she turned around, Ned knew he would see brown eyes of considerable depth. Now he saw interest and even recognition.

"You were in the depot a few nights ago," she said to Ned.

At least, he thought that's what she said. Her accent was charming, but nearly incomprehensible and made him shake his head.

She must have seen that reaction several times since she had left wherever it was she came from. She repeated herself more slowly, and the words came out stilted and exaggerated, but understandable.

"I was," he replied. "Beg pardon, ma'am, but where are you from?"

"The US, same's you," she said. "Maine." She spoke slowly and distinctly. "Maybe you would introduce yourself?"

Of course. Lord, he was a ninny. "Um, Edward Avery, ma'am, and you are?"

"Katherine Peck," she said. Still standing on the box, she set the wet rag in the bucket, swiped her hand across an apron many sizes too large for her, and held it out to him.

He shook her hand, enjoying the firmness of her damp handshake.

Ned had always been a man of swift decision. Perhaps Wyoming, with its vagaries and harsh living had pounded that into him. Maybe he even prided himself on his ability to size up someone. He took another look at Miss Katherine Peck, she of the impenetrable accent and no prospects, if she was washing windows for a preacher, and wasted not a minute.

"Miss Peck, I'll pay you thirty dollars a month to be my chore girl."

## Chapter Two

"What makes you think I need a job?" she asked, her eyes going from the rancher wearing a canvas duster, to the round little minister who had so kindly taken her in a few nights ago.

"Well, Mr. uh, Reverend, uh. He said…" Mr. Avery stopped. "Maybe I was wrong." He turned to go.

Katie could tell she had embarrassed him, and she wondered again why she carried around so much resentment. Things weren't good and she did need a job. She needed *something.* A man had offered her employment and she had snarled at him like a homeless pup with nothing going in its favor.

"I do need a job, because I am not going back to Massachusetts," she said.

He stopped and turned around, but his eyes looked wary now. "You said Maine."

"I work in Massachusetts," she said in a rush, unwilling to apologize for her sharpness, but equally unwilling to embarrass him further. "I'm a mill girl. I regulate four looms in Lowell at the Chase Millworks. I came West to get married, but I don't think that's happening."

The rancher nodded. "The preacher told me a little."

Katie could tell he was unwilling to ask any more, which touched her heart. Maybe people didn't pry out here. Maybe others came West on a shoestring like she had, with their own histories to leave behind.

She could tell he was a patient man—something in his eyes—but she could also see that he had no time to waste, the way he slapped his gloves from one hand to the other. And she needed a job.

Katie stepped down off the box and seated herself on it. "Mr. Avery, you tell me what you need, and I'll answer your questions." She indicated the other corner of the box, as if they sat in the parlor at the dormitory at the millworks, and not the back wall of a half-painted church.

He sat down, hat in hand, which he set on the ground beside him, and didn't dillydally. "My father is, well, he's dying of heart disease. He can't do much except lie in bed and chafe about the hand dealt him. He won't want you there, even though he knows he needs you."

"Just the two of you?" Katie asked. "You don't have a wife?"

"I have a little brother," Mr. Avery said. He made a wry face. "He's not altogether. I mean, he's polite and kind and generally follows orders, but…"

He looked away, and she saw the muscles work in his face. She knew she sat with a private man, one not accustomed to telling anyone much of anything, and here she was, a stranger.

"You can't quite trust him to take care of your father while you do the outside work," Katie filled in.

His expression changed and his shoulders relaxed. She could tell he was relieved that he didn't have to say more.

"I'll pay you thirty dollars a month, in addition to your room and board," he said, not looking at her. She saw the red rise in his face, and she knew there was more.

"Will I have a room?"

"No, ma'am," he said finally. "Pa built the place a room at a time, as we needed it. It all connects and there's nothing for a chore girl."

She couldn't take his offer, even as she knew she wanted to. As it was now, she shared a tiny room with two other women of questionable virtue who were, as Reverend Peabody whispered in a low voice, "Trying to get out of the life." The collection plate on Sunday yielded very little revenue in a railroad town like Cheyenne that was just starting to think about respectability, but not too hard. The meals were almost as sparse as they had been at home in Maine, and the minister had a wife and two hopeful children.

"It doesn't have to be a large room," she surprised herself by saying. "A corner of the kitchen?" *Try a little harder, Mr. Avery*, she thought, encouraging him silently to think of something, because she couldn't burden the Peabodys any longer.

Silence, then, "I could partition off the sitting room. No one sits there."

He was quiet again. Kate could tell he had no intention of begging or pleading. He wasn't that kind of man.

She knew it was going to be a poor, hard job, but she was used to those. She put out her hand. "I'll do it."

He shook her hand for the second time in barely ten minutes. She felt relief cover her like a blanket and made no effort to release his hand. He chuckled and hung on to her hand, too. "I get the feeling that we're both really relieved by this turn of events," he said.

"Ayuh."

"What?" he asked.

"Yes," she translated. "I'll try to remember that you don't speak Maine."

She let go of his hand and stood up. "I... I'd better finish this window," she said, shy now. "I promised the preacher."

He stood up, and put on his hat, which made him loom over her. She stepped back instinctively, teetered on the edge of the box and felt his firm hand in the small of her back to steady her.

"Be careful!" he admonished, but kindly. "Train leaves at seven tomorrow morning. Can you meet me at the depot?"

Katie nodded and applied herself to the window. He tipped his hat to her, and left as quietly as he had come. In another minute she was singing again, something a little livelier than the reverend's "Rock of Ages."

Satchel in hand, Ned was waiting at the depot by six thirty

the next morning, wondering if Katherine Peck would come, or if she had changed her mind. He had already bought her ticket to Medicine Bow, but he knew he could exchange it if she changed her mind. *I need you*, he thought, looking through the depot doors toward Fifteenth Street. He hoped she would see him as an ally, and not just a boss. Pop needed to be handled delicately.

And there she was, coat too light for this climate slung over her arm, tugging a battered tin trunk after her. She shook her head when one of the other passengers offered to help her. Maybe she thought she would have to tip them, and she had no money.

He took it from her, surprised how light it was. He thought of Mrs. Higgins's own daughter, and her two trunks full of clothing and household goods, when she married a rancher near Sheridan, plus furniture. Katherine Peck had next to nothing. Maybe she saw Wyoming as a step up from the mills.

He gave her her ticket and tipped a young boy a quarter to wrestle her trunk aboard the westbound train, which steamed and waited—just barely—acting like a horse ready to race and held in check with some effort.

She followed him down the aisle and sat where he pointed. He sat next to her, after removing his duster and stowing it overhead, along with her coat. That coat would never do, but he didn't feel bold enough to tell her.

They had some time to wait, and he did want to know more about her.

"I was wondering if you might have second thoughts about accepting my offer," he said, more as small talk than serious conversation.

"No second thoughts," she said. "Nay, not one."

*Nay?* He asked himself. *That's quaint, but I can understand her better.* "Will you go back to Massachusetts or Maine when you accumulate some savings?" he asked her, even though it pained him. He was not a man to pry.

"Not either place," she said firmly. "I don't aim to back-track."

There was so much he wanted to ask her, and it must have shown on his face. She stifled a little sigh, then folded her hands on her lap with an air of resolution. "I am, or was, a mill girl, from Lowell, Massachusetts," she said. "I went to the mill at twelve years."

"You have a fellow out here?" he asked.

"One of the mill's floor managers has a cousin who farms near Lusk."

"Ranches," he corrected. "No one farms anything in Lusk."

"Saul Coffin went there four months ago. He and I had an understanding."

"Going to marry you?"

"Ayuh. A month ago he sent me part of the train fare. He was supposed to meet me here." She looked at the back of the seat in front of them. "The Reverend Peabody said he told you what we think happened to Saul, uh, Mr. Coffin."

"Lots of reasons a man can miss a train," he said, suddenly not wishing to crush her with the likelihood of her fiancé's death, even though she had already heard the worst. "Something delayed him, that's all."

"The reverend told me the same thing," she said, looking at him now. "After you left, he and I walked to the sheriff's office and told him where I would be, if someone came to inquire."

"Wise of you. You may hear from him yet," Ned said.

He could tell that she didn't believe him, which made him wonder if she'd ever had a nice thing happen to her. He didn't think there were many.

"Boooard! Boooard!" the conductor called.

Ned thought Miss Peck might look back at Cheyenne as they pulled out, but she kept her gaze directly in front of her. The town obviously held nothing for her except disappointment, something that she seemed to possess a lot of.

"Nothing here for you," he commented, mostly just to fill an empty space.

"No, sir," she agreed promptly.

"Christmas is coming," Ned told her, then felt like a complete idiot. Of course it was coming! So was the Fourth of July and Thanksgiving. New Year's, too.

His chore girl saw right through his lame attempt at conversation. "That'll do, Mr. Avery," she said so kindly in the accent he was finding more charming, by the minute. "I don't require idle chat. I'll be your chore girl. You don't need to worry any more."

Maybe it was the saying of it, her quiet sort of confidence that intrigued him almost as much as her accent. He sat back, inclined to think she was right.

# Chapter Three

Katherine Peck was not a talkative woman. He pulled out a copy of *Roughing It* he had bought in Cheyenne, but she had nothing to read. He stopped the candy butcher who came swaying down the aisle as the train picked up steam, and asked about his magazines.

"What would you like to read?" Ned asked.

Miss Peck shook her head. "No money."

"I have some. What would you like?" He leaned closer. "You *can* read."

"Ayuh," she said, a little starch in her voice.

Ned picked out a copy of *Ladies' Home Journal*, paid for it and handed it to her. "This do? May I call you Katherine? Most people call me Ned. A whole winter of you calling me Mr. Avery just might give me a case of the fantods."

"Fantods?" she asked as she carefully placed the magazine on her lap, almost as though it were valuable beyond comprehension.

"What? No fantods in Maine?"

"Not that I know of."

"The creeps. The heebie-jeebies. The fantods," he explained. "When people call me Mr. Avery, I just naturally look around for my father. Call me Ned."

"I will, if you'll call me Katie," she told him.

Her hand caressed the magazine. He could tell she was eager to start reading, but she was also polite, and he was her boss. "Katie? I thought you preferred…"

"I want a different name. Am I allowed?"

"Certainly. Many shady people come West and change their names."

"I am not shady," she told him. He thought he saw amusement in her eyes for the first time.

"Didn't think you were, Katie."

She turned her attention immediately to the treasure in her lap. He couldn't help watching her from the corner of his eye, how she caressed the magazine, then turned the pages so slowly. Her satisfied sigh touched his heart.

He couldn't help smiling through the first few chapters of *Roughing It*. He gave himself over to the story and had just finished the fifth chapter when the conductor shouted, "Laramie!"

He put down the book and stood up. "I'll be right back," he told Katie. To his amusement, she barely glanced up from the magazine.

He dashed into a hardware store on the block next to the depot and bought a doorknob with a key and two hinges. A quick lunge for a bag of lemon drops completed his stampede through Laramie. He made it back to the train just as the conductor was calling, "This train is ready to depart!"

He handed her the parcel. Without a word, she untied the twine that bound it and spread out the hardware.

"I can knock together a wall and a door," he said. "Until your room is done, my brother and I will sleep in the barn. Shouldn't be more than a day."

Katie ducked her head, staring hard at the parcel in her lap. "When I was ten, my stepfather started to beat me," she whispered. "When he thought to do other things more grievous, I ran away. I was twelve."

*God forgive me when I whine*, Ned thought, appalled. "Won't happen here," he told her. "Have a lemon drop. Things are going to get better."

Eyes still lowered, she took a lemon drop from the proffered bag. "You still want me to work for you?"

"Yes. Girls of ten or twelve don't have much say in things, do they?"

She shook her head. "I walked to Massachusetts, sleeping in barns and doing odd jobs, and became a mill girl. I'll be a good chore girl and I won't run away."

Kate put aside the magazine, and looked out the soot-grimed window, as if searching for scenery.

"You're looking in the wrong direction, if you're after scenery," Ned told her, impressed with her bravery. He pointed across the aisle. "That seat's empty. Take a look."

Intrigued, she did, and was rewarded with an eye-filling view of a mountain rising out of all that empty space.

"Elk Mountain," he said, coming across the aisle to sit beside her. "It's the northernmost mountain in the Snowy Range. My ranch is by that river over there. We're seven miles from Medicine Bow."

"Practically next door to a town," she added.

He liked her smile and her handsome high cheekbones. He liked even more that she thought to tease him. "Out West, that's the truth," he replied. "Pa was here early, so we have river acreage. He came with a railroad crew, laying this track that we're riding on. He liked what he saw, and stayed."

"How many acres?" she asked.

"Better question is, how many cattle do we run?"

"Well, then…"

"One thousand, all behind bob wire, because we learned our lesson sooner'n three years ago, when we had a bitch of a winter and the cattle all drifted and died. Pardon my language."

She made a little gesture with her hand, and he continued. It still wasn't a good memory. "Some of the ranchers twitted us earlier about fencing our property. Sure we lost cattle in '87, but not as many as the stockmen whose beeves drifted."

"What happened?"

"They're mostly gone."

"The tough survived?"

*Just like you*, he thought, impressed. "Guess so. You should do fine, Katie Peck."

## Chapter Four

To Katie's eyes, Medicine Bow looked no better and no worse than Laramie, only smaller. She let Ned Avery take her tin trunk and followed him from the train. She waited on a bench by the stable while he and the liveryman hitched one horse to a small wagon, such as she had never seen back East.

"It's a buckboard," he said, as he helped her in. "One stop and we'll head home."

He pulled up in front of Bradley's Mercantile. He must have ordered everything before he left Medicine Bow, because he came out in a few minutes with more wrapped packages, plus a paper bag, which he set in her lap.

*"Pirozhki,"* he said. "Some Roosians moved here from Nebraska and we can't get enough of them. Two for each of us. Hand me one, once I get us over the tracks."

She did as he said, enjoying her pork roll while he coaxed the horse across the railroad track. She handed him one, which he downed quickly, then the other, which disappeared about as fast. He protested when she offered him her second one, but not for long.

"Apples in the barrel behind you," he said, and she produced two. "Barrel at home is nearly empty." One satisfied her, but Ned needed two more apples.

"Just seven miles, so we're practically in town," he told her as they bumped along. She tried to brace herself so she wouldn't nudge his shoulder, but the seat was so narrow. "I wanted to take my pa to Medicine Bow, where he could stay with the doctor and get better care, but he won't have it."

"Yours must be a nice place, if he won't leave it."

He shrugged. "Pa fought for the Confederacy, and came out here with nothing."

"Your mother, too?"

"A little later. I was born in Mississippi. As soon as he had a holding out here, he sent for us."

"Mr. Ave…"

"Ned."

"No, it's a Mr. Avery subject," she insisted, which made him chuckle. "Mr. Avery, I can probably manage without a room of my own. I'm asking too much."

He stopped the team. "Have you ever asked for anything before, Miss Peck?"

Embarrassed, she thought a moment. "I never dared."

"I think maybe you're overdue. It won't kill Pete and me to spend a night in the barn."

She opened her mouth to protest, then closed it, because she wanted that room. "Very well."

"Is the matter closed?"

"Yes."

"Good thing, because I don't like to argue about stuff that needs to happen." Ned pointed to a spot where the road turned toward the river they had been paralleling. "We'll be on Avery land soon."

She hung on to the seat and pushed hard against the footboard as Ned guided his team into the river. She looked around, pleased with the bright yellow leaves that seemed to shiver as they passed. She thought of winter to come, and suppressed an involuntary shiver of her own.

"You need a warmer coat. Didn't anyone ever look after you?"

"No." She winced inside at how bleak and bald the word sounded, and she wondered just when she had gotten used to mostly nothing.

They topped a small rise, then Ned coaxed his horse down into a lovely valley. October winds may have been blowing cold, but she liked what she saw, except for what had to be Ned Avery's home. She pointed.

"Yep. It's a real sow's ear. I guess we just got used to it," he said, and she heard all the apology in his voice.

*A body gets used to a lot of things*, she thought, and wondered just when she had given up. Another thought struck her. For the first time since she couldn't remember, someone was looking after her. It was a pleasant thought. She doubted Mr. Avery saw it that way, since he had made a business deal with her, but she felt herself relax, somewhere inside her body, or maybe it was her mind. She waited for the feeling to leave, but it seemed to settle in, like a cat on a hearth.

In a short time, she stood in the middle of a little kitchen, being introduced to a woman who looked as capable as Ned. "Pleased to meet you, Mrs. Higgins," she said as they shook hands after Ned's introduction.

A few whispered words to Ned, and Mrs. Higgins waved a cheery goodbye. In a few minutes, Kate heard hoofbeats.

"She watched Pa for me. This is Peter," Ned said, and pulled a younger man closer, one with the same blond hair and build, but vacant blue eyes, with the same dark rim around lighter blue, but none of the intensity. "He does the best he can, most days."

"Hi, Pete," Katie said, and got a vague smile in return.

The rancher indicated the next room. "This is the sitting room." He held his hands out, as if measuring the space. "I can build you a room right here. There won't be a window— that would make it too cold."

She followed him through the next connecting room. This room had a bed, and crates stacked on top of each other for clothing. "Pete and I sleep here. Wait. I'll see how Pa is."

She stood there, Peter beside her. He cleared his throat.

"Ned was looking for a chore girl."

"He found one."

"You can cook?"

"Pretty much anything you want to eat, Peter," she told him. "You do like to eat, don't you?"

Pete nodded, and then looked away, as if that was too much conversation.

She looked through the connecting arch to the next room, where Ned stood looking down. She went closer and saw Daniel Avery.

He was so thin, and probably not as old as he looked. She had already observed that the men out here had lots of wrinkles on their faces, sort of like sea captains from back home.

"Pa, this is our chore girl, Katie Peck," Ned was saying. "She'll be looking after you, after all of us, I guess."

The older man looked at her, then carefully turned himself toward the wall. Kate sighed, wondering what it must feel like to be strong one day, then brought low by a heart ailment another day.

"Never mind, Mr. Avery," she said. She touched his arm, then pulled the blanket a little higher. "I am here to help and that is all."

"Don't need…" the old man began, then stopped. His shoulders started to shake. "…help."

Kate quietly left the room. Ned followed her, his expression more troubled than she wanted to see.

"I was afraid he might do that," he said in apology. "He knows we need you, but his dignity…"

"Doesn't matter," she assured him. "You hired a chore girl and I will do my job."

She said it quietly, as she said most things, as she had lived her own hard life that bore no signs of getting easier. She looked down at her hands, surprised to see that she still carried the doorknob and hinges. She knew other people must have epiphanies now and then—the minister said so—but she never expected one of her own. Here it came, filling her with peace. She handed the hardware to Ned Avery.

"I can do this," she told him. "Just watch me."

# *Chapter Five*

Kate began her work in the morning, after a surprisingly comfortable night in the bed usually belonging to Pete and Ned Avery. Ned had insisted on changing the sheets the night before and she was glad of it, considering how dingy they seemed.

His eyes wide with surprise, Pete watched his brother make the bed. "He never tucked in anything before," he told Katie.

Ned had turned around with a smile. "I can't even trust a brother to watch my back," he said. "Pete, you're toast."

Pete laughed out loud. Something in Ned's eyes told Kate that no one had laughed in the Avery household in recent memory.

"No respect whatsoever," Ned said with a shake of his head. He gathered up the nearly gray sheets, put his hand on Pete's neck and pulled him from the room, but gently.

There wasn't any privacy, not with the rooms connecting the way they did. As Ned tended to his father's needs, she winced to hear Mr. Avery insisting that no chore girl would ever touch him.

"I don't know how long it will take, but he'll come around," Ned had told her as he put on his coat. Katie heard the doubt in his voice. "Come on, Pete."

*I have many things to prove to Mr. Avery,* Kate thought. She began in the kitchen, laying a fire in the range, a black monstrosity that, like everything in the house, needed a woman's touch. She knew there would be Arbuckle's and a grinder; soon the aroma of coffee spread through the house.

She made a pot of oatmeal. By the time the brothers opened the door, ushering in frigid air with them, toast was out of the oven and buttered, and the oatmeal in bowls.

She stood by the table, her hands behind her back, pleased with herself, even though the meal was many degrees below ordinary.

"Don't stand on ceremony," Ned said as he sat down. He dumped the milk from a bucket into a deep pan and covered it, after taking out a cup of milk. "Join us."

"I can wait until you are done," she said.

"Maybe you could if you were the czar of Russia's chore girl. I mean it. Get a bowl and join us."

She did as he said. He pushed out the empty chair with his foot.

"Barn's getting cold and Pete isn't much fun to cuddle," he said, as he took a sip of the coffee, nodded and raised the cup to her in salute. "Damn fine, Katie Peck. I'm going to build you a room today."

And he did, after instructing her to move what little furniture the sitting room possessed to the other side of the doorway arch that cut the room into roughly two-thirds and a third. She did as he directed, coughing from the dust she raised.

"The only problem I have noticed with housework is that five or six months later, you have to do it all over again," he commented, gesturing for Pete to pick up the other end of a settee.

Once the furniture was moved and the floor swept, Ned worked quickly, measuring and marking boards he had dragged from the barn with Pete's help. When he gave her no assignment, Katie decided to tackle the stove, which hadn't seen a good cleaning in years.

She found a metal pancake turner in the depths of a drawer of junk and scraped away on the range top until her shoulders hurt. All the time, Ned and Pete walked back and forth, bringing in more boards. After the fifth or so trip, Ned stopped to watch.

"Funny how this stuff built up and I continued to ignore it," he told her, sounding more matter-of-fact than penitent, which scarcely surprised her. She was coming to know Ned Avery.

"A little attention every day—not much, really—keeps the carbon away," she said, and surprised herself by thinking, *Kind of like people.*

"Tell you what," he said. "We'll surprise you. No peeking, now."

She stopped long enough at noon to fix everyone jelly sandwiches and canned peaches, then continued into the afternoon until the stove was clean. The hammering continued, punctuated with laughter, which soothed her heart in strange ways.

With his own shy smile, Pete borrowed the kitchen broom.

"How does my new room in there look?" she asked, pretty certain that Pete would spill the beans, because his mind was too simple to keep a secret all the way from breakfast to supper.

Pete surprised her. "Not gonna tell. You have to wait."

Impressed, Kate built a fire in the stove, determined to cook something better than sandwiches. Ned had already pointed out the smokehouse next door. She sliced off several steaks as her mouth watered. Even in her more enlightened place of employment in Massachusetts, meat was a rare treat administered only on holidays. Soon steaks and sliced potatoes sizzled. She opened another can of peaches and poured them into a bowl this time. She had found some pretty dishes that only needed a rinse.

She was about to call the brothers to the table when they came into the kitchen. Ned held out a key to her, just an ordinary skeleton key for a simple lock that anyone could pick, but which meant more to her than Ned Avery would ever know.

"Take a look." He gestured her into the sitting room, or what remained of it.

She stared in surprise. "I… I thought you were going to

carve a tiny space out of *this* side of the doorway," she said, delighted. "Where will you sit in the evenings?"

"I already told you we use the kitchen for everything," he reminded her, his eyes on her face.

Ned had turned the larger side of the sitting room into her bedroom, leaving only a small area on the other side of the open archway for a chair, settee and a table, the kind for books or magazines. She stared at the new wall and door, then opened the door and sighed with the pleasure of it all.

The bed was just a cot, perhaps an army cot scavenged from somewhere. Because her boss had given her the lion's share of the former sitting room, it included the potbellied stove. He and Pete had dragged in one of the stuffed chairs and a footstool.

"I have another washbasin somewhere, and I can put up some pegs for your clothes. Sorry I don't have a bureau."

What could she say to such kindness? She barely knew this man, and he had given her something priceless—a room of her own, a safe one.

"Thank ye," she managed, hoping tears wouldn't well in her eyes. No employer wanted to hire a crybaby.

"Try it out," her boss said.

She walked inside her room, her own room. She sat down in the chair and put her feet upon the footstool. *I can sit here and reread my Ladies' Home Journal*, she thought. *This might be the best winter of my life.*

# Chapter Six

Kate spent a peaceful night in her room, sitting for a while in the chair and reading, as she suspected wealthy people did. Her new bed was narrow and the mattress thin, but she had no complaint.

She debated whether to lock the door. Key in hand, she had the power, but the urgency was gone. She closed the door, and that was enough.

In the morning, she woke to angry voices in the back bedroom. Kate opened her door slightly and listened as Ned and his father argued about leaving him alone to the mercies of "a dratted female I can barely understand" while his sons rode fence today.

"Try a little harder, Dad," Ned said.

"What for?" his father shot back. "You know I'm dying, I know I'm dying, and that…female with the damn fool accent knows I'm dying!"

"I guess because it's the civilized thing to do," Ned replied, and he sounded so weary.

"You don't need me," Daniel Avery argued. "You can run this ranch."

"Did it ever occur to you that we love you?" Ned asked, sounding more exasperated than weary now, and driven to a final admission, maybe one hard for a man not used to frills, if love was a frill.

Katie dressed quickly, pleased to see that Ned or Pete— likely Ned—had laid a fire in the cookstove. While the argument about her merits and demerits continued in the back room at a lower decibel, she deftly shredded potatoes and put them in a cast-iron skillet to fry.

She silently ordered the argument down the hall to roll off her back. She was the chore girl and she was getting through a winter doing something she hadn't planned on, because Saul Coffin, drat his hide, had a temper. *Sticks and stones*, she thought. *That's all it is.*

Breakfast on the table brought a smile to Ned Avery's set expression. He asked for the ketchup, then ate silently before finally setting down his fork.

"I'm sorry you had to hear that," he told her.

"I'll set his food on that little table by his bed and just leave him alone with it," she said, getting out another plate.

"I can take it to him. Maybe I had better," Ned said, starting to rise.

"Eat your breakfast," she said, as she started down the hall with Daniel Avery's steak and hash browns on a tray.

Mr. Avery was staring at the ceiling, which she noticed for the first time was covered with newspapers. Just standing there, she stared up, too.

"'Archduke Crown Prince Rudolf of Austria, heir to the Austro-Hungarian crown, is found dead with his mistress Baroness Mary Vetsera in Mayerling.' Oh, my," she said, then sat the tray of food on the table where he could reach it and left the room. She thought she heard him laugh.

She sat down in the kitchen to oatmeal, which she preferred to steak in the morning, and was just spooning on the sugar when she heard, "Ned!" from the back of the house.

"You should have let Ned take Dad his breakfast," Pete told her.

"That's enough, Pete," Ned snapped, as he got up from the table. "Maybe I appreciate a little initiative."

From the vacant look on the younger brother's face, Kate could see he did not know the word, and felt surprisingly sorry for him.

Ned came back and took the ketchup off the table. "He wants this."

"Stubborn man," Kate said.

"I'm just pleased not to see the whole thing on the floor," her boss said, and he sounded more cheerful. "He wants some of your coffee, too."

"I'll take him both," Kate said. "Sit down and finish your breakfast."

He did as she said. "Are you as stubborn as he is?"

"Ayuh," she said, which made him laugh.

She took ketchup and coffee down the hall, pausing inside the last bedroom to read something else from the ceiling that looked a little newer than Crown Prince Rudolf's misfortune. "Mr. Avery, it appears that Christine Hardt has patented the first brassiere. If you need anything else, just ask. I intend to earn my thirty dollars a month."

She returned to the kitchen and finished her breakfast as Ned poured himself another cup of coffee, gave her an inquiring look, and poured her one, as well.

As she ate, he filled her in on the day's task, which included the mysterious "riding fence" he had mentioned earlier. She had spent a lifetime cultivating an expressionless face, the kind that mostly encouraged people like her stepfather to forget she was even in the room. Ned Avery seemed to see right through it.

"I can tell you have no idea what I'm talking about," he said, elbows on the table.

"I *am* curious," she admitted. "I don't think anyone rides fence in Maine."

"Probably not. I've seen Maine on a map and it looks pretty squished together. We'll just be riding down the fence line to make sure the bob wire is tight and all the strands are in place."

"If not?"

"We'll fix them. I'll have a roll of wire and staples with me, and the straightener. Up you get, Pete."

Pete shook his head. "Don't like to ride."

"I need your help."

Ned gave his brother a push out the door. Ned looked back.

"Can you fix us some sandwiches from the leftover steak, and stick some apples in that bag?"

Kate wiped her hands on her apron, ready to begin.

"I'd do it myself," Ned said, sounding apologetic, "but I've noticed something about sandwiches."

"Which is…"

"They always taste a little better when someone else makes them. Back in a minute," he said.

Pleased with her boss, Kate made sandwiches, adding pickles from an earthenware crock to the thick slabs of beef between bread. She found waxed paper in a drawer and made two sandwiches apiece. Four apples went in the bag on the bottom. She put the rest of the coffee in a canteen she noticed by the canvas bag and handed the whole thing to Ned when he returned to the kitchen, bringing in more cold weather with him.

"Pete's pouting in the barn," he announced.

"He really doesn't like to ride?" she asked.

"Afraid of horses." Ned leaned against the table. He shrugged. "I still need his help."

"Maybe I could help," she offered.

"Can you ride?"

"I can learn," she replied.

"I believe you would try," he told her. "Just keep an eye on my father. I set his, well, his, well you know, close to his bed."

She nodded. "I'll remove his breakfast dishes later. Maybe I'll read to him."

"I doubt he'll let you."

"I can try."

He gave her an appraising look, one part speculation, two parts evaluation, and another part she didn't recognize. He slung the bag over his shoulder and startled whistling before he shut the door.

*Poor Pete*, she thought, wondering what the slow brother would really rather do, given the opportunity.

She thought about the Averys as she set a sponge for bread. She glanced down the length of the cabin through the arches, wondering if she dared risk the wrath. *Why not?* she asked herself.

Mr. Avery pretended to sleep as she gathered up the empty dishes, and tucked the ketchup bottle under her arm. Back in the kitchen she busied herself with the bread dough, then cleaned through layers of debris and ranch clutter while the loaves rose to impressive height. What was the use of ropes she could not have guessed, but there were enough partly used liniment bottles stuck here and there to make her wonder just how troublesome the cow business could be.

The fragrance of baked bread filled the little ranch house. When it came from the oven still hot and not entirely set, she cut off a generous slice, lathered it with butter, put it on a plate and carried it down to the last bedroom, where Mr. Avery immediately pretended he slept. She left the bread on the table and washed her hands of that much stubbornness.

She slathered her own slice and propped her feet up on another of the kitchen chairs to enjoy it. The wind blew and beat against the one small kitchen window. She eyed the window, and wondered where she could find material for curtains.

Sitting there in the kitchen, wind roaring outside, she felt herself relax. The whine and clank of the industrial looms that had been her salvation from mistreatment, but the author of headaches, had never seemed farther away. No matter what she decided in the spring, she never had to go back.

If only Daniel Avery, rail-thin and suffering, would agree to a truce. She glanced at the calendar, the one with a naked woman peeking around a for sale sign—*where* did Ned get these calendars?—and resolved to find better calendars, and while she was at it, a better job for Pete and comfort for Mr. Avery. What she would do for Ned escaped her, but she had time.

## Chapter Seven

Not in years had Ned Avery come home to a house fragrant with the twin odors of fresh bread and cinnamon. Ma had been dead so long he could not remember much about her, except her lovely eyes. Katie had eyes like that—brown and appealing.

Pete decided to sulk in the barn, so Ned shut the kitchen door and breathed in the pleasant fragrance, aware that this might mean something delicious to eat, but just savoring an unexpected, simple pleasure.

He watched Kate Peck come down the hall from her father's room, carrying an empty plate. She smiled her greeting—another unexpected pleasure—and put the plate in the sink. Without a word, she cut off a slab of bread, slathered it with butter and handed it to him.

"Your father pretends to be asleep, but he ate a lot of bread and butter," she said. "Your turn."

He ate the bread, embarrassed to be uttering little cries of pleasure, but nearly overcome with something as simple as warm bread and butter. "Best thing I ever ate," he said, and meant it.

"You're an easy mark," she teased, which made him smile. "I have something even better."

What he couldn't imagine, unless it was to strip and stand there naked in the kitchen. *That* thought earned him a mental slap. "Hard to imagine anything better," he told her, grateful people couldn't read each other's thoughts.

In answer, she opened the warming oven and took out a cinnamon roll the size of a dinner plate. "Sit down."

He sat. Without a word, he plunged in, wondering how lucky a man could be, to find out that he had inadvertently hired a cook, along with a chore girl.

"Words fail me," he said finally. "I didn't know we had any cinnamon."

"It's a little weak. I found it stuffed in the back of that cupboard, along with a stack of napkins, a hacksaw and a rope with dried blood."

"That's where it went!" Ned said. "I use that rope for pulling calves."

He could tell she had no idea what he was talking about. "When Mama Cow has trouble, a little noose slipped around her calf, plus a mighty tug, finishes the job."

Kate pointed to the rope, hanging from a nail near the door. "Keep it in the barn, the hacksaw, too."

"You're a bit of a martinet," Ned replied.

She gave him a startled look that settled into a thoughtful expression. "Two days ago, I wouldn't have imagined such a thing."

He started for the barn, when she surprised him by walking along beside him. She stopped and he stopped, too, waiting for her to speak.

"Your father may have a bad heart, but he needs something to do," she said. "I didn't want him to hear me talking about him."

Eyes troubled, she looked back at the house, which suddenly looked too small and shabby to him. Couldn't they afford something better now?

"He's lying there waiting to die," Katie said. "How is that better than death?"

It felt like one accusation too many. "Do you have some bit of wisdom to change things? You think you're telling me something I don't know?" He didn't mean to shout. He regretted the look in her eyes. "Sorry. That was unkind."

"He still needs something to do," she repeated softly, and left him there.

Ned Avery watched the sway of her skirt, wishing—not for the first time—that someone else was in charge of his life.

He stayed in the barn until the cold started to seep through his coat, watching his horse eat. Pete, still unhappy with his day spent riding fence, pointedly turned away from him, much as a cat with a gripe would.

*I am satisfying nobody,* Ned thought. "Pete, what would you really like to do?" he asked.

"Work someplace warm," Pete said with no hesitation, as though he had been considering the question for years. Perhaps he had been.

"I'll see what I can do," Ned told his brother. He patted Pete's shoulder. "Come inside. Katie has made cinnamon rolls."

"Will I like them?" Pete asked, as they walked toward the ranch house.

"Yeah, you will. If you don't, I'll eat yours, too." He stopped. "Ride with me tomorrow to check the fence in the other direction, and then I really will see what I can do."

Dinner was another unimaginable feast, nothing more than beef stew, but much more because of spices or whatever sort of alchemy seemed to be coming from a kitchen he knew too well.

"Tucked beside the cinnamon, I found some thyme. And do you know, there is bush after bush of sagebrush right outside your door," Katie said.

He could tell she was teasing him, and it felt good, reminding him how long it had been since he had laughed about something, anything.

There was no humor in the last bedroom, where his father lay, staring at the ceiling. Ned helped him sit up to eat, but Pa said nothing about the wonderful stew. Pa seemed determined not to have anything good to say about Katie.

*Stubborn old man,* Ned thought. He imagined himself condemned to lie in bed until death finally nosed around and found him. He had to admit Kate was right—this was not living.

After helping his father through slow and painful bedtime rituals, Ned said good-night and wandered back through the house. In the next room, Pete was already asleep. He kept going, passing through the small sitting room now, and by the room he had built for Kate, who just wanted to feel safe.

She was drying the last of the dishes. He eyed the remaining cinnamon roll, which she pushed toward him, along with a just-dry fork. "I can make more tomorrow."

She sat down, and he found himself enjoying the novelty of someone sitting with him. Before Pa got so weak, they sat at this table together and he missed that.

"I have to find something for Peter to do," he said, halfway through the roll.

"You'll think of something," she said.

"I wish there was someone else around here who could think," he said, ashamed to whine.

"The whole burden is yours, isn't it?" she said, her voice soft. "That's hard."

She surprised him then. "Tomorrow, I'm going to start reading to your father." She chuckled. "He'll just pretend to sleep and ignore me."

"Sorry about that," Ned murmured, embarrassed at such stubbornness.

"No need. I'll sit by the arch into his room, and read just loud enough to hear, but not easily. Maybe he'll invite me into his room to read."

"Could be a while," Ned said. "He's damned stubborn."

"So am I."

## Chapter Eight

Katie began her campaign after a breakfast of baked oatmeal, helped out with a tin of peaches. If she fed the fire in the range carefully, the roast Ned had sliced off from the steer hanging in the smokehouse would be done in late afternoon, when he and Pete rode in again.

She had taken Mr. Avery's breakfast to him instead of Ned, tightening her lips when the old man pretended to sleep. She said a cheerful "Good morning," before she retreated to the kitchen.

An hour later, she went to Ned and Pete's room and picked up Ned's copy of *Roughing It* he had been reading on the train. He had left it on the bed, as she had asked him to, when she explained her campaign.

"Good luck," he had said, and she heard all his doubt.

She positioned the chair right by the archway that led into Mr. Avery's room. She made herself comfortable and started to read aloud.

"'Chapter One. My brother had just been appointed Secretary of Nevada Territory—an office of such majesty…'"

The chapters were short, which obviously suited Mark Twain, and suited Katie, too. She found herself laughing out loud after a very few pages, even when her captive audience began to snore, or pretend to. *Stubborn man*, she thought, but with sympathy. He was in a bad situation and they both knew it. She kept reading, and found her enjoyment growing at Twain's depiction of the West in which she now lived.

The snoring stopped by Chapter Five and Twain's description of a coyote as "'…always hungry. He is always poor, out of luck, and friendless.'" Katie took that as a good sign and kept reading.

She hardly knew how long she read, but her stomach growled around noon. She turned down a tiny corner of the page and said, "'The city lies in the edge of a level plain.' Remember that, Mr. Avery, for it is where I shall begin again. I'm hungry. Are you?"

Silence. At least he wasn't pretending to snore. She fixed herself a beef sandwich, ate it and made one for Mr. Avery. She set it on the little table close to his bed, and watched him for a moment as he pretended to sleep.

The book lay on her chair. She picked it up and turned a few pages. "Let's see…did we finish? I'm certain we did. Must be here on Chapter Six," Kate said. She ran her finger down the page. "Chapter Six it is. 'Our new conductor (just shipped) had been without sleep for twenty hours…'"

"No! Start with, 'The city lies in the edge of a level plain,'" Mr. Avery said from his bedroom. "And for the Lord's sake, come a little closer."

Kate smiled so huge that she felt her dry lips crack. She tugged the chair into Mr. Avery's bedroom, pulling it close enough to the stove for warmth, since the day had turned cold.

"Very well," she said. "'…the edge of a level plain.' Here we are."

She read until the shadows of late fall stretched across the page she was reading and at the same time the aromatic roast in the kitchen made itself known. She stood up and put the book in the chair.

"Thank you for letting me read to you," she told the quiet man, who lay on his back now, deeply veined hands clasped together. "You know, Mr. Avery, if you have trouble understanding my accent, I can read slower."

"I understand you," he growled. "Silly of you to think I wouldn't."

"I have to prepare supper." She was tying on her apron when the brothers came indoors, bringing with them October and geese calling to each other, and a rush of sage before the door closed.

"One more day will finish up the near fences," Ned told her.

"Pete's more agreeable?" she asked.

Ned shrugged. "Well enough. I promised him I would think of something else for him to do." He started toward the back of the house, but stopped. "You think, too," he said and gave her a little salute with his finger to his forehead.

Kate couldn't help feeling pleased to be included in likely what was a hopeless task. She sliced potatoes for frying on the stovetop, and found enough good apples in the nearly empty barrel to make applesauce. She looked into the window and gave her reflection a little salute, too.

She already knew the evening routine. Ned kept a pile of old newspapers by the stove. Once his father was taken care of, he retreated to his room with a newspaper and read the articles, no matter how old they were.

Pete sometimes stayed in the kitchen with a bucket of blocks. He created towering buildings carefully, losing himself in the simple task. After a few days of wondering what to do, Kate took an old newspaper, too, and read it in her room. Sometimes Ned took a deck of cards to the kitchen and played solitaire.

And then in the morning another day began and became much like the one before, a day of riding fence for the Avery brothers, and her reading to Mr. Avery, who at least didn't pretend to sleep anymore, even if he never spoke.

Ned surprised her two days later by inviting her to come to town with him. "Didn't I hear you say something about material for kitchen curtains? I'll leave Pete here with Dad. We won't be gone much more than half a day."

She had her doubts, but agreed. While he hitched the horse to the wagon, Katie peered into Ned's shaving mirror. There wasn't much she could do for her straight hair, but she was pleased to see that the bloom wasn't entirely gone from her reflection.

"May I get you anything in town?" she asked Mr. Avery, who lay on his bed, turned to the side facing the wall. He ignored her and her heart dropped, wondering if he was back to his silent hostility.

"I'll read twice as long tomorrow to make up," she cajoled. Nothing. It was as if she had never read to him, as if they had never started even the simplest of conversations.

"You are a stubborn man," she said finally, when she heard Ned calling her name from the kitchen.

"I want to go, too," he said, softly.

Katie heard his disappointment. "I wish you could. I truly do."

Silence. Ned called for her again, but she moved closer to his father instead. She sat on his bed. "Is there something *else* I can do for you, besides what you really want?"

She looked over her shoulder to see Ned approaching. She put her finger to her lips and he said nothing.

"I want a window," Mr. Avery told her finally. "If I have to lie here, may I look out at…at…something?" He opened his eyes, and Kate saw all the torment. "Can you do that? Can you?"

Kate glanced back at Ned and saw a serious face with no anger in it. He nodded. His look changed to a thoughtful one, as though he was already planning how he would do it. He turned quietly and went back through the house.

"I believe we can," she told Mr. Avery.

She heard his enormous sigh. "Make it a big window and make it low enough for me to see out of, just as I am now."

"Done," Kate said as she stood up. "Call Pete if you need anything."

"I can't imagine he wants to stay here," Mr. Avery said, a touch of humor in his voice.

"No," Kate said, "but it's my turn to go to town."

She hurried toward the kitchen. Ned stood there, something in his hand. He held it out to her. "I found this in the box of oddments you wanted me to go through. Mama used to stick it in her hair. You take it."

"I shouldn't," she said, coming closer to look at the tortoiseshell comb.

"I think you should. Mama was never one to waste things. Here. I'll do it."

He stepped into her private space, and she felt no automatic need to step back. "Where should I put it?" he asked.

She touched the side of her head where strays seemed to come from. "Right here."

With no hesitation, he slid the comb right above her ear, slanting it up a little and then more, until he was satisfied. She held her breath at his nearness, thinking of times when her stepfather had yanked her around, or even when Saul Coffin leaned in for a kiss. She felt no urge to step back or dodge Ned Avery.

*I trust you*, she thought, and the feeling was warmer than late autumn.

"That'll do, Katie," he said, nodding his approval. "I didn't know you had freckles on your nose."

"And I didn't know you did, too," she told him.

"I'm not exactly full of surprises," he said as he opened the door.

*I'm surprising myself*, Katie thought, pleased in a way she had never been pleased before.

## Chapter Nine

Both of them were silent on the ride to Medicine Bow, but it was a comforting silence to Katie, the kind of quiet when you share space with a friend, or so she thought.

Ned stopped the wagon in front of Bradley's Mercantile and helped her out onto the board sidewalk. "Go inside and look around," he said. "They may or may not have anything resembling what you think we might need, but that's Medicine Bow." He straightened his Stetson. "I'm going to the Watering Hole for a drink."

"Don't you get likkered," she teased.

"My mother used to say that," he replied, and she saw good humor in his eyes. "Haven't heard it in years." He tipped his hat to her. "Thanks for the reminder."

She nodded and went into the mercantile. The odor of dried fish, leather and coffee, with a hint of molasses drifting in from some dark corner made her wrinkle her nose.

"Can I help you, miss?" the man behind the counter said.

"Ayuh," she said, which made him smile. "I mean, yes." She handed him the list Ned had given her.

He scanned it. "Hmm. More sugar. Cinnamon, cloves and nutmeg? Ned's never given me a list like this."

"Christmas is coming," she reminded him. "I intend to do something about it."

That announcement brought another smile, accompanied by more thorough appraisal. "Tell me now—did Ned Avery find himself a wife?"

Katie felt her face heat up. "He needs a chore girl to help

with his father," she explained, lowering her voice. "I fell on hard times, and he ended up hiring me."

"I did hear he had a mission to accomplish in Cheyenne," the man—probably Mr. Bradley—told her. "How *is* Daniel?"

"Bored, mainly. He thinks I am unnecessary, but he lets me read to him," she replied.

"I can't imagine this state of affairs sits well with him," Mr. Bradley said. "He used to be so strong and capable. Well, like Ned. Let's see that list."

Kate went through her own list quickly, adding each item to a growing pile on the counter. She stood by the cash register while Mr. Bradley toted up her purchases, and noticed the help-wanted sign for the first time.

"What sort of work do you need help with, Mr. Bradley?" she asked, when he came to the end of the list.

"Simple stuff—stocking the shelves, sweeping out, keeping things tidy," he said. He rang up the total. "Fifteen dollars. I'll box these and get them out to the buckboard."

"Are you thinking of bailing out?" he asked as they carried the boxes to the buckboard. "Need a job?"

They walked back to the store together. "No, sir, I promised I would help out and I don't go back on my word."

"Why are you interested?"

"I'm asking for Pete Avery," she said. "Mr. Bradley, Pete doesn't like ranch work, and he can do all those things you listed." She clasped her hands together and gave the merchant her kindest smile. "He would feel so useful, and he would be dependable."

"I don't know," Mr. Bradley said, and she heard all the doubt in his voice.

"Could you think about it?" she asked.

"Think about what?"

Startled, she turned around to see Ned standing in the doorway. As she looked at him, her confidence dribbled away. It was probably a stupid idea anyway.

"Your chore girl here is wondering if your brother might

be a good store clerk," Mr. Bradley said, pointing to the help-wanted sign.

Ned stared at the sign, then glared at Kate. "There's no need to joke about Pete."

"I'm not joking," she replied, stung by the disbelief in his voice. "Pete can put cans on shelves. He can sweep and tidy up. He's polite, and I'll wager he knows a lot of people here in Medicine Bow."

"He doesn't need to work here." Ned turned away to count out the money he owed. "Unlike you, the Averys aren't charity cases."

That stung. Kate felt the familiar prickle of tears behind her eyes. Some imp made her keep talking. "He can do this work, and you know how he feels about riding fence." She turned to Mr. Bradley, who was watching the two of them with real interest. "If you hire Pete, is there a place he could stay?"

"Right here. There's a little room off the storeroom," he said, for some reason taking her side. "I can tell you I wouldn't mind having someone down here at night. He could eat upstairs with us."

"It's out of the question," Ned replied, but he sounded neither determined nor irritated now.

"Why?" Kate asked softly. "Pete can work and earn money, same as you and me."

"I'm liking this idea more and more," Mr. Bradley said. "Why not try? If it doesn't work after a week or so, we'll know." The merchant turned the force of his enthusiasm on Ned. "Your ma used to tell my wife that all she wanted was for Pete to have a chance at something. What could be better than this? He knows Millie and me. Hell, Pete knows everyone in town! What do you say?"

"Just don't say no so fast, Ned," Kate urged. "Can we think about it?"

*"We?"* Ned asked, exasperated again.

*You're not going to make me angry*, she thought. She took

a deep breath. "Yes, *we*. If Pete goes to work here, we'll have to work a little harder to take care of your father."

"You don't mind?" Ned asked, and she knew she had him.

"Of course not. Nothing changes for me. You're the one who won't have any extra help outside."

Ned sighed. "As it is, with Pete I'm dragging around a boat anchor. He'd rather do anything than get on a horse and ride all day."

"There you are," Mr. Bradley said cheerfully.

Silence for a moment, as Ned looked from her to the merchant and back. "All right. I'll bring him to town tomorrow and we'll try it for a week."

"Shake on it?" Mr. Bradley asked, holding out his hand.

They shook hands, and Kate wanted to do a two-step around the pickle barrel.

Mr. Bradley beamed at them both. "Your chore girl and I loaded the food in the buckboard. Millie and I will tidy that little room tonight. Bring Pete by anytime before noon, will you?"

"You got me," Ned told Katie after he helped her into the buckboard and went around to his side.

"I saw the sign and thought of Pete," she said simply, determined not to apologize for a good idea acted upon.

He didn't say anything for half the journey home, and then he started to chuckle. Kate felt the tension leave her shoulders.

"We'll try it out," he told her. "Pete used to milk the cow morning and night. You up for that?"

"If you'll remind me how. It's been years."

"My pleasure." He started on his tuneless whistle that she was already familiar with. She relaxed some more when Pete met them at the front door—the only door—of the worst place she had ever lived. Funny that she was already thinking of it as home.

# Chapter Ten

Katie gave Ned credit for impressive self-control that night when Pete kept asking every few minutes if he was really going to work in town for Mr. Bradley. He asked it from the stew to the muffins, and only stopped when Ned told him to put a lid on it or he would take it all back.

Reasoning that he hadn't made any promises to Katie, Pete then asked her over and over, when he was supposed to be teaching her to milk the cow, a rangy little number that didn't appear to suffer fools gladly, if all those looks she gave Kate were any indication.

"Pack your clothes in that old carpetbag of Pa's," Ned said finally. "And don't drive Pa nuts!" he called after his brother.

"I should have just stuck him in the buckboard tomorrow and told him on the way to town," Ned grumbled to Kate. He sat down beside her on the stool and nudged her over. He told her to watch him milk and she did, aware of how close he sat and that he smelled of hair oil.

"You got your hair cut," she said. "I was hoping you didn't spend all that time in the Watering Hole," she teased.

He gave her another nudge, which sent her off the stool and frightened the patient mama cat waiting for her turn.

"Beg your pardon," he said in mock contrition, but he moved over a little and she sat again. "Put your hands beside mine."

She wondered if she should tell him she had milked cows when she was a little girl. Her step pa had hit her when she didn't do a good job, but Ned Avery didn't need to know that.

"You try it now," he directed.

She did as he said and he watched her. For one small moment, that same irrational fear came over her, but the ending was different this time.

"You'll do," he said, and touched her shoulder. He returned to the other side of the barn and finished his chores. He carried the bucket of milk into the house when she finished and told her that his father wanted to see her.

"Don't look so worried," he exclaimed.

"My step pa used to beat me when I didn't do chores the way he wanted," she told him, embarrassed to admit it, but wanted him to understand her own fear.

"That will never happen here," he said quietly, then stopped so suddenly that the milk slopped over a little. "In fact, I know something about you that you probably don't even realize."

"What could that possibly be?" she asked, half amused, half wary.

"I've thought about this while I was riding fence," he began, shaking his head. "Riding fence is so boring that my flights of fancy sometimes amaze *me*!" He turned serious then. "You've told me what you've been through at the hands of a very bad man."

Even when he said no more, she understood what Ned wanted. "Are you wondering why I agreed to work for you?"

"I'm wondering more than a little. How did you know I wasn't a bad man, too? You didn't even know my name."

They stood there in the empty space between the barn and the house, no one else in sight, the sky dark, snow threatening. She did not know how he would feel about her answer, but it was the only one she had. "Something about you told me I could trust you," Kate said finally. She thought some more. "You didn't crowd me. You just stood there so respectful, your hat in your hand."

"Pa says I'm too serious. He says ladies want someone exciting."

Katie shook her head. "Not me! Something told me I could trust you."

He followed her into the kitchen, setting the milk into pans and covering it with a clean cloth. Tomorrow she would skim off the cream and add it to the cream of the day before. In another day she would churn it. She had found a small glass rose, stuck in that same cabinet with the calving rope, that she intended to press into the still soft butter to make a decoration.

"I should have asked you before I promised Pete to Mr. Bradley," she said.

"Maybe, maybe not. Just thinking of that conversation embarrasses me," he said. He sat down at the table and patted the chair beside him. "You notice how quick I was to say no, without even thinking?"

"I noticed," she told him, "but you make the decisions."

"No excuse for not considering something before I shut it down," he said. He touched her hand lightly. "Thank you for not giving up on a good idea that I probably would have strangled at birth."

She couldn't help but feel flattered. "Everyone is taking a chance with this idea."

"Glen Bradley will let me know if it's not working," he said. He gestured down the hall. "Pa wants to talk to you. Want me in there, too?"

Pride nearly made her say no, but as Katie looked into his eyes, she saw the kindness there. "I do," she whispered.

Mr. Avery told her to take a seat and she did, pulling up the one chair in the room until it was closer to his bed. Ned stood behind her chair, his hands on the back of it.

"Ned, I'm not going to scold her," Mr. Avery said. "You can leave."

She was too embarrassed to look around, but heard Ned's laugh as he backed out of the room. He didn't go far, because she heard the rustle of his mattress in the next connecting room.

"You did a good thing for Pete," Mr. Avery told her. "None of us knew what to do, but you did."

"I got lucky," she managed to say.

"It's more than that," he contradicted. "You're looking out for Pete, same as we are, but you're looking at him from a different angle. Thank you."

"You're welcome," she said simply.

He motioned her to lean closer. She did.

"My other boy needs to find a wife," he whispered. "He's thirty-one. Got any good ideas for him?"

Kate felt her face grow hot. "Surely he can find a wife by himself," she whispered back.

"He hasn't so far," Dan said. "Think about it and do what you can. I'm going to sleep now. Good night."

Laughing inside, despite her embarrassment, Kate stood up and went to the door. Dan called her back. "I'm getting a window tomorrow. You mentioned that to him, didn't you?"

"I did, Mr. Avery. When will he do it?"

"As soon as he gets back from dropping off Pete." Mr. Avery smiled at her, and her heart turned over. "'Cept for finding a wife, he's a prompt fellow. Good night now."

# *Chapter Eleven*

Ned got Pete to town, gave him all sorts of admonition and advice that probably rolled right off his back, if the amused look Mrs. Bradley gave him was any indication.

"We'll watch out for Peter," she said as they stood on the sidewalk. "You've been a good brother, but he's growing up and needs duties of his own."

It always rolled around to duty, he thought, on the ride home, after purchasing a pane of glass at the lumberyard and anchoring it safely between two-by-fours. He'd had this conversation with himself before, especially during hard times. To his gratification, there wasn't much sting to this duty. Pa wanted a window and he could install one. He'd have to ask Kate if he could borrow her room for Pa, because he doubted he had time to finish the window today, what with winter bringing darkness so much sooner.

He could put Kate in his room and he could bundle up and sleep in Pa's bed for the one night it might take him to finish the little project and caulk the new window against the bitter winter headed their way soon. Ned knew the doctor had warned Pa not to exert himself at all, but the more he thought about that injunction, the more he wondered about it. Sure, Daniel Avery's battered heart might last longer if he never did anything more strenuous than sitting up, but to what end?

He wanted to mull it all around with Katie Peck, and see what she thought about helping Pa walk down to the kitchen, or maybe even outside. One of the more pleasant byproducts of his impulsive hiring of her was the discovery that behind her solemn face was a sensible brain.

He glanced at the two-story Odd Fellows Hall as he crossed the tracks and rode south toward home, wondering if Katie knew a few dance steps. Mrs. Bradley had mentioned a dance there in mid-December and asked, "Who are you saving yourself for, Edward Avery?"

He was saving himself for no one and he thought Katie might help. She was a woman and she could probably dance. Would it hurt to ask for help?

As he passed through the gate onto Avery land, Ned's thoughts took him in another direction, one that surprised him. For years, Pa had promised Ma a real house. Once she died, Pa had lost interest. Just thinking of a house instead of a log cabin made Ned stop at the top of the little rise and stare down at his home. The logs were stripped of bark now, the result of hungry deer and elk during many a bleak mid-winter. He'd been meaning to paint the door, and even had the paint to do it, but hadn't bothered.

It was time for a real house. He'd humor Pa by putting in a window so he could see a sampling of Avery land through it, but maybe in the spring he could draw up some plans. Kate would probably have good ideas.

With the buckboard driven into the open-sided wagon lean-to, and his horse rubbed, grained and watered, Ned went inside, sniffing appreciatively. Kate had a way with beans, beef and onions. He served himself a bowl of stew. Kate had found the ceramic bowls from somewhere and re-tired the tin cups.

He heard laughter as he walked down the hall, bowl in hand. He saw his copy of *Roughing It* in Kate's lap, and wondered how it was that a quiet mill girl from Maine knew just how to handle his father. He sat on the edge of Pa's bed and ate as she finished the chapter.

"One chapter left," she said. "What will we do then?"

"I'll find you another book," he promised. "Got one somewhere."

She held out her hand for his now empty bowl and he

shook his head. "I can probably struggle all the way back to the kitchen with this."

"I'm the chore girl," she reminded him.

Suddenly, as if some cosmic hand had flicked his dense head with thumb and forefinger, he knew she was more than that; Katie Peck was a friend. He wondered if she felt his friendship. Never mind. He had all winter to figure it out.

When Ned returned to Pa's bedroom, he outlined his ideas for the window.

Between the two of them, they helped Pa walk the short distance to Kate's room. He was breathing heavy from the mere steps from one room to the other, and Ned felt his own heart sink.

Ned watched his father until his color returned and his breath became less labored. "I need Kate to help me with this window. Rest now."

Pa nodded and closed his eyes. Ned stood looking down at his father, remembering earlier days and wishing for them like a child. Kate touched his shoulder, recalling him to the project at hand.

Kate moved things out of the way as he measured the window glass, the log wall, and his two by fours, which he took to the barn to finish. It took longer than he thought, because after a while he heard the sound of milk in a bucket. He looked over the partition to see Kate milking his cow, resting her head against the animal's flank.

She looked so pretty, her dark hair pulled back in that jumbled, untidy way that he liked. He couldn't help smiling when she began to hum. Ma used to do that. God knows he never hummed to a milk cow.

She finished before he did, and gratified him by coming to his impromptu workshop to perch on the grain bin and watch him groove the wood.

"I like your company," he blurted out, then felt his face grow warm.

"I like yours, too," she replied in her sensible way, and

his embarrassment left. "You can do a little bit of anything, can't you?"

"That's part of running a place like this," he said, as he blew sawdust from the frame he was building. He tossed her an extra cloth and she wiped down the wood, blowing off sawdust, too.

"There's a dance at the Odd Fellows Hall in a couple of weeks," he told her, after a few minutes of working up his courage. "I want to go, but I don't know how to dance. Do you?"

"Ayuh," she said. He grinned because she only said that now when she felt playful. "I can two-step and waltz and do something Mainers call a quadrille. I doubt you'll need that."

"Would you mind teaching me?"

"Not at all." She cleared her throat. "Your father thinks you should find a wife, and it'll never happen playing solitaire in the kitchen."

"Not many ladies in Wyoming," he said. Her pointed look wouldn't allow excuses. "All right! Maybe I'll find a wife at the dance. I'll get married and next year you can go to the dance while we watch Pa, and find yourself a husband." He laughed at her skeptical look. "Stranger things have happened, Katie."

He picked up his work and she fetched the milk pail. They walked together to the house, neither in a hurry.

"Does my father talk a lot?" he asked.

"Mostly he listens as I read," she said, and gave a satisfactory sound between a sigh and an exclamation. "We've come a considerable distance in the past few weeks."

Ned helped her with the milk, even though she didn't really need his help anymore. When he finished, he picked up the wood frame and she held up her hand to stop him.

"Ned, he wants to eat at the table and not in bed," she said.

"The doctor said he shouldn't exert himself," he told her, wondering why he had to even mention the obvious.

"I know, but that's no fun," she replied.

"It's not a matter of fun," he said, maybe a little sharper

than he meant to, because the subservient look came back into her eyes. He took her arm, but gently. "Katie, I want him to live longer."

"Maybe it's not living," she said, her voice gentle. "He needs some say in what he wants."

"I'm not convinced." He released her arm. "Help me get this frame in the window?"

She nodded. He snuck another look at her, and didn't see a woman convinced. Something told him the discussion wasn't over, and that he might not win this one. The idea pained him less than he thought it would.

Pa insisted on watching, so they bundled him up and Ned carried him to his bedroom, over his protests that he was capable of walking. He glowered at them both, then resigned himself to sitting silent as Ned planed down the rough logs, then set in the frame for the window glass.

At his request, Kate brought in more kerosene lamps to counterbalance the full dark. The room was cold and she shivered until he went into his room, found an old sweater of his and draped it around her shoulders.

"I'll fit in the glass now, and glaze and putty it tomorrow," he said.

It took little time, which was good, since Pa had started to fade. He offered no objection to being carried back to Katie's bedroom.

Ned went back to his father's room, where Katie was wiping more sawdust off the new window ledge.

"Looks good," she told him. "He'll see the trees and that little rise with sagebrush."

"Maine and Massachusetts are prettier, aren't they?"

"Different, but maybe not prettier," she said, and he admired her diplomacy.

"Tell me something, Katie. Would you marry a rancher around here?"

She gave it more thought than he believed the matter needed. But that was Katie. She thought things through.

"I guess not," he said, which made her laugh, something she didn't do too often, so it charmed him.

"I haven't decided!" she said in humorous protest. "P'raps if I was raised here I might be tempted."

"I mean, you were going to marry…uh…"

"Saul Coffin," she supplied.

"And *he* came out here." He stopped, noting her dismay. "I'm sorry. I shouldn't have reminded you of Mr. Coffin."

"That's not it," she said.

"What is it?" *Good God*, Ned thought. *I am turning into a nosey person.*

"I have to be honest. Some days I'm sorry he's gone, and other days, I wonder if he is alive."

"The sheriff in Cheyenne knows where I live, Katie. If he's alive, we'll hear."

She shook out the sawdust onto the floor and started to sweep, then stopped, giving him the clear-eyed look of a realist. "I could live here in Wyoming." She sighed. "Saul thought he could, too. You should have heard him talk about Wyoming."

"Like it was the Garden of Eden?"

"Sort of," she agreed. "It's not, but I still like it." She leaned the broom against the wall. "That's it, Ned. You'll meet a nice lady at the dance."

He wondered just how much store to put into one holiday dance at the Odd Fellows Hall. "Better teach me to waltz, Katie. This could be a long ordeal."

## Chapter Twelve

Since Katie had forgotten all about purchasing material for curtains in the excitement of Pete's job, the next day Ned had found a length of blue-and-white gingham, in a box of Ma's old things in the barn. No one had sewn anything since Ma, so he had to help her look for the flatirons, once she had cut and hemmed and trimmed the curtains and declared they had to be ironed.

He had no trouble finding the time to help Katie search for the flatirons because she was starting to interest him. He wanted to ask her if she ever wasted a motion or even an hour, but he thought he already knew the answer.

"I vow everything is in this odd little room," she said, as they both squeezed themselves into the storeroom off the stalls.

He heard her exclamation of delight when she found a copy of *A Tale of Two Cities* on a shelf with liniment bottles, a gallon or two of vinegar and unidentifiable bits and pieces of ranch life. "I wondered where that book went," he said.

Katie's search for flatirons stopped with the discovery of something new to read, now that she had finished *Roughing It*, and Pa was getting tired of her *Ladies' Home Journal* stories. Hardly aware of Ned, she took the book into the kitchen and sat down at the table, where she carefully wiped away the dust. He sat down next to her with the flatirons and held them out. He clapped them together and made her laugh.

She set down the book with some reluctance, and nodded at the flatirons. In another minute, she had them warming on the stove. Back he went to the storeroom for the ironing board.

"When I iron these, we can string them on that dowel, and your Pa will have curtains," she said. "Since I have this ironing board up, I can press a white shirt for the dance."

"We have to go to that much trouble? I'll be wearing a vest. Who'll see my shirt?" he asked.

"Who will ever marry you if you don't look presentable?" she asked. "And please tell me you have a collar and cravat somewhere."

While she ironed, he found a pathetic collar and a cravat in even worse shape. She frowned at the collar, but she shook her head at the cravat. "I'll make you one," she told him.

"Out of what?"

"I have some fabric," she said. He knew he heard something wistful in her voice, and thought perhaps he shouldn't ask.

When she finished ironing, they each took a panel of fabric to Pa's room and strung them on a dowel Ned had cut and sanded. Katie clapped her hands in approval and Pa smiled from his bed.

Katie had crocheted ties to hold back the fabric, giving the curtains a certain elegance he never thought to see in their jury-rigged, add-on-as-needed cabin. *Ma, you would have liked this*, he thought, then smiled at Katie who held her hands together in delight. *You'd have liked Katie, too.*

"After you find me a shirt, sit with your father," she said.

He did as she asked, then perched on the edge of his father's bed.

"You have a view," he said. "Look there."

He had seen cows all his life, but there was something nice about looking at them through a window. Here they were now, just nosing in what little snow there was, searching for nourishing grass that made this hard land cow country.

Pa patted the spot beside him on the bed. He pulled out the extra pillow behind his head, doubled over his own, and left a place for Ned beside him.

Ned tugged off his boots and did as his father asked, wondering when he had become too busy to do this. Never mind. He sprawled out beside his father, savoring the moment.

"You built a good ranch, Pa," he said. "I'll take care of it."

Maybe he shouldn't have said that. Tears came into Pa's eyes.

Ned started to apologize, but changed his mind when Pa took his hand and kissed the back of it. He felt the years slip away, and some of the cares. All that he lacked now was to see Ma come into the room, put her hands on her hips and in her soft drawl, declare them useless layabouts, which was acres away from the truth.

He heard footsteps coming closer and looked up in anticipation, thinking of Ma, but it was just Katie. She had folded his ironed shirt so carefully. He watched her put the shirt on the top apple crate in his room, smoothing out what by now had to be imaginary wrinkles.

"We'll have steak and potatoes in a few minutes," she told them. "Ned, help your father to the kitchen."

"I don't think…"

"Mr. Avery, would you like to eat with us?" she asked, ignoring Ned.

"More'n anything."

"Give yourself plenty of time," she admonished, but kindly. He knew she was right. An old rancher with a new window and a view of the valley ought to have some say in where he ate supper.

It took Pa three pauses to get to the kitchen. To Ned, his look of triumph when he finally sat in the kitchen was close kin to his expression when he won a cow penning at the local rodeo a few years back. Maybe it was more than a few years. Time had crept up on them all. Ned couldn't remember the last time Pa had sat at the table with him, and he wondered why it had taken the gentle insistence of a chore girl to give him enough courage to let Pa do what he wanted.

"Pa, I've been treating you like a China doll," he said finally, pushing away his plate. He nodded to Katie, who took the plates to the sink. "I owe you a debt, Miss Peck," he said.

She sat down again. The way Pa looked at her suggested that they had planned it this way. He knew better than to question whatever it was that had turned them into confederates. *What is it about you, Katie Peck*, Ned wanted to ask.

After the dishes, Katie told Pa to settle in. "Ned, we're going to waltz," she told him. "One two three, one two three. It's simple."

She came close and put her hand on his shoulder with no hesitation. "Put that hand on my waist, and I'll take the other one," she directed. "I'll lead, until you figure it out. Mr. Avery, you may do the one two three."

Pa did, waving his hand, as Katie Peck directed Ned around the kitchen. She told him not to look at his feet and he tried to do as she said. Her waist was small. His hands were large, and he felt like he was encroaching a bit on the pleasant swell that began her bosom. She made no objection, which relieved him, because she felt so good.

They banged knees a couple of times, and he stepped on her feet, but at least he had taken off his boots and wore only his stockings.

When Katie said, "You're supposed to carry on pleasant conversation," he stopped dancing.

"Like what?" he asked.

"The weather, the price of two-year heifers," Pa teased.

Katie sighed, but there was no overlooking the fun in her eyes, and the soft way she looked at Dan Avery. "Mr. Avery! Instead of that, Ned, ask your partner what book she's read lately, or maybe inquire about her family."

"I'm supposed to do that and dance at the same time?" Ned protested.

She nodded, and put her hand on his shoulder again. "That's why we're going to practice the waltz every day until the dance. When is it, by the way?" she asked, standing there poised and ready to push off.

"A week from Friday." He whispered in her ear. "Pa's getting tired."

"I know," she whispered back. "Mr. Avery, Ned's going to lead now. He can *think* one two three."

He towed her around the floor to his silent one two three. They narrowly avoided the cooking range, but he kept one hand firmly on her waist, and the other clasped in hers. Around again, without stepping on her, and once more.

"I'm ending this dance," he said. "How do I stop?"

"When the music stops, you give a little bow, and thank her," Katie said. She turned to his father. "What do you think, Mr. Avery?"

"I think he might find a wife yet," Pa said. "Do the two-step now."

"It had better be simpler," Ned told her.

"It is. And it's fast. Hand on my waist again—oh, you never took it off—and take my hand again. It's just one and two and."

Off they went. It *was* simpler, Katie nimble and smiling the whole time. Third time around the room, he picked her up and she laughed.

"I hope…you're not…expecting…conversation," he managed to gasp.

"Only…if the building…catches on fire," she said, which made him give a shout of laughter and grab her up.

He held her that way, so they were on equal eye level, breathing hard. She put both hands on his shoulders, not to ward him off, but to remind him. He let her down, and she stepped away, her face red from exertion, but her eyes bright.

They both looked at Pa, who nodded. "That'll for sure find him a wife, unless he's dancing with another man's missus." He laughed. "Then we'll have a shoot-out and a hanging!"

"We'll practice every night," Katie assured Ned. She started sticking hairpins back in place, but gave it up for a bad business and shook the rest of her hair down.

Ned hadn't realized how long it was, almost to her waist,

and the prettiest shade of just ordinary brown, with little bits of red glimmering in the light of the lamp.

He looked at Pa, whose eyes were closing. "No objections from you, Pa," he said, as he carried his father back to his room. Katie trailed along behind, watchful, and Ned began to realize the strength of her attachment to his father.

"I'll help him from here," he told her. She went into her room and closed the door. He listened for her to lock it, then realized with a start that she had never locked her door, not even the first night when he handed her the key.

*We're doing something right*, he thought.

## Chapter Thirteen

They danced every night, and soon Katie had no fears for her toes. Ned's conversation still suffered, but she knew him as a reticent man. A dancing partner would have to appreciate taciturnity, Katie decided. She knew *she* didn't mind his silences. He had a lot on his mind.

"Did you mill girls have dances?" he asked one night.

"Ned, you're wonderful!" she exclaimed. "You asked me that and didn't look down at your feet."

"Did Saul Coffin dance with you?"

"Now and then, but he was mostly all business around the looms."

"Maybe I shouldn't bring him up," he said after another turn.

"Doesn't matter," she replied. "We may never know what happened."

She didn't mind the silence that followed, because she had a moment to reflect on how seldom she thought about Saul Coffin, the man who had partly paid her way to Wyoming Territory. She knew the truth, though: hard life had taught her not to expect anything. When Saul Coffin had been notable by his absence in Cheyenne, she quietly set about forgetting him.

She looked up at Ned, struck by the knowledge that she would miss him, when he didn't need her any longer. Ned made another turn, and she glanced at Mr. Avery, sitting at the table and looking healthier. She decided that lying alone all day in a back bedroom wasn't designed to cure any ailment, even if a bad heart is a fragile thing.

It struck her that a good heart was a fragile thing, too,

and she hoped that Ned Avery found someone to share his life with. Maybe a wife, the right one, would ease his way in this hard land.

The day of the dance, she took the piece of forest-green brocade from her traveling case to make Ned a cravat. The matter gave her less of a pang than she thought, considering that the fabric was the only item remaining from her real father, a sailor lost at sea during the China run. Besides a pittance so small that Mama was forced to remarry, the skipper had given her a length of green brocade. She had no use for it, except to parcel it among her four children as their only legacy from their father.

After morning chores, Katie picked apart his old cravat, ironed the pieces and angled them here and there on the brocade to be her pattern. She hesitated only a moment before cutting.

"That's mighty elegant," Ned said, as he came into the kitchen, prepared for a day in the saddle. "You didn't find that in Wyoming."

Without thinking, she told where it came from and noted the dismay on his face. "You needed a new cravat, and I have the material," she pointed out.

"It's a treasure," he protested. She had already cut into the fabric, so a man as practical as Ned knew the argument was over.

She continued cutting. The long strip remaining to her could easily be hemmed and turned into a bookmark for her Bible. That would do. As it was, she barely remembered her father.

That day, Kate skimped on reading from *A Tale of Two Cities*, which raised a protest from Mr. Avery. "Bad as he is, we cannot leave St. Evrémonde with a knife through his heart," he reminded her.

"I fear we must," she said. "If I am to finish the cravat, we'll have to leave the marquis weltering in his gore."

"You sound remarkably like Dickens," he told her, but gave her no more argument.

She sat with Mr. Avery and sewed, determined to have the pretty thing finished by the time Ned carried in the milk bucket late in the afternoon. He had insisted on doing her chores so she could finish the cravat, even though she knew it was seven miles to Medicine Bow and the dance started at nine o'clock. She handed the cravat to him after the last stitch.

"No one will have a cravat this fine," he said, and held it up to his neck. "I have an ironed shirt, too."

Her heart nearly stopped when he took her hand and kissed it. Impulsively she put her free hand on his head for no reason, except that she wanted to touch the man who had been so kind to her. He had helped her when he had no idea if she would steal the spoons in his house and vanish the next day, and he had built her a room. Her heart was full.

Kate wiped her eyes. "Go find someone nice," she whispered. "I'd better read to your father while you take a bath in the kitchen."

"You won't scrub my back?" he teased.

"Not for thirty dollars a month," she said, and he laughed.

*A fellow could hope*, Ned told himself, after he filled the galvanized tub in the kitchen and eased himself in for a quick soak, which turned into a longer one, because he had not enjoyed such luxury since his visit to Cheyenne. Ordinarily, a fast wash at the bowl and pitcher in his room sufficed. He sat so long in the cooling tub that he could have used one more bucket of hot water from the cooking stove's reservoir. He doubted Kate would pour him one, but he could ask.

She surprised him by coming to the doorway of the kitchen, her head averted. "Another bucket?" she asked, and he heard the timidity in her voice.

"Yes, please. I'll cover up. Just pour it behind my back," he said, and hunched over his middle, his washcloth in place.

She did as he said. His hair was already damp so he lathered in soft soap. "If you could dip out half a bucket of hot water, and add an equal amount of cold from the kitchen pump, I can rinse this."

"I'll help," she said, sounding businesslike. "A body can't rinse his own head."

Kate rinsed his hair without a complaint, even though it took two buckets to meet her apparently exacting standards.

"There. If you can't manage the rest of this bath, you're too young to go to a dance," she scolded.

He sat a little longer in the water, wishing he could stay at home and listen to more of Lucie Manette, Charles Darnay and Sydney Carton, too, as read by his chore girl to his dying father who had taken on a new lease on life. Ned had enjoyed the book years earlier, but there was something almost royally sinful about having enough time to listen to another read it. Ned almost resented losing an evening at a dance, when he could be home, lying beside his father, listening to Katie read.

Or maybe he just didn't want to dress up and ride through the dark to a dance where there might not be anyone young and even remotely eligible, Wyoming being what it was. *I'm getting set in my ways*, he thought. *Kate is kind to rescue me.*

Katie had managed to repair his one pathetic collar, stiffening it, and sewing it together to fit on his shirt. He called to her to button his new cravat in the back. He sat down on the corner of his bed so she could reach him. When she finished, she told him to stand up and turn around so she could adjust the handsome bit of brocade to suit herself. She stood back for a better look, and finally nodded her approval.

"You'll do," she told him as he put on his vest. She helped him into his black coat, smoothing the back of it near his shoulders. He liked her touch, but what man wouldn't?

"*You'll do?* That doesn't sound like a ringing endorsement," he teased.

"It is in Maine," she assured him. "I mean what I say."

Ned stood in the doorway of his father's room, hesitant to leave. He understood his reluctance as Katie looked back at him. He saw the pride in her eyes that looked a little like ownership, which bothered him not at all. He owed this whole evening to her.

As he mounted his horse and started for town, he had another idea, one that bore some thought: he really didn't want to go dancing without Katie.

# Chapter Fourteen

Medicine Bow must have grown during the past year. Ned Avery had no trouble filling out a dance card with a new schoolteacher in town, the banker's daughter, a widow roughly his age who danced even better than Katie and the Presbyterian minister's cousin from Ohio.

He remembered not to mumble *one two three* when he waltzed, came up with enough small talk to get him through a dance and stepped on nothing except the wooden floor.

By the time the dance ended, Ned had the name and address of the banker's daughter, and had promised to take Sunday dinner with the minister's cousin before she left for Ohio in the spring. The schoolmarm spent more time dancing with a rancher ten miles farther out of town; she'd find out soon enough he was a widower with five rowdy children.

Still, they weren't Katie. Besides, if Katie had come with him, she could be filling up a dance card and looking over the local bachelors. She could also be dancing with him. He missed the sweetness of her breath on his neck when he whirled her around the kitchen.

He found himself comparing his dancing partners with Katie. Excepting the widow, none were as light-footed. The schoolmarm appeared as trim as Katie, but the whalebone corset he felt against his hand suggested otherwise. On the plus side, they were all easy to understand. He made a joke with the schoolmarm at Katie's expense, imitating her Maine accent until the lady laughed, then felt ashamed of himself. Katie couldn't help where she came from.

At three in the morning he went to bed in the hotel. He sat

for a while on the edge of the bed, looking out at a full moon. He had a breakfast invitation from the Bradleys, provided he showed up by seven, so both Pete and Mr. Bradley could eat before they had to open the mercantile at eight.

He lay back finally, pleased with the way the evening had gone. He could tell Katie he had danced, conversed and looked over Medicine Bow's promising females. He learned there would be a party on Christmas Eve with a real tree, sponsored by the Presbyterians.

He knew Katie would urge him to go, but as he lay there, the dissatisfaction which had dogged him all evening finally focused on the source of his discontent—Katie couldn't go to the Christmas party, either. He had hired her to take care of his father, and there was no one else. His nearest neighbors had chatted with him at the dance, telling him they would attend the Christmas party, too.

He turned over, irritated at the unfairness of the deal he had struck with her. For a moment, he resented his father's frailty. Pa had hung on so long, and now he even seemed to be getting better on Katie's watch. She had promised to stay as long as his father needed her. What had sounded so simple a deal in Cheyenne wasn't.

Once she was released, she would leave. There was nothing to tie her to his ranch. She had no burden of calving time, and beef prices and the fear of a dry summer.

He flopped on his back and stared at the ceiling. Pa had built the ranch from scratch, working horrible hours under difficult conditions, struggling through long winters, hot summers and Indian threats.

"I don't have it in me," Ned said aloud, voicing a fear that had teased him for months, ever since his father took sick.

The unfairness of his life bore down hard as he lay there. Because he lay there alone, Ned admitted to himself that he wanted to get on the train tomorrow and leave everyone behind. He could get a job in a warm place that didn't require every ounce of his strength. He didn't want this life his father had dumped in his lap.

Ned sat up and swung his bare legs over the side of the bed, disgusted with himself for such cowardice. He wanted to talk to Katie about it, to pour his troubles into her lap, simply because he knew she would listen. Maybe he just needed to share his misery with someone else.

By skipping his daily shave, he made it to the Bradleys' store and up the stairs in time for breakfast. There he sat, stupefied with exhaustion and trying to look interested as Pete described a typical day at the mercantile. Gradually, as what Pete was saying sank in, Ned pronounced a silent, grateful thank-you on Katie for acting on that help-wanted sign, something he would have ignored. Was he too stubborn to change?

"Pete suits us," Mr. Bradley told Ned as the three of them trooped downstairs to the mercantile. "Don't you, Pete?"

Pete nodded shyly, with a sidelong look at Ned.

"Then you're all doing what the Lord intended," Ned said, glad Pete had escaped from endless ranch work. No sense for both of them to be tied to the place.

He picked up a box waiting for him at the post office, the one bright spot in a day already going nowhere. "Hope you don't think I'm getting ideas," he said, looking down at the Montgomery Ward label.

"Ned, are you talking to parcels now?" he heard, and looked around to see the sheriff heading his way with something close to purpose in his stride.

"Only now and then, sir," he said and waited for the sheriff.

"You need to know something," the man said. "Name of Saul Coffin ring a bell with you?"

## Chapter Fifteen

"Last I heard, he was dead and buried in Lusk," Ned said.

"Turns out the guy in the coffin was someone at the Lucky Dollar who made fun of Mr. Coffin's decidedly different accent," the sheriff said. "Apparently the law in Lusk decided Mr. Coffin was acting in self-defense, when the drunk came at him." He shook his head. "Drunks in a bar. Who is sober enough to know what went on?" The sheriff reached into his vest pocket. "Here's a note from Mr. Coffin. Give it to the chore girl. Maybe she'll straighten him out."

*My job just got harder*, Ned thought. He gave the sheriff two fingers to his hat brim, and started home down a road that seemed suddenly unfamiliar.

*I can't lose her. How will I manage?* fought with, *This will please her no end.* He patted the note in his pocket and decided that it could wait until he felt like handing it over. He knew he didn't feel like it now. His whole middle-of-the-night irritation came crowding back.

*Give it to the chore girl*, the sheriff had said. Ned asked himself when she went from being a chore girl to being Katie, the woman who wanted a room of her own, but never locked her door; who used the last tangible memory of her real father to make him a cravat; who read *A Tale of Two Cities* aloud to his father; who took care of things at home so he could ride to Medicine Bow for some well-deserved fun, and all for thirty dollars a month and a place to stay.

He wondered what would happen when she came to the end of Dickens's novel, where poor Sydney Carton sacrificed himself for another woman's husband. He knew Katie would cry. To his knowledge, she hadn't cried over Saul Coffin, but he knew she would cry over Sydney Carton. Because he knew that, Katie was his responsibility, too.

Never had a responsibility sat so lightly on his shoulders. He wanted to be there because she was in his house, taking quiet care of his father and him. She never complained. She did what was asked of her and slept in her bed each night, securely safe because she knew he would do her no harm. She had said as much and she was right.

What had gone from an impulsive agreement for her help until his father died had changed into a longer game. His father was getting better under Katie's good care. The window he had cut into his father's room was only one of Katie's changes. She had taught Ned to dance, found Pete a job that suited him, dug into the dark recesses of the clutter of cabinets and found his mother's old spices. She was making them all better because she cared. *I owe her a great debt*, he thought.

His well-being lasted until he rode his horse onto the stretch of grass between the house and the barn. The object of his thoughts must have been watching for him because she threw open the kitchen door and ran into the yard, waving her arms.

He wanted to leap from his horse and grab her, until she got close enough for a good look at her face.

"My father?" he asked, as larger worries took over. "Is he dead?"

She shook her head, but there was no disguising her distress. She stood there, looking so small and alone, almost as if she feared what he would do to her. He reached out to her, and she backed up.

"Katie, hold still," he said. "He's alive?"

She nodded, but he saw all the worry and tension in her whole body. He wanted to put his arm around her, but she wasn't having any of that. They walked side by side to the wide-open door, Katie giving him fearful glances as if to determine his mood. He had certainly never known her step-father, but Ned Avery suddenly hated the man.

"What happened?" he asked. "Tell me now before I go back to his room."

She took a deep breath. "Last night. I was reading out loud. He grabbed his chest and said he couldn't breathe." She bowed her head. "I've never been so scared!"

He didn't care what she thought as he flung off his coat and put his arm around her. "I shouldn't have left you alone," he said, but she stopped him with a thump to his chest.

"Don't do that!" she exclaimed. "You never get away." Her head went up. "I did as you told me to do. I…I found that bottle of glycerol…glycerol…"

"…trinitrate…" he finished, and started them both down the hall. "You put a tablet under his tongue?"

"Just like you said," she told him. "He calmed right down."

He stopped her at her room and put his hands gently on her shoulders, not willing to startle her, but not eager to let her go. "Then you did everything I would have done, Katie Peck," he said. He saw the dried tears on her face and wanted to touch them. "But you felt pretty lonely, didn't you?"

She seemed to know exactly what he was telling her. The fear left her face, replaced by tenderness. "And you've been doing this for how long?" she asked softly. "All alone, even with Pete here?"

"All alone."

She gave him that level look, that calm glance of a real-istic woman. She knew exactly how hard life was, and she had borne up under it, just as he had.

"As long as I am here, you're not alone," she told him.

He wanted to hold her in his arms, but his father called to him. Ned hurried down the hall to his father's room.

His father lay there, eyes half-open, but calm. He had stuck his finger in *A Tale of Two Cities*, probably where Katie had dropped the book when she heard his horse.

"Madame Defarge spends all her spare time knitting and watching aristocrats lose their heads," Dan Avery said, by

way of greeting. "Did you meet any promising women? I
hope Katie didn't gussy you up for nothing."

Ned lay down beside his father, his boots on the bed,
which he knew would irritate Katie. Yes, he had met a promising woman. She lived in his house, he paid her thirty dollars
a month and he had a letter in his pocket from her fiancé. *I
live a life too simple for so much drama*, he thought in mild
amusement. *And what did I do but fall in love?*

"I have a dinner invitation and an address I'm not sure
what to do with. The schoolteacher resisted my charms, but
you should see the preacher's daughter. Pete is doing fine at
the Bradleys, and you gave Katie quite a fright, Pa."

"Couldn't seem to help that," his father agreed, and rubbed
his chest.

Ned took a good look at Pa, wondering when he had got
so thin. He took the book from his father. "Looks like the
French Revolution is too much for you."

His father managed a laugh. "I'll tell you about Chickamauga and the Battle of Franklin sometime, and then we'll
see what's too much for me." His father rose up a little to look
down the hall. "She did everything you would have done.
You really just hired her on a whim?"

He nodded. "She stay up all night with you?"

"She did. I'm glad you're home so she can sleep."

He looked around. Where had she gone?

He found her in the barn. Katie sat at the milking stool,
her head against the cow's flank. Ned walked around to see
her face, and her eyes were closed.

"Katie, go to bed," he said softly.

She opened her eyes. "I'm not…"

She didn't even get the word out before her eyes closed
again. He moved her off the stool and into the hay and finished the morning milking, done late because she hadn't left
his father's side. When he was done, he nudged Katie awake.
Without a word, she stood up as dutifully as a child and followed him from the barn. The wind caught her and he heard
her intake of breath.

After a glass of warm milk, some meat and broth from the stew simmering on the hob, Katie walked down the hall to her room and closed the door. He listened for the lock, and heard nothing except a yawn.

He brought his father a bowl of stew, and one for himself. Dan Avery finished first, after only a few mouthfuls.

"I scared her," he said, "but you should have seen the determination in her eyes." He chuckled. "She reminded me of you, and I knew then that I would live."

What could he say to that? "I've been scared, too, Pa," he admitted finally.

"Guess that's three of us," Pa replied. "Thing is, you don't quit."

*You have no idea how much I want to*, Ned thought.

## Chapter Sixteen

*I should get under these covers*, Katie thought. *I really should.* She lay where she was, stupid with exhaustion. She thought she heard someone knock on her door, just a quiet tap.

"Yes?"

"Ned. Let's talk."

"Come in," she said and sat up. Maybe her boss wouldn't mind covering her feet at least. She asked herself why she wasn't afraid to have him come into her room, especially after her insistence that she have her own room in the first place. She was either more tired than she thought, or she trusted him.

He came in, apology all over his face, that changed to a smile as he looked at her. "Too tired to get in bed?"

"Yes. You would never be so indecisive."

"There have been times." He left the room and came back with a grey blanket, draping it over her and tucking in the bottom to cover her feet. At least she had taken off her shoes.

He left again and came back with a chair. He sat down hunched over, legs wide apart, arms dangling between his legs, and looked at her. "You did everything right."

"I was certain he was going to die," she confessed.

"I won't leave you alone again."

"How will you ever find someone to love and marry, if you don't get off this ranch?"

He shrugged. "That could be the least of my troubles." He reached in his inside vest pocket and pulled out a letter.

"The sheriff gave me this. I…I almost wasn't going to give it to you."

Katie didn't want to touch the letter. When had anything good ever come from a letter?

"Katie…"

She knew the handwriting on the envelope. "I thought he was dead," she said, appalled that it sounded like an accusation.

He didn't leave the room. She wondered for a moment if he felt more than mere concern, then told herself that he had a vested interest in a letter from Saul Coffin. The deal was thirty dollars a month, at least through the winter, and he must think this letter had the power to change that.

She took out the single sheet of note paper, read it to herself and handed it to Ned.

He read it. "At least he apologized for not being there."

"Killing a man in self-defense?" Katie said. "And in a bar? I thought I knew him better than that. Now I am to meet him in Cheyenne." She took another look at the letter. "I'm to send a telegram in Medicine Bow to Lusk to let him know when I will be in Cheyenne."

"I won't stop you," Ned told her.

"I made you a promise," she replied, wishing he were not so noble, maybe someone more like Saul Coffin. "Maybe I don't want to be ordered about."

"He is a bit demanding," Ned said. He sounded cautious, as if gauging just how much he could say against Saul without angering her.

"He always was demanding," Katie said. "I never really noticed just how much until…" She stopped. "…until this letter."

"We'll get Pa into Medicine Bow," he said. "Can't leave him here alone while we go to Cheyenne."

"No need," Katie replied. "Your neighbor can sit with Mr. Avery until you drop me off at the depot in Medicine Bow."

"And let you take the train to Cheyenne on your own?" he asked, as if she had suggested somersaults in the corral.

"I got here by myself," she pointed out.

The skeptical look he gave her told Katie all she ever wanted to know about Ned's opinion of *that* journey.

"I'm coming with you," he insisted. "I won't let a lady ride alone from here to Cheyenne."

He was beginning to sound as demanding as Saul Coffin, but in a better way. "I'm no lady," she insisted. "I'm a mill girl. I'm a chore girl. You know that!"

He leaned over and kissed her forehead, then left the room, causing her to wonder who had told her men were simple creatures.

As tired as she was, she could not return to sleep. Katie closed her eyes and thought through the last few months, from her fear when Saul wasn't in Cheyenne to meet her, right down to his insistence now that she do what he wanted. Her fear left, mainly because of Ned Avery's strong presence. He was a man without doubts, and she had so many.

Since she couldn't sleep, she walked down the hall and shared her letter with Mr. Avery, who agreed that she wasn't going to Cheyenne alone. He also had no objection to their plan to bundle him into the buckboard to Medicine Bow and stay with the doctor. Katie felt her own objections to Ned's help growing weaker by the minute. *No one is listening to me*, she thought.

Katie remained silent when Ned said he would go to Medicine Bow to send a telegram, telling Saul she would be in Cheyenne in four days. "That gives him time to get there," Ned explained. "He can meet you in the lobby of the Plainsman Hotel. While I'm in Medicine Bow, Pa, I'll tell the doctor to expect you."

"Why must I go to Cheyenne?" Katie burst out, surprising herself. "I *promised* you I would stay."

Ned folded his arms across his chest. "You came to Wyoming to marry Saul Coffin, didn't you?"

"I suppose I did," Katie said, "but you are an aggravating man."

"I am a realist," he said simply. "Let's get these dishes to the kitchen."

Angry with herself, she followed him down the hall, and plunked the dishes in the sink.

"What do you think?"

She turned back to her boss, who held out a woman's coat.

"I hope I got the size right. Try it."

Numb, she slid her arm in one sleeve and then the other, as he held out the coat. Tears welled in her eyes and she couldn't do a thing about it. It was too late to press the bridge of her nose, or take deep breaths; she was past those measures that had served her so well through life. She let the tears fall as he turned her around and buttoned her coat.

"You needed a new one" was all he said, right before he took her in his arms.

She knew better than to trust men, but all that painfully earned knowledge flew away as she hugged him back, wondering about the kindness she had found in an unlikely place.

He pulled away first, his eyes bright with amusement. "You're a watering can, Katie."

"Am not," she declared as the tears fell faster. "Why…"

"Christmas came early. I ordered it two months ago when we got here from Cheyenne. "You needed it then, so I know you need it now."

*I need you more*, she thought.

He helped her out of the coat, which she folded carefully and placed on the table. She wanted him to leave, because she wanted to cry. Drat the man; he sat down at the table.

"There's going to be a Christmas party on Christmas Eve," he said.

He was changing the subject, so she knew *his* heart wasn't wounded beyond repair. "You can drop me in Cheyenne, and certainly make it back in plenty of time," she said. "And your father will be there to enjoy it, too. Where?"

"Mrs. Bradley says this one is in the Presbyterian Church. She says there's a social hall, with a high ceiling for a tree all the way from Minnesota. There'll be candy canes and ribbon candy and turkey. Christmas carols, too. Mrs. Bradley says the little children in town will have a Christmas play."

His enthusiasm touched her heart. "You've never seen anything like that before, have you?" she asked, setting aside her own sadness that she would miss both it and him.

He shook his head. "There wasn't anything in Mississippi. Yankees burned it all. And when we got here, it was just hard living. Medicine Bow is getting civilized, Katherine."

Why had she ever thought Katie was lovelier than Katherine? It sounded so beautiful on his lips. "Do...do...do you think Lusk is civilized?" she asked.

"I doubt it," he replied promptly. "People over there in Niobrara still bay at the moon."

She smiled, because she knew he wanted her to. "We should do something here at the house," she told him.

He stood up and shook his head. "I don't have the heart for it," he said and left her there in the kitchen.

## Chapter Seventeen

The four days shot by, to Ned's chagrin. He wanted them to draw out and give him courage to say more to Katherine Peck, before he took her to Cheyenne and let Saul Coffin reclaim her.

But every morning he woke to find his father sitting up, usually with a cup of coffee in his hand, because Katherine knew how to take care of people.

Ned asked her how she knew so much, and she gave him an answer for the ages, one that put heart into his exhausted soul. "I do what the day demands," she told him. "That's enough."

He thought about that as he rode to the Higginses, who assured him they would look after his milk cow for a few days. A ride into Medicine Bow gained him the assurance of the doctor, who saw no problem with Dan Avery "coming for a visit," as he put it.

"I'm honestly surprised he is still alive," the doctor said.

"You wouldn't be if you saw how well my chore girl is taking care of him," Ned said. "He told me last week he's not going to die until she finishes reading *A Tale of Two Cities*."

He sent a telegram to Saul Coffin, General Delivery, Lusk, Wyoming, telling the man to look for Katherine Peck on the evening train, and to meet her in the Plainsman Hotel. It gave him grim satisfaction to sign Edward Avery, Eight Bar Ranch. It was a well-known name and brand in these parts.

As he rode home, snow was blowing sideways in all directions, a feature of Wyoming winds that he took for granted.

He was tired of it all, and unwilling to think how sad his life would be, once Katie left.

"I can't do everything," he told the darkening sky. "I can't even get through this winter."

Katie waited for him at the kitchen door, her eyes anxious. He assured her he knew how to get home, which made her go all quiet. Perhaps he could have said it in a nicer way; maybe he'd raised his voice. Angry at himself, he strode to his father's room, feeling two inches tall and most unmanly.

He stopped short to see the Christmas tree. No one could have done this but Katie. She must have trod out into the knee-deep snow and chopped the tree herself. He came closer and saw his mother's old ornaments, dredged up from some dark corner. Katie had crocheted a chain that went around and around the tree. He looked at the cardboard star and swallowed. Damn his hide, but she had taken the green brocade strip, the last memory of her father, and found a way to glue it to the star.

He couldn't even face his father. "I snapped at her for worrying about me."

"The tree is taller than she is, but she dragged it in here somehow. She spent the rest of the day decorating it, and the last two hours just walking back and forth and worrying about your sorry hide. I couldn't even get her to read me another chapter."

Ned lay down beside his father. He raised up on his elbow to look at him, someone with a bad heart but lots of wisdom.

"Why do women even want to have anything to do with men?"

"I've wondered that," Pa replied. He glanced down the hall to make sure he wasn't going to be overheard. "They do like the lovemaking, and once we get 'um with child they see the necessity of sticking around." He sighed. "They need us when the babies are little, and then they just stay."

"Hoping we'll change?"

"I never had the nerve to ask," his father replied, which made them both laugh.

Ned lay there a moment longer, relishing quiet time with the man he frankly adored. Why hadn't he seen that sooner? Why had he let all those years of unremitting labor sour him?

He knew he owed Katherine an apology. "You already eaten, Pa?" he asked as he stood up.

"Yep. Go down there and say something nice to the kindest person on the Eight Bar."

"On my own, eh?" Ned teased.

"Time you learned something from someone besides me, son," his father told him. "Maybe this chore girl is the best thing that ever happened to you."

"I'm taking her to her fiancé tomorrow," Ned reminded him.

"You're going to let that stop you?"

Ned couldn't think of anything to say that wouldn't sound cowardly and whining. The woman had purposefully come West to marry the man. "I probably am," he said finally.

His father just sat there, hands folded across his stomach. "You could ask her how she feels." He shook his head. "But you're afraid."

"I am," Ned agreed. "I can at least apologize for being an ass."

"Son, look in the top drawer of that bureau, under my handkerchiefs."

Ned took out a small box.

"Look inside."

Among mismatched cufflinks he saw a ring. He took it out, "This?"

"Hand it over."

Pa held up the ring. "I took this off a dead Yankee at Chickamauga. Lord, you should've seen them run! He wasn't fast enough and I shot him. Tried to give it to your mother, but she refused to wear it."

"You kept it."

"Your ma was always funny about this bauble. When I told her I was going to sell it to pay our taxes, she set up such a racket. I said if I couldn't keep what little property we owned, even a nasty ring from a damn Yankee, we had no choice but to go West. *Let's do it*, she said, so you can blame her for Wyoming."

"You never told me this."

"Never saw a need." He set the ring down and reached for Ned's hand. "I know you haven't been happy here."

"Pa, I…"

"Shut up and listen! Your ma knew there wasn't any life in burnt-over, ransomed Mississippi. She had some money that wasn't rebel money and we bought land here, plus homesteaded." He picked up the ring again. "She wanted you to give this to your woman." He laughed softly, the kind of memory laugh that Ned knew he wanted someday with a woman. "She told me, *If Ned marries a damn Yankee lady, she'll not mind this.* So there you are, son."

The conversation had worn out Pa. Ned pocketed the ring, tucked the coverlet higher around his father and returned to the kitchen for penance.

Katherine sat at the table, her eyes stormy, her lips tight together as she clasped her hands. Better begin at once.

"Katherine, I was rude and I'm sorry," he said. "I'm not used to having someone worry about me, and I know the road home."

She glanced at him, then looked away, her stormy expression gone. "I shouldn't have worried," she said finally. She looked around as if she was seeing all the wide-open, wind-scoured mountains and valleys in his territory. "This place frightens me a little. You know your way around it and I don't."

He had to know something, because he was curious. "Do you like it here?"

Silent, thinking, she served him roast and those crisp potatoes of hers that he liked so well. "I believe I do," she said. "I'd have to see it in summer to know for sure." She hesitated. "What's it like around Lusk?"

He wanted to tell her it was an awful place, but it was just

Wyoming, take it or leave it. "Never lived there. Couldn't tell you." Damn, here he was again, sounding like a fool.

She said nothing else and he ate supper, thinking about women in ways he had never thought about them before. He wondered what it was like to have a woman around all the time, one that was his alone. He had never wanted to inflict his hard life on anyone, but now he did.

He watched Katherine at the sink. She had such a pleasant sway to her hips as she worked. He admired the blue-and-white kitchen curtains she had sewed. All the racy calendars were long gone. The stove was blacked, the floor swept and the food was good. His chore girl had turned the godforsaken cabin into a home.

And now like a fool he was taking her to Cheyenne to meet her fiancé. If there was a more stupid man in the territory, Ned had never met him.

# Chapter Eighteen

On the morning of their departure for Cheyenne, Katie reluctantly accepted sixty dollars in wages for the last two months, even though she knew she had earned it. Ned seemed so certain that she wouldn't be returning to the Eight Bar with him that he almost convinced her. She had listened to father and son talk about finding a hired man. *What about me?* she wanted to ask, but it wasn't her place.

She knew a hired man would be more useful, but who would read *A Tale of Two Cities* to Mr. Avery? Could Ned even cook? She could see Mrs. Avery's spices, tablecloths and dishes being shoved back into their cubbyholes, and it pained her.

She packed, then looked around her room one last time, this room of her own. She had slept here peacefully with no fear. She thought about Saul Coffin and his admittedly hot temper. She had accepted his proposal because she felt some affection, and yearned to leave the mill.

She thought about Ned Avery: his constancy, his family loyalty, his willingness to tackle everyone's burdens, his thoughtful gift of a coat because he saw how ill-suited hers was for Wyoming. She even liked his looks, scoured as they were by wind and sun.

Saul Coffin didn't measure up, not now. She had been making the best of bad bargains all her life and she was tired of it. Still, the man has to ask and Saul had asked. Ned had never done more than hug her and kiss her forehead once, but she never wanted to leave his side.

"Are you ready?"

"Yes. Would you like me to sit in the buckboard bed with your father? I can keep an eye on him."

"Thank you. I won't have to worry then," he said.

He came into her room for her battered traveling case, hefting it easily, because she had come with little. What she was leaving with far outweighed any baggage. Maybe the best life had to offer was intangible.

Instead of following Ned outdoors, she went to Mr. Avery's room. She was going to miss reading to him. At least he had a Christmas tree, more tree than she ever had. He had been deprived of so much by his illness, and what she was doing felt like abandonment.

She turned around to see Ned in the doorway, watching her in that quiet way of his. "You make sure there is water in that bucket, if you want the tree to last through Christmas," she said.

"Ayuh," he replied, which meant she had to turn away because she had no proof against that.

His hands went to her shoulders. He turned her around, uncertainty written all over his capable face, the one she had thought so weatherbeaten and hard but which was exactly right. "Just teasing."

"I know that," she whispered. "It's hard to leave friends."

They arrived in Medicine Bow with time to settle Mr. Avery into a pleasant room on the ground floor of the doctor's office. "I'll be back tomorrow, Pa, or maybe the day after, if it takes me more time to find a hired hand," Ned said.

"Shouldn't," Mr. Avery said. "I'd be surprised if there weren't a whole brace of out-of-work hands eager to sign up."

"What about you, Katie Peck?" Mr. Avery asked her. "You know you don't have to leave, if Saul Coffin isn't quite the man you remember."

She nodded, too full of love to speak, and kissed Mr. Avery's cheek. "We'll see."

Mr. Avery motioned her closer. "My boy's a little slow, and I'm not talking about Pete. You might need to do the nudging."

She left before she started to weep. A few deep breaths righted her equilibrium. She wondered what had happened to the capable mill girl who never cried. *I've changed*, she thought. Whether for better or worse, she didn't know, because change was hard.

The Union Pacific was on time for once, although the conductor mentioned that past Cheyenne that would change because of the snow, or so he had heard via telegraph. Ned seemed disinclined to talk, which hardly surprised her. He touched her heart when he leaned against her and slept. She did the same, peaceful at last when his arm went around her, too.

Full dark came an hour before the conductor announced their arrival in Cheyenne. She stood up, grateful Ned had insisted on accompanying her to the Plainsman Hotel. Other ladies in the train car had their escorts, none finer than hers, she told herself. She looked as good as they did, with her handsome navy blue coat. Her hat wasn't much, but it was an Eastern style.

In the dark, she admired Ned's capability and courage, well aware that these qualities were found in his generous heart, hers alone to see. She tightened her grip on Ned's arm, which made him look down in surprise.

"Things'll turn out better this time," he said. "Someone is waiting for you."

Someone was. She looked around when they entered the hotel lobby and there sat Saul Coffin. He stood up when he saw her, but stayed where he was.

"Don't leave me here," she said, suddenly afraid he would disappear. "Not until I know."

"I'll wait here," Ned said. "Go on now. He's expecting you."

"Don't you want to meet him?" she asked, then held her peace when she saw the look of distrust in Ned Avery's eyes. She glanced at Saul, and saw the same look.

Katie took a deep breath and walked toward Saul Coffin. He looked the same, but it had only been six months since she had last seen him. He had left the mill long before her, the better to get things set up for her arrival, he had told her. How many times had he bragged to the others about his cousin out in Wyoming who wanted him to go into the ranching business with him?

He was more handsome than Ned, and he dressed so well. The closer she came, the more she knew something had gone wrong. She saw it all over his face.

She held out her hand. "Saul, I suppose late is better than never."

"You didn't make it easy for me to find you," he complained, and stepped back when she raised up on tiptoe to kiss his cheek.

"I was here when you said, just as I am now," she said, stung that he chose not to accept her affection, and not willing to apologize for something that wasn't her fault. "Mr. Avery over there left my name and his address with the sheriff. That's how you found me, wasn't it?"

"You were pretty quick to go with him," he said, still standing apart from her.

"I knew no one here. I had no money. He offered me a job to tend his father. I'm the chore girl."

They looked at each other; he looked away first.

"What now, Saul?" she asked.

He sighed so loud Katie wondered if Ned could hear him. "I am *not* staying here," he announced. "It's too hard. The house my cousin promised is a two-room shack." He held out his hands. "I have these callouses and blisters."

She stared at him. "Think of what you said in Massachusetts! How your cousin's ranch was the perfect place for a man with ambition to get ahead."

"I'm glad *you've* never been mistaken about anything in your life," he said, sounding more sulky than a schoolboy sent home with bad grades. He took an envelope from his coat pocket and she recognized the lettering—Chase and Sons Textiles, Lowell, Massachusetts. He slapped it in her hand.

She scanned it quickly. David Chase was willing to offer Saul his old job back. Shocked, she read the next paragraph, giving her back her old position, too.

"We can leave tomorrow morning, provided you can help out with your ticket, same as before," he told her. "I assume that man paid you wages."

"He did," she said, the roaring in her ears making his voice seem distant. "You...you won't even give Wyoming a year's trial?"

He shook his head and took the letter back from her. "You'd hate the place, too. Nowhere to go, too much work, an old cabin with a dirt floor."

The roaring in her ears stopped. The Eight Bar cabin had wooden floors, even if they were uneven. The pump brought water right into the house. Maybe in fifty years there would be gas or electricity. She couldn't help smiling.

"What is so funny?" Saul Coffin demanded. "I'm offering you the opportunity to go back to Massachusetts to our old jobs! This...this whole state smells like a bog pit!" He lowered his voice, "Everyone makes fun of the way I talk! They won't stop teasing me!"

"Same thing happened to me," she said, sure of herself now, confident and happy. "I got over it. I like it here. I'm staying."

She turned and walked away without a backward glance. She sat down beside Ned Avery, her boss, her friend, the man who bought her an overcoat because he cared, the man she taught to waltz and lost her heart to. There wasn't going to be any delicate way to declare herself, but she didn't care. If she was wrong, then she was wrong. She had no doubt she could find a job in Cheyenne. Maybe Ned would come around, and maybe he wouldn't, but she knew she could manage. His strength had made her stronger.

Ned stared at her. "Better tell me what happened."

"Saul Coffin is a milky boy who can't stand the smell of manure and has a deathly fear of hard work," she said. "He is going back to Massachusetts and his old job, and demands I come along, too, if I pay part of my way. I said no."

His expression softened. Katie held out her hand, only to discover that his hand was already extended. They clasped hands.

"I have a confession to make," he began. "I've been doing my own whining. I never liked the ranch, I'm tired of hard work and I wish for an easier life. I'm no more a prize than Mr. Milky Boy over there, who looks like he can't believe that you walked away from him."

"Could you really sell the ranch?" she asked, wanting to know his heart.

"I could in December and January," he told her. He had moved closer and his other arm circled her waist. She watched his expression soften. "But then the calves come in late February, and I'm busy through March. April storms dump snow on the little fellows, and I have to keep them close to home."

"And?"

"Spring comes, and you wouldn't believe how green the pastures are. The calves that made it through the storms are strutting their stuff. I have new colts by then, too. I'm growing more and more grass for hay, and it smells so good along about July. I'll be eternally riding fence and coming home late." He paused and took a deep breath. "You have to promise me not to worry so much."

She heard what he was really saying, and her hand automatically went to the bridge of her nose to stop her tears. "I really couldn't leave your father, either, because we haven't come to the end of *A Tale of Two Cities*." She leaned closer, enjoying the fragrance of his aftershave. She pressed her cheek against his and heard his sharp intake of breath. "Besides, before I said goodbye to your father, he said you had a Christmas present for me."

He chuckled, the soft sound for her alone. "I suppose I do. Hold out your hand, Katherine."

She did. Ned fumbled in his vest pocket, which meant

she noticed for the first time that he was wearing the green brocade cravat she had made him, along with a white shirt and his good suit. Probably his only suit. What did a stockman need a suit for, except for weddings and funerals and the occasional dance, where he was supposed to find someone to marry and didn't?

The ring was gold, with a smallish green stone. It fit on her middle finger, so that's where it stayed.

"One of us should propose," she told him. "I'm willing."

"Even when it's December and January and I'm ready to sell the place and move somewhere warm?" he asked, suddenly serious.

Katie touched his face and his lips automatically went to the palm of her hand. She kissed his hand in turn. She wanted him, plain, simple and soon.

"You won't sell the place *this* December and January," she whispered. "Not with me there loving you. I know your bed will fit the room you built me."

He laughed at that, a quiet laugh so intimate that she wanted to drag him to the desk clerk, demand a room and take the stairs two at a time. "Katherine, would you believe me if I told you that earlier this week when you were out milking, I measured my bed against your bed? It'll fit."

They laughed together. She looked around. Saul Coffin was gone. "He was going to make me pay half my fare again."

"What a pup. He'll be better off in Massachusetts. Tomorrow morning, you and I will toddle over to the courthouse when it opens, for a license to wed. I will pay the entire amount, and we'll find the justice of the peace."

She giggled at that.

"We'll stay a night or two here in the Plainsman." He gave his timepiece a long look, then cleared his throat and looked remarkably young. "Uh, about tonight... We'll be jumping the gun by about twelve hours. Do you really, seriously mind?"

Katie put her hand over his watch. "No! I have a better

idea than the justice of the peace. That Christmas party in the Presbyterian Church is tomorrow night? Why don't we…?"

"…wait to get married in Medicine Bow?" he asked. "Turn it into a wedding party?"

"Your father will be there," she reminded him, which made his eyes fill with tears. "Don't, my dearest," she said, trying out the words and liking them. "He's alive to see you married." She touched his face. "Maybe he'll live to see our first child."

Ned put his hands on her cheeks and touched her forehead with his, then pulled her close. His overcoat was unbuttoned, so Katie put her arms inside it, enjoying the feel of his back.

He kissed her several times, until she wanted to push as close against him as she could. The lobby was deserted, except for the desk clerk regarding them with considerable attention. He rented them a room for the night, and Katie never even thought to be afraid when Ned locked the door to the room and pulled her even closer.

No words were spoken for a long time; none were needed. Not until Katie relaxed into his arms, enjoying the warmth of his so quickly familiar bare embrace, did she have a question for him. It had nothing to do with what they had just done, the first of many times, she knew already.

"You've been calling me Katherine," she whispered into his neck. "Why?"

"It seemed like a wife's name," he whispered back. "I started that a while back, didn't I?"

She kissed his chest, closing her eyes as his hand rested so lightly on her hair.

True to the conductor's predictions, the westbound Union Pacific was delayed by snow east of them. Not until well into the next evening did the train pull into Medicine Bow. They left her luggage at the depot and walked toward the Presbyterian Church, well lit and with blanketed horses tied to hitching rails. Someone played the organ. The strains of

"Silent Night" made their way into the night, where snow had begun to fall again.

They walked slowly, matching each other's steps, stopping to watch the stars overhead, kissing now and then, and in no hurry, because their lives together stretched before them.

They stopped at the church's front door. "I'm almost afraid to go in," Ned told her.

Katherine tightened her grip on his arm. "This from the man who breaks horses, brands anything that holds still long enough, and tells *me* not to get tight-mouthed if he's late for supper?"

"That one," Ned said.

There was just enough light for Katherine to see he was smiling. "The man who had better marry me since I did extraordinary things last night without benefit of clergy?"

"That one, too," he said and joined in her laughter. "Oh, hell, let's give this door a push."

They started to push and nearly fell inside because some-one must have heard them laughing on the steps. Welcoming hands pulled them inside the warmth of the church's vesti-bule, decorated with artificial ivy, probably because no one considered Wyoming sagebrush appropriate.

The Bradleys, Peter with them, pulled them right inside the chapel, and up to Mr. Avery, who sat close to the front beside the doctor. Katherine waited for her nearly almost husband to speak. A glance showed her how Ned struggled, so she knelt beside the man she was so soon to call father.

"Mr. Avery, we decided to get married right here and right now," she said. "Ned has a license and I'm thinking you can produce a minister."

She noted with amusement that many partygoers gave her quizzical looks, so she repeated herself, using a little less Maine and a little more Wyoming. General applause followed, reminding her just how much she knew she would love this place.

And then they stood in front of the minister, who looked just a little silly in his Saint Nicholas costume, but only just a little. Ned had taken his brother by the hand, pulled him close and pronounced him best man, which made Mr. Avery nod in appreciation.

Katherine paid close attention to *Dearly Beloved*, then closed her eyes and felt gratitude seep into her heart. She said "Ayuh" instead of "I do," which made her really almost husband shake with silent laughter. The ring came off and went back on, with a whispered promise from the now husband to find one that fit, and soon.

The minister urged a little kiss, which occupied them a brief second. She already knew from sound, recent experience that Ned Avery was capable of a much longer and deeper kiss, but that wasn't information anyone in the chapel needed.

Katherine looked into Ned's eyes then, knowing it lay in her power to make him happy well beyond the Decembers and Januarys of his hard life. From the look of real contentment on his face, he knew it, too.

* * * * *

# CHRISTMAS IN
# SALVATION FALLS

## KELLY BOYCE

To my own Christmas Crew, thanks for always making the holidays a time of laughter and wonderful memories—ShayFaye and Bone; Craig, Joanne, Owen, Natalie and Dylan; Alyson, Allan, Malcolm, Maggie and Gabriel; Riley (Rileymas!); and, of course, to John and Cedar. Love you all and Merry Christmas!

Dear Reader,

When the opportunity to take part in this year's Harlequin Christmas anthology came about, I jumped at the chance! Not only is Christmas a huge event in my family, but also I was thrilled with the idea of getting to spend it in Salvation Falls with past characters and new ones searching for their own kind of Merry Christmas.

The idea for Morgan and Willa's story came from the image of a woman sweeping the porch and a man watching her from a distance. I began to wonder who she was and why he seemed so shocked to see her there. After that, the story and the characters gradually unfolded, telling me their secrets, past and present.

I love the idea of second chances, and thoroughly enjoyed spending Christmas in Salvation Falls. I hope you will, too.

*Kelly Boyce*

# Chapter One

*Salvation Falls, Colorado, 1877*

Years had passed since Morgan Trent had seen her last.

So many, in fact, he had convinced himself his memories of her had dimmed. He'd worked hard to shove them into the recesses of his mind where he kept all the things he preferred not to think about. But now, sitting atop Buckeye, saddle sore and in desperate need of a place to rest his travel-weary bones, those memories stood not two hundred feet away, bright as day, mocking him. Turns out he hadn't locked them away as tightly as he'd hoped.

Maybe coming to Salvation Falls had been a mistake. He'd spent over half a decade running from the pain of his past. From mistakes he didn't care to admit to. Now here he was, face-to-face with it—with her—once more.

When Uncle Bertram had asked Morgan to join his law practice in Salvation Falls, it had taken a full year for him to make the decision to accept. It had been years since he'd practiced the law. Since he'd done much of anything that required brain over brawn, or which meant staying in one place for too long.

What his uncle had failed to mention in his letter, however, was that the woman Morgan had loved and lost would be here waiting for him when he arrived.

Well, perhaps *waiting* was the wrong word. After all, she'd stopped waiting, then up and married another man. The pain of losing her had filled him with such hurt and anger, he'd turned his back on lawyering. There hadn't seemed to be much point. It was because of her he had been determined to set down roots, make himself a success. He would have been perfectly happy to have left Mississippi to head West and set up a small practice like his uncle, but one did not marry the daughter of the great Lyle Stanford and expect her to live an ordinary life in an ordinary town with ordinary things. That much was made clear the moment he expressed an interest in courting the timber baron's daughter.

So what the blue blazes was she doing here—in Salvation Falls of all places—sweeping the porch of a boardinghouse that bore her name?

A sane man would turn tail and ride right back out of town on the road he came in on. But night fast approached, bringing with it a bitter wind and impending storm. He could feel it on his skin. Taste it on his tongue. He'd spent enough time on the trail to judge the change in weather.

Besides, he'd come here for a reason. The life of a drifter had grown old quickly. Uncle Bertram's offer allowed him a chance to start over and he'd be an idiot not to take it. Leaving wasn't in his plans. But upon arriving, he'd found his uncle's office and living quarters charred by fire. The idea he'd come all this way only to find a grave had twisted his stomach into knots. Thankfully, the proprietor of the Klein Hotel had assured him Bertram was alive and well and currently living in a room above the jail. Morgan had gone there next, but the room had been empty with no sign of his uncle. With night and the storm fast approaching, he'd set his mind to finding shelter, but both hotels and boardinghouses had been full with ranch hands and other drifters like him hunkering down to wait out the weather. Maybe partake in some Christmas cheer. He planned on doing the first. As for Christmas, he'd stopped celebrating that holiday a long time ago.

The remaining boardinghouse at the end of Main Street was his last hope. He stared at the sign, painted white with bright red letters. It swung in the breeze, mocking him.

Red's Boarding House.

He pulled Buckeye up short, earning an irritated snort from his horse.

*Red.* He'd been the only one to call her that. Hope of receiving a warm welcome surged inside of him, unwanted and uncalled for. He tamped it down. No point going there. Too much had happened to be thinking that way. Besides, fate had a way of treating Morgan with contempt when it came to the woman standing on the porch.

Regardless, Red at least owed him a room at the inn after breaking his heart by marrying Clancy Barstow when she'd promised to wait for him.

Granted, maybe leaving town three days before their wedding hadn't been the best timing on his part, but he'd needed to get out from under her father's thumb. Lyle ruled with an iron fist and didn't always walk on the right side of the law while doing so. The part of Morgan that believed in truth and justice couldn't keep working with a man who showed such disrespect for the law.

Red had claimed to understand when he'd climbed through her bedroom window to give her the news. Cocky and self-assured, he'd told her it would take him six months to build his practice and make his fortune. Ah, the ego of youth. He'd thought success would simply fall into his lap because he wished it so.

Six months had turned into eight and then twelve. The pressure to attain the kind of success needed to give Willa Stanford the life she was accustomed to mounted and instead of answering her regular letters, he'd avoided them. A cowardly move, he admitted. Truth was, he hadn't wanted to admit his failure. Couldn't stand the idea of looking into the eyes of the woman he loved to find disappointment staring back at him.

Besides, what were a few more months? She'd promised to wait. They'd sealed it with a kiss beneath the mistletoe she'd hung in her bedroom. Morgan breathed out. He could still recall the taste of her on his tongue.

But the kiss had meant nothing. Nor had her promise to

wait. A fact clearly highlighted when a year later she'd sent him a letter informing him she was marrying her father's second in command—Clancy Barstow.

He'd received that particular letter on Christmas Eve, six years ago.

A burst of wind sliced through his sheepskin jacket. Buckeye snorted once again, shuffling his feet to announce his annoyance at the delay.

"Fine," Morgan muttered. He nudged the horse forward. What other choice did he have? Red was his last hope of finding lodging and he was just brazen enough to demand she make room for him. The well-bred Willa Stanford he remembered would be too polite to turn someone in need away.

As he drew closer, it struck him how quickly he'd recognized her, even from a distance. Would she recognize him as easily? Likely not. The clean-cut lawyer she'd known was long gone, shucked off and left in pieces on the trails he'd traveled, as far north as Montana Territory and as far west as Nevada. But he wasn't a young buck any longer. Pushing thirty, he was saddle-weary, having spent the years exhausting himself body and mind with physical labor, the kind that kept him busy enough so that he didn't think about the life he'd dreamed of. The life that had been within his grasp before it had all come crashing down.

Morgan watched Willa as he approached. She'd turned her back to him as she swept the dusting of snow off the front porch of the boardinghouse. Her wild mahogany hair was hard to miss, the deep red standing out like a beacon. Or a warning.

He kept riding toward it either way.

His brain churned, trying to determine what convergence of events had brought her here. She'd known about Uncle Bertram. Morgan had shared his uncle's regular letters with her. Morgan's parents had died when he was fifteen and an elderly cousin had taken him in, but it was Bertram who'd sent money to ensure he had proper schooling and his uncle's love of the law had inspired Morgan to follow in his footsteps.

When Lyle Stanford had offered him a job, he thought he was well on his way. He'd work hard, make a name for himself, save up some money—then he'd head West and join his uncle in Salvation Falls. He'd find a good woman, settle down and have a family. Live a good life, a simple life, filled with the kind of love and laughter he'd known until scarlet fever had swept through his home and robbed him of his parents.

But plans of a simple life were put on hold the moment he'd laid eyes on Willa Stanford. He'd known that if he wanted to marry her he would need to prove he could provide her with a life of comfort and plenty. Willa hadn't been the type of young lady you packed up and dragged out West.

And yet…here she was.

It made no sense. Had she come here hoping to find him? Unlikely. She was married to Barstow now. He gritted his teeth at the thought of seeing that rogue again. They'd been rivals at Stanford Timber, each vying for the boss's praise, the next promotion, Lyle's daughters' attentions… The eldest daughter, Lettie, was considered the jewel of the family— blonde and delicate with a vivacious nature that commanded everyone's attention. Willa on the other hand was quiet and sensible with a tender heart Morgan had been determined to keep and protect.

Even if it meant working for a man as crooked as Lyle Stanford. But swallowing his conscience proved a harder task than Morgan had imagined. As their courtship continued one thing became clear—if he married Willa now, Lyle would own him for good. There'd be no breaking free.

With each passing day the fear of such a fate had gripped him harder until he feared it would strangle him. He had to leave, to make his own way, or he'd never be able to sleep at night. Willa had held no delusions when it came to her father. He ruled his daughters much as he did his business. She'd given Morgan her blessing, more or less. Maybe less once she'd learned it meant him leaving town. But regardless, she had promised to wait for him.

Yet, instead, she'd broken her promise and married Barstow. Morgan spent the next six years drifting from town to town, picking up work where he found it and never staying anywhere long. The only company he kept was a posse of regrets that traveled with him wherever he went.

The tired clomp of his horse's hooves on the frozen dirt road was a reminder of how far they'd come. Cold wind whistled through the alley between the boardinghouse and the post office next door, cutting through his coat like it was nothing. All he wanted was a hot meal and a stiff drink—maybe two—a warm stable for Buckeye and the oblivion of sleep.

But he had to get through Red first.

He dismounted and hitched Buckeye to the post near the bottom of the steps leading up to the porch. He took off his hat and rested a booted foot on the first step. His muscles protested even that small movement and exhaustion threatened to drop him where he stood. Lucifer, but he was tired.

"Hey, Red."

Her shoulders stiffened and she froze midsweep, the broom hovering a few inches off the porch. When she turned to face him, any hope he'd had that he'd find her in a generous mood blew past him on a bitter breeze.

Words jammed in his throat. Sweet mother of mercy. When he'd left her, she'd been a wispy thing with pale skin, freckles and a mass of mahogany hair he longed to sink his hands into, but the vision before him now—well that was something else. Her hair hadn't changed, but the rest—well, it left him thinking about things he had no business thinking about.

Morgan took a fortifying breath. "Hi, Red."

The use of her nickname caused a fire to kick up in her hazel eyes. Not a *happy to see you* fire either. More like an *I'll skewer you with the pointy end of my broom* kind. He cleared his throat and took another step. The fire blazed brighter and by the third step, self-preservation kicked in and Morgan stopped.

He'd given her that nickname. She'd come into her father's

office one day, a quiet young girl of sixteen and gifted him with the sweetest smile he'd ever seen. He'd never stood a chance. The nickname wasn't all that original, he admitted, but it seemed a far sight better than calling her Freckles or String Bean, and it had been bestowed with affection in the way only a nineteen-year-old boy with limited experience could manage. The other men had teased him, but he hadn't cared. He'd liked her. Then he'd loved her.

And then he'd left her.

He pushed the memory and the shadow of guilt that came with it away. In the grand scheme of things, his sins were nowhere near as egregious as hers.

One dark eyebrow lifted. "I'm afraid you have me mistaken for someone else. My name is Mrs. Barstow."

His mouth tightened. As if he could have forgotten. As if the pain of her marrying another man had dimmed over the years. Morgan advanced another step and Willa gripped the broom in front of her with both hands. If he made it to the top of the stairs without getting bayoneted with the broom handle, he'd consider himself lucky.

It was his turn to glare. "We really gonna pretend like we don't know each other, Red?"

"We *don't* know each other," she said, standing above him on the porch with strands of her wild hair blowing in the hostile breeze. "The man I knew could be counted on to keep his promises. Are you that man?"

"I remember you promising to wait for me," he shot back, then turned his gaze toward the door of the boardinghouse. "Where is your dearly beloved, by the way? Perhaps I should pass along my belated felicitations on your nuptials."

"He's buried six feet under." The words came out clipped and cold and something passed through Morgan that he hadn't been prepared for. Shock? Hope?

"I'm sorry, Red." The words rang hollow and she didn't acknowledge them. Instead they stood staring at one another, a field of all the things left unsaid lying fallow between them.

This was not going well at all.

Morgan pulled off a leather glove and rubbed at his eyes. They burned from the cold and grit of a long day's ride. He didn't have the stamina to go a few rounds with her, to try and convince her he was the injured party here. What did it matter anyway? It was a lifetime ago and they had both moved on. Or, at least, she had. He'd mostly just moved around.

He let out a long breath, white puffs of air clouding the space around him. He was minutes away from collapsing where he stood and like it or not, he needed a hot meal and warm bed more than he needed to persuade her she'd been in the wrong, not him.

"You got a room or not, Red?"

"Not." The one word summed up her feelings toward him. "You best try somewhere else."

"The other boardinghouses and hotels are full up. You're my last chance."

She let out a harsh laugh, a sound he'd never heard from her before. "That doesn't bode well for you, now does it?"

The wind buffeted him and Willa's skirts pressed against the new curves that were proving to be a distinct distraction. He looked away. He needed to focus. To reason with her. Convince her to let him stay before his legs buckled from sheer exhaustion right here on her step. He changed tactics, focusing on the present and not the past. He motioned toward the boardinghouse. "You and Clancy seem to have done all right for yourselves before he passed on."

"Clancy had nothing to do with this." The bitterness in her voice caught him off guard and her eyes flashed, enhancing the sharp angles of her face. "He got himself killed in the Black Hills. This place is my doing. No one else's."

Morgan struggled to imagine how the pampered daughter of a timber baron had managed to go from widowed in the Black Hills of South Dakota to owning a boardinghouse in Salvation Falls, all of her own accord. He came up blank. The young woman he'd known had had everything done for her. It was one of the reasons he'd been determined to earn his fortune, to keep her in the only lifestyle she'd ever known. The fact that she hadn't needed that was a punch to the gut.

He left the subject of Clancy alone. It was a sore spot for both of them by the looks of it. "Look, Red, I've got nowhere else to go and the storm's comin' in fast." He nodded toward the distance where dark clouds tumbled over the tips of the mountains heading straight toward them like a dark omen. "If I ride out and get caught in it, that'll be that. Looks like my life is in your hands."

The tension in Willa's shoulders gave way a little and relief swept through him. She wouldn't send him out to meet his death. At least not this night.

"There's a room on the top floor. You can stay until the storm passes. Then I want you gone. Huck will check you in." She nodded toward the door then turned her back on him as she continued sweeping, moving to the far corner as if to put as much distance as possible between them.

# Chapter Two

Willa stared out of her bedroom window at the whiteness swirling about, making it impossible to see the mercantile on the opposite side of the street from her boardinghouse.

Fate mocked her.

The storm Morgan had claimed was coming had arrived hard and fast through the night. Not that him being right offered any solace. The weather rendered her housebound while Mother Nature unleashed her fury, hurling it down upon Salvation Falls from the tip of the mountains to where the town nestled in the valley below.

She closed her eyes, but the sudden darkness offered no relief, only memories.

*Once I get my feet under me, I'll come back for you, Red. I'll come back and I'll kiss you right here underneath this mistletoe and make you my wife, just like we planned. But I can't do it now. I can't live a life ruled by your father.*

At first, his words had broken her heart. They were supposed to be married in three days. But then he'd kissed her. The touch of his lips seared into every part of her. His mouth had been soft and gentle at first, then hungry and desperate. He'd never kissed her like that before and something inside of her had awakened—something she hadn't even known was asleep. When he'd pulled away, she'd known he felt the same. Shock had brightened his blue eyes and he'd stood motionless, staring at her as if seeing her for the first time.

In that moment, she'd known for certain, he wouldn't leave her. Not now. Not ever. Not after a kiss like that.

She'd been wrong.

A soft knock on her door pulled her away from the mess swirling outside the room and inside her heart. Likely Huck had come to fetch her. With most of her boarders stuck inside for the day, they would need all hands on deck to keep things running smoothly.

"Coming," she called out, as she passed through her bedroom into the sitting area beyond. Huck was a sweet boy. She'd taken him in after his pa had died, but at fourteen years of age, he weighed no more than a hundred pounds soaking wet. He'd be no match for the rowdy cowpokes if they got out of control. During the storm they'd had last February, some of the men had kicked up a ruckus that had left her with broken dishes, a cracked window and two bloodied cowpokes. She did not need that kind of headache again.

She pulled open the door and came face-to-face with a broad chest dressed in faded flannel, blocking her view of the narrow hallway.

Definitely not Huck.

She glanced up and her heart gave a swift jolt when she fixed on a pair of eyes the shade of a summer sky, making her forget all about the storm raging just beyond the walls of the boardinghouse.

By ginger, it wasn't fair how handsome he'd become!

She gripped the door handle but stopped short of slamming it in Morgan's face. She would not give him the satisfaction of knowing his presence here rattled her as much as it did. Not that he would care. Likely he hadn't given her a moment's consideration since he'd jumped out of her window six years ago, stomping all over her tender heart as soon as his feet had hit the ground below.

"Is there something I can do for you, Mr. Trent?" Keep it formal. She was the proprietor of this establishment and he nothing more than a paying guest. "Is the room not to your liking? You are more than welcome to leave if you find the accommodations lacking."

Morgan looked over her head to the window beyond and raised one golden eyebrow. "Don't think that'd be advisable."

"It wasn't advice. It was a suggestion." She smiled sweetly. At least she hoped that's what she was doing. Her head buzzed standing so near to him after all this time. The feeling was about as welcome as a rattlesnake.

Morgan leaned against the doorframe, his hands loosely pushed into the front pockets of his denims, a study in lean masculinity that surrounded her from every direction. Much to her dismay, time had not diminished the effect he had on her. Standing here, separated by mere inches, her disobedient heart trembled at his nearness. How she hated her weakness where he was concerned. Shouldn't the years have dulled that at least a little?

"The room is fine," Morgan said, in that slow, hypnotic drawl of his that always reminded her of slipping into a warm bath. "Just thought I oughta give you this."

He pulled one hand out of his pocket and drew out several bills, folded in half. He held them out to her.

She crossed her arms over her chest. "What's this?"

"Room and board." He shot her a half smile and her hands fisted, pressing her knuckles against her ribs. The effect of that smile sped through her like a lightning strike, down into places she hadn't given much thought for several years. "Didn't figure you'd let me stay out of the kindness of your heart."

He had that much right. She unfolded one arm and reached for the money, but Morgan didn't release it, forcing her fingertips to rest against his. They were rough on the edges—a working man's hands. Not like Clancy's. He'd never done a hard day's work in his life. Morgan's touch invaded the blood in her veins and burned through her like venom.

He tugged at the money and pulled her attention back to his handsome face. "How about we call a truce, Red?"

"A truce? I wasn't aware we were at war." She dropped her gaze and it landed on their hands. Warmth spread up her arm and threatened to invade her heart. She needed to let go, but she couldn't seem to get the message from her head to her hand.

"You know what I mean. We didn't part on the best of terms."

She glanced up at him sharply. "Then you remember it differently than I do, because I distinctly remember us parting with a kiss and you promising to return."

Anger blazed in his eyes. That was ridiculous. What did he have to be angry about? "And I remember *you* promising to wait for me."

"I did wait!"

"Is that a fact, *Mrs. Barstow*?"

His insinuation knocked the wind out of her. His letters had stopped months before her father had forced her to marry Clancy. She'd balked at the idea, even going so far as to flat-out refuse to do the great Lyle Stanford's bidding, but her father would not countenance such behavior. He'd threatened to disown her, to toss her out onto the street with nothing but the clothes on her back unless she did his bidding. What other choice had she had?

"You made your interest in marrying me clear by your continued absence. An absence that was your decision, Mr. Trent, not mine. But if it gives you any solace, marriage to Clancy proved a miserable experience and I've learned my lesson in that regard. I make my own way in this world now. I don't spend time fretting about you or the past." The lie tripped off her tongue and left a sour aftertaste.

Truth of the matter was, she thought of Morgan all the time. When she saw happy couples like the Becketts or the Donovans, when she heard children running about laughing and playing and when Morgan's uncle, whose twinkling blue eyes were so much like his nephew's, came to dine at her establishment. Her memories lived just below the surface and made their presence known on a regular basis.

Morgan's finger brushed against hers. The simple touch sent an onslaught of longing and hurt through her veins until her blood sizzled and burned. Her heart whispered its need to know what had happened to him—why he hadn't come back for her, why he'd stopped writing. She ignored it. It wasn't

fair the way his presence, his touch, still spoke to her heart
in that secret language they'd once shared.

"I don't want to fight, Red."

"Fine."

He shifted his feet, but did not break the connection where
their fingers touched.

"Thank you for sending up the bath last night. It was
kind of you."

She still didn't know what had possessed her. He didn't
deserve it, but he'd looked so cold and weary and her heart
had overridden her common sense. Then she'd spent the rest
of the night tormented by images of him soaking in the big tin
tub, the ends of his hair curling and rivulets of water wind-
ing down his neck onto his chest before beating a path to—

Willa jerked her hand away, pulling the money with her.
Mercy, this storm could not wear itself out soon enough for
her liking! It had been difficult enough dealing with all these
urges for him when she was nothing more than an innocent
girl, but she was a widow now, and while Clancy had definitely failed to elicit any excitement in that particular area,
she knew instinctively with Morgan, it would be different.
He had a knowing about him, an ability to make her quiver
with the smallest of touches and the way he looked at her
now, with that sad, lopsided grin that made his clear blue eyes
sparkle like newly fallen snow kissed by sunlight...well, it
did not bode well for one's state of mind, is all.

"Breakfast is being served downstairs if you're hungry.
Good day, Mr. Trent."

Willa stepped out, pulling her door closed with more force
than she intended. With her jaw locked, she brushed past
him and made her way to the stairs. She needed distance.
She needed to break this crazy connection that crackled between them like dry wood near a hot flame.

Frustration filled her. Was this how she would spend the
holiday, with the specter of Christmas Past haunting her
every move?

Before she could answer that question, the hum of voices

from the dining hall rose in volume, sharp and angry. Her heart sank.

"Oh, not again!" She picked up her skirts and rushed down the stairs and into the dining hall, Morgan Trent temporarily forgotten.

Morgan had been in enough rooming houses and saloons to recognize the telltale signs of a brouhaha kicking up. It was clear that was exactly what was occurring on the other side of the archway Willa had just run through as if her skirts were on fire. What the blazes did she think she was doing charging into the middle of that? When a bunch of yahoos got to throwing punches, they weren't about to stop and reassess their behavior because a woman told them to do so. No matter how beautiful that woman was.

He rushed down the steps after her. It hadn't taken long for the ruckus to turn into a full-blown melee. Inside the dining area, the boy Huck cowered in the corner behind an overturned table, cringing as a plate crashed against it. In the middle of the room, standing on top of a table, was a large beefy man with coal-black hair and arms thick as tree trunks. He had one man in a headlock and brandished what appeared to be a ladle in his other hand.

The situation would have been comical if Red hadn't suddenly lost her mind and run straight into the fracas. The girl he had once known would have run in the opposite direction and found a safe place to hide until it was over. She sure as heck would not have thrown herself into the middle of it. The fool woman was going to get herself killed!

Morgan fought his way through, pushing and punching in an effort to reach her and pull her to safety. Someone slammed into his back and he staggered sideways, regaining his footing. Where was she? He turned around, looking for Red and ducked just in time to keep from getting cold-cocked in the jaw but as he straightened, something hard and unforgiving crashed against his skull, rattling his teeth. Stars exploded inside his head then everything faded to black.

A cold cloth pressed against his forehead but it offered little relief from the pounding in the back of his skull. What in blue blazes had happened? A hand tapped his cheek, gentle at first then with a bit more force.

"Morgan?"

*Red.* What was she doing here? Where was he? His memories had scattered and he struggled to piece them back together. He was in Salvation Falls. Red was here. She'd run into the middle of a dustup like a mad woman and he'd gone after her. The memories stopped there.

He opened his eyes and stared up at her, waiting for his vision to focus. She didn't have a hair out of place. Well, at least no more than usual. Oh, but she was a pretty thing. The years had definitely been kind in that regard, though her personality was far more acerbic than he recalled. Had marriage to Clancy Barstow made her that way?

"You okay? Are you hurt?"

She raised an eyebrow. "I'm not the one lying on the floor."

He swept his gaze around to survey the damage but he couldn't see much past the other two bodies crouching on either side of him. One was the beefy bear of a man who still held his ladle. Strange thing to bring to a fight, Morgan thought. The other man, with brown hair, a felt hat and a couple of days' worth of stubble shadowing his jaw appeared untouched by the melee. Unlike him, apparently.

"What happened?"

The man in the hat spoke. "You got hit by a chair."

"A chair?" Taken out by a piece of furniture. How valiant.

The man nodded, then held out his hand. "Caleb Beckett. You new in town?"

Morgan hesitated, then reciprocated because he didn't seem to have much of a choice unless he wanted to be rude. "Yeah. Morgan Trent."

Beckett tilted his head to one side, studying him. "Bertram's kin?"

"Nephew."

"Hmm."

The man clearly didn't waste breath on excessive words.

The man Morgan compared to a slab of beef crouched to his left, chucked him in the shoulder with a meaty paw. "Ya think ya can stand, then, boyo?"

"Yes. I'm sure I can stand." He'd been hit on the head, he wasn't an invalid and his pride didn't particularly take to the suggestion he was, especially in front of Red.

"Well, up ta your feet, then."

The man grabbed his arm and hauled him up in one fluid motion like he weighed nothing, but as soon as Morgan's feet were under him the room started tipping one way then the other. He blindly reached out in an effort to steady himself.

"Whoa, there," Beckett said, disappearing, then something scraped against the floor behind him. The ladle-carrying bear of a man put a heavy hand on Morgan's shoulder and pushed him down. He dropped like a stone into an awaiting chair.

Red sighed. And not out of relief that he was okay, given the frustrated twist of her lips. "Just sit tight for a minute. Fritz, give me a hand up."

A hand up?

Before Morgan could make sense of what she'd said, Red climbed on top of one of the few tables that remained upright and shouted out to the men in the room. While he'd been out cold, the ruckus had quieted down and the rowdies were littered about the dining hall licking their wounds.

"Excuse me, gentlemen. May I have your attention, please?"

The murmur in the room faded away. Morgan sat mute. When had the quiet, proper girl he'd proposed to become this woman who jumped on top of tables and commanded the attention of everyone within earshot using a tone of voice that brooked no disobedience?

Willa cleared her throat and glared at the men like a stern schoolmarm. "Seeing as the lot of you have just destroyed my dining hall, no further meals will be coming from the kitchen until you have rectified the matter and put this room back to rights. Anything busted must be repaired, and funds collected should be given to Fritz to replace any broken dishes. I want the floor swept up and this room looking the way it did before you all decided to misbehave like spoiled children. Do I make myself clear?"

Silence reigned across the room.

Morgan blinked. What had happened in the ensuing years to transform her from a rich man's daughter to this? That strange feeling from yesterday—a bitter mixture of guilt and hope—resurfaced and poked at him. He shook it off. He didn't have anything to feel guilty about. And he sure as shootin' didn't have anything to hope for, not where Red was concerned.

Willa put her hands on her hips accentuating those sweet curves. Morgan swallowed. Lord help him. Despite everything, he wanted to haul her off that table and carry her back upstairs to discover all the changes he'd missed out on, inside and out.

Her sharp voice quickly cut off that recalcitrant thought. "If any of you are unwilling to fix this place back up, you can pack your bag and leave. Immediately."

"But it's stormin' out there, Mrs. B," one rowdy whined.

Willa shrugged, unmoved. "Then you best dress warmly, Ted."

The room filled with sighs of contrition and a few grumbles, but soon, everyone who could stand did, and the sound of wood scraping against the floor made it clear no one questioned the seriousness behind their proprietress's threat.

Morgan looked at Willa with newfound respect. It took a lot of guts to stand up to a roomful of men who had torn up her dining hall and demand recompense. But she hadn't flinched and the men had hung their heads like sulky children.

What would have happened had she shown that spark of confidence when he'd told her he was leaving? If she'd demanded he take her with him, would he have? Damn! Think of all the heartbreak and misery they could have avoided if she'd only shown this side to him sooner.

*Or if he'd only taken the time to look beyond who she was in the moment to see who she had the ability to become.* He scowled at his conscience, wishing it'd keep its own counsel.

When Willa turned to step down from the table, Morgan pushed himself to his feet and reached for her. She hesitated for the briefest second before placing a hand on his shoulder. He grabbed her waist and helped her down, her body sliding against his, creating a riot of sensation that made his head spin. At this rate, he'd find himself flat on the floor all over again. Though if she landed on top of him, he wouldn't complain.

It felt good to hold her in his arms. He hadn't thought he'd ever experience that again. He closed his eyes and savored the moment.

"Let me go," she whispered, pushing against his chest.

He didn't acquiesce right away. He couldn't. Letting her go, well, that seemed about as wrong as a thing could get.

Willa, unfortunately, disagreed and gave him another shove. Reluctantly, Morgan relinquished his hold, his hands sliding away from her narrow waist. She ducked her head, but not before he saw her cheeks were thoroughly flushed. He smiled. Perhaps she wasn't as immune to him as she pretended to be. What that meant exactly, he couldn't figure out. Fact was, he was having trouble making sense of anything at the moment. Between the riot her closeness caused and the way the room insisted on spinning, he was having trouble thinking lucidly.

She cleared her throat and avoided his gaze. "Are you certain you're feeling okay, Mr. Trent?"

He smiled down at her. "Parts of me are feeling just fine."

Granted, those parts were all south of his belt buckle and strongly hinting that he needed to kiss that lovely mouth of hers. Perhaps the blow to the head had left him more addled than originally thought.

"Morgan?"

She said his given name. Hell, but that sounded sweet. He was getting a bit tired of the whole *Mr. Trent* business. He just couldn't understand why she sounded so far away, like she was drifting away from him. "I feel a little funny."

"Morgan!"

His view of the room shifted, tilting somehow and then he was falling once again as black dots rushed his vision. He tried to reach for Red, but the darkness claimed him before he could find her.

# Chapter Three

Willa sat next to Morgan's bed where he lay propped up against a bevy of plump pillows. She'd doctored the cut on the back of his head as best she could. Once the storm eased she'd send Huck to fetch Doc Whyte, but until then she feared leaving him alone. Mick Fontana had taken a blow to the head not three months past, he'd gone to bed that night and never woken up again. She wasn't taking any chances Morgan would suffer the same fate.

She didn't bother examining why. She'd do the same for anyone. It didn't make him special. But the worry in her heart refuted this claim. She rubbed at her chest to make the feeling go away but it proved as stubborn as the other parts of her that were convinced that Morgan showing up in Salvation Falls meant something.

"He didn't come here for you," she reminded her foolish heart, letting out a frustrated huff as she sat back in the chair next to Morgan's bed. He hadn't come back for her six years ago like he'd promised, so the notion that he'd traveled West to find her now bordered on ludicrous. Still, when she'd entered the ruckus, she'd heard him behind her, calling out her name. His voice had been filled with urgency. No, not urgency. Fear. Pure, unadulterated fear. For her. Did he still care, maybe even a little? And what if he did? What did that mean exactly?

She wished she could say she felt nothing for him—that time had healed the wounds and faded the memories, but it hadn't. When his eyes had rolled up into his head and his legs had given out beneath him, the same fear she'd heard in his voice rocked her. In an instant she'd realized he might die. That, this time, she would lose him forever.

She pinched the bridge of her nose. This would not do. At all. She needed to wash her hands of him. Send him on his way and pretend he'd never arrived at all. That nothing unusual had happened.

Except something unusual *had* happened.

Morgan had returned. To the wrong place at the wrong time, but he'd returned.

"Why come here now?" she whispered at his inert form. "Why didn't you come back six years ago? If you had, Father wouldn't have forced me to marry Clancy. We could have been together. Happy. I needed you then, not now."

She'd forged her own way in the world since then. It had been hard, and some days she hadn't known if she'd make it through. But she had—the determination to never leave her life in the hands of someone else kept her going. Now she relied on no one but herself. Counting on others only resulted in hurt, heartbreak and humiliation.

Maybe it wasn't the life she'd envisioned. A life that included a home, a husband and a passel of children. She'd accepted that. Sometimes that was just the way things went. But the life she'd built was dependable and constant. This life would never leave her, or disown her or cheat on her. And that was a far sight better than the life she'd had before, so she accepted her lot and was glad for it.

Morgan groaned, a quiet rumble from deep inside his chest. Willa held her breath as his eyelashes flickered. He had the longest lashes, black at the base and tipped with gold at the ends. He opened his eyes and stared at her. Her breath caught as it always had whenever she looked into those eyes, so reminiscent of the Colorado sky on a brilliant summer's day. Not much had changed in that regard, though thin lines that hadn't been there before now fanned out from the corners of his eyes, giving him a bit of a weathered appearance.

What had happened to Morgan after he'd left her? The last letter she'd received indicated his law practice was doing well and then, nothing. The silence had turned deafening as the months wore on. What had occurred after his last letter that turned him from a successful lawyer into a drifter with only a saddlebag full of belongings to his name?

"Please tell me I didn't faint." Morgan's voice, warm and deep, interrupted her thoughts. Relief swept through her. He was fine. He'd have one beast of a headache for a day or two, but he was fine.

"More like passed out."

He winced. "Fantastic. Very heroic."

"Were you trying to be a hero?"

He turned his head and looked at her, the effect potent and exhilarating. "Were you? You went charging in there like a raging bull. What did you think to accomplish?"

Was he chastising her? Had he forgotten this was her establishment? What did he expect her to do—just stand there, wring her hands and fret about it? "I had hoped to diffuse the situation before it got out of control."

"Darlin', it was already out of control before you started running toward it."

*Darlin'*. The term slipped past the barriers around her heart like a thief. She beat it back. Closed the doors. Checked the locks. "So I discovered."

"You scared the hell out of me." He gave her a censuring glare as if he cared what happened to her. A wave of heat rushed through her. She felt too many things when he was near. Time might have softened her memory of the effect he had on her, but this was no memory lying a few feet away. This was reality, and not one she had been prepared for.

"I wasn't thinking about your feelings in that particular moment," she said. Though it might have been the only moment since his arrival when he hadn't dominated her thoughts.

"You weren't thinking at all, from what I saw."

As if he was in a position to take her to task! "I wasn't the one who ended up knocked to the floor, was I?"

The corners of his beautiful mouth turned downward into

a scowl and her lips twitched in response, knowing she'd hit a nerve. Other parts of her body responded too, but she ignored the sensation. It had a bad habit of getting her into trouble where he was concerned.

Willa stood and stretched the muscles in her back. It was best she leave. Too much time spent in Morgan's company had a negative effect on her ability to think straight. "I need to ensure everyone is doing their part to put my dining room back to rights."

"Hold up." His hand wound around her wrist. Heat spread through her like a brush fire, swift and out of control. "Sit for a bit, Red. Talk to me."

"I can't imagine there's anything left to say." Suddenly she did not care to stand here and have him provide an itemized list of the reasons he hadn't come back for her. To hear why he had changed his mind and decided he didn't love her enough after all. "Unless you want to tell me why you're here?"

"I came here to work for Bertram. He sent me a letter about joining his practice. I guess his office was damaged by fire and I was told he is now living above the sheriff's office, but he wasn't there when I went over. I have no idea where he is."

"I suspect Hunter and Meredith took him out to the ranch. Hunter Donovan is the sheriff. Bertram and Hunter's wife, Meredith, are quite close. She's been trying to convince him to move in with them, but so far he's perfectly fine staying in the one room above the jail."

"Sounds like close quarters. Might be I need to stay here for a bit longer until I can find more permanent accommodations. If you'll allow it?"

Nothing good could come of that, but what other choice did she have? He'd been injured in her establishment and a beast of a storm raged outside. "You can stay until you can speak to Bertram and work out an alternative."

"Appreciate it, Red." His grip on her wrist loosened and slipped downward until he held her hand, the intimate touch battering her flagging will. Once upon a time, that touch had meant security to her. A way out from under her father's dictatorship. An escape from a life where she had no say, no choice. Where she was nothing more than a pawn in her father's games. Back then, Morgan had been a safe harbor, a promise of a new, different kind of life. But one day, that safe harbor was gone, leaving in its wake a rocky shore filled with the jagged edges of broken promises and the crashing waves of lost dreams. "You haven't told me how you ended up here yet."

"You haven't asked."

He squeezed her hand. "I'm asking now."

She pursed her lips. He'd lost the right to hear her story after he left her high and dry. But even as her brain made this decree, her knees gave way and she lowered herself back into the chair.

"After Clancy got himself killed in the Black Hills, I had nowhere to go and no one to turn to. He'd tried to swindle Father a year after our wedding and so we were cast out."

Shock registered across his handsome features. "Your father disowned you?"

She nodded. "A year after that, Father died. Lettie's husband Ernest took over the business and subsequently ran it into the ground. Lettie managed to send me a little money before that happened, but it wasn't much."

"I'm sorry, Red. I had no idea."

"Why would you?" She tried unsuccessfully to keep the accusation from her tone, unwilling to accept his sudden concern. "Anyway, I managed to keep the money from Clancy and when he died, I used it to come to Salvation Falls. I suppose after all the stories you told me about the place, it felt familiar."

"Was it what you expected?"

A sharp laugh, devoid of mirth, escaped her. "Nothing was what I expected at that point. I was frightened and alone for the first time in my life. The woman who originally owned this place took me in. And when what little money I had ran out, she allowed me to work for my room and board. A couple of years ago, she passed on and left the place to me."

Morgan stared at her, an unreadable expression darkening his eyes. "That's quite a story, Red. Can't say I ever expected you to be the one to land on your feet. Guess you proved me wrong on that account."

She stood and pulled her hand from his. His lack of faith in her abilities pricked her pride, but the truth was, when she'd arrived here, she'd been as green as could be, despite everything she'd been through. But she'd learned fast. Necessity was a master motivator. "I wasn't trying to prove anything to anyone. I was just trying to survive. What other choice did I have?"

He shook his head and a look of respect settled upon his features. "Some people would have faltered. You didn't. Look at this place, Red. You didn't just survive. You thrived. You should be proud of yourself."

"I am. But everything comes with a price." The words were out before she could stop them. Talking to Morgan had always been so easy and she'd told him all the things she could never tell anyone else. He had a way of listening to her as if he really heard her, as if he took what she said to heart.

Willa stood and straightened her skirt. She'd stayed too long. She couldn't afford to slip back into these easy patterns they'd once shared. It brought her too close to having her heart broken all over again.

"Leaving?"

"I've work to do." She walked to the door and opened it, turning before she left. "Oh, and don't be surprised if you see Lettie."

He sat up sharply then winced, holding a hand to the side of his head. "Your sister? She's here?"

"Arrived six months ago. Turns out Ernest didn't care to live life as a pauper. He's petitioned for divorce and is now living with a wealthy widow."

"So you took her in?"

She shrugged. She and Lettie had never had the easiest

# "FAST FIVE" READER SURVEY

Your participation entitles you to:
✴ **4 Thank-You Gifts Worth Over $20!**

*Complete the survey in minutes.*

## Get 2 FREE Books

*See inside for details.*

Dear Reader,

Since you are a lover of our books, your opinions are important to us... and so is your time.

That's why we made sure your **"FAST FIVE" READER SURVEY** can be completed in just a few minutes. Your answers to the five questions will help us remain at the forefront of women's fiction.

And, as a thank-you for participating, we'd like to send you **4 FREE THANK-YOU GIFTS!**

Enjoy your gifts with our appreciation,

*Pam Powers*

▲ If offer card is missing write to: Reader Service, P.O. Box 1867, Buffalo, NY 14240-1867 or visit www.ReaderService.com ▲

**BUSINESS REPLY MAIL**
FIRST-CLASS MAIL    PERMIT NO. 717    BUFFALO, NY

POSTAGE WILL BE PAID BY ADDRESSEE

**READER SERVICE**
PO BOX 1867
BUFFALO NY 14240-9952

NO POSTAGE
NECESSARY
IF MAILED
IN THE
UNITED STATES

of relationships. Lettie had always blamed Willa for their mother's death that had arrived so soon after her birth. But she was all the family Willa had. "If it hadn't been for the money Lettie had sent me after Father died, I don't know what would have become of me. In a way, she saved me. It only seemed right I return the favor."

"Does she help out around here?"

Willa twisted her mouth into a semblance of a smile. "Only if you consider constantly criticizing everything helpful. Now, I need to go. Once the weather clears, I will send word to Bertram that you've arrived."

The sooner she could do that, the sooner Morgan would be out from underfoot and she could get on with her life.

But even as she told herself that, her heart whispered something different. It whispered that her life had just done an about-turn and there was nothing short of leaving town on the next train that she could do about it.

Morgan spent a good portion of the day drifting in and out of sleep. By the time he finally woke for good, the storm had burned itself out. Orange and purple streaked across the sky beyond his window, the last of the sun's light illuminating the snow-covered tips of the mountains in the distance. The scene robbed him of breath and for a few minutes, he simply lay there and watched the sun kiss the day goodbye. It was moments like this when he knew coming to Salvation Falls to finally put down some roots had been the right thing to do. Not that he'd expected to have the life he'd once imagined. That dream had been destroyed long ago.

Or so he'd thought.

But now Red was here. And the dreams that had burned to cinder and ash all those years ago sparked anew, like tiny embers that had yet to give up and fizzle out. All he'd ever wanted was to build a home filled with life and love like his parents had had, but somewhere along the way he'd got caught up in the idea that he'd achieve that with success and money. That's what Lyle Stanford had drilled into him and he'd been young and stupid enough to listen.

And then it had all come crashing down around him when he'd lost Willa.

Why had his uncle never mentioned her in his letters? Did he fear learning Red was in Salvation Falls would send Morgan heading in the other direction? Maybe. And maybe he would have been right on that account. The letter that had broken his heart had sunk him deeper than he'd ever been. He'd spent the next week trying to drink his pain away before he'd wised up and decided it was better to head back to DeSoto County and restake his claim. But he'd arrived too late.

If only he'd returned when he'd first received her letter instead of drowning himself in whiskey. If only he'd answered the letters she'd sent before then instead of putting it off.

If only.

He shook his head and winced, both at the pain throbbing beneath his skull and the one lancing his heart.

He never delved too deep into his own part in the breakdown of their relationship. Why bother? Sure, he should have been more attentive, gone back and visited a time or two. Replied to her letters. But her marrying Clancy Barstow had been permanent, a clear end to their relationship.

Her betrayal had raged through him until there was nothing left but bitterness and regret. He'd walked away from his law practice and thrown away the future he'd worked so hard to build for her. What was the point? It had all been for her. To go on without her would only be a caustic reminder of his loss.

And nothing could ease that loss. He couldn't quite remember how to live in a world that didn't have her in it. Each time the thought of settling down popped up, the idea soured in his gut. Settle down to what? With whom? The cold, hard fact remained that the only woman he'd ever loved—still loved—had married someone else. So he tucked the notion away and moved on to the next thing, only staying a little while until things began to feel comfortable and then moving on once more, constantly searching for that missing piece.

He never found it.

Until now.

The second he'd set eyes on Willa everything had fallen into place. At least it had for him. Though she didn't appear to share his belief that this was fate's way of handing them a second chance. To hear her tell it, she had her own life now and he didn't fit into it.

Maybe she was right, because while he'd moved from one place to the next, she'd come here and put down roots, made a life, become a part of the town he'd always dreamed of settling in. And grown into a competent and beautiful woman in the process.

Did he even stand a chance at convincing her to give them a second try?

Someone banged on the opposite side of his door, shaking the thick oak on its hinges. The sound reverberated through his skull like someone swinging a pickaxe. Whoever stood on the other side didn't bother waiting for an invitation. The door swung open, banging against the wall with another resounding thud and the beast who'd brandished the ladle barreled in with a tray of food. If he was a cook, it explained the ladle, Morgan supposed. The scent filled the room and he immediately forgot his irritation at the disruption as his stomach grumbled, announcing its displeasure over not being fed since the night before.

"Here ya go. Eat up. Willa wants ya strong like an ox so ya can get outta her hair." The man sat the tray across his lap and tossed a cloth napkin onto Morgan's chest.

Morgan glanced up from the tray. "She say that?"

"It was inferred." The beast gave him a look that was hard to decipher given the bushy eyebrows and thick beard covering his wide face, but Morgan would bet his last dollar that irritation factored in heavily. Apparently this two-legged bear had elected himself Willa's protector. Great.

"Is she around?"

His uninvited guest crossed his arms, which seemed a chore in itself given their size. "Can't see that'd be any of your business, boyo."

"The name is Trent. Morgan Trent. Not *boyo*." Beast or not, the man was grating on his last nerve. He took a bite of the succulent roast beef smothered in gravy. It was so tasty he nearly wept.

"Hmm. Speakin' of, Bertram's on his way up. Don't see the resemblance though. And you can call me Fritz."

Morgan would prefer not to call the man at all. Unless he brought more meals like this. He hadn't eaten mashed potatoes this good since his ma had died. "Then, Fritz, you didn't answer my question. Is Willa around?" He preferred not to call her Mrs. Barstow if he could avoid it. The name didn't suit her and saying it felt like a punch to the gut.

"She's over at the church helping with the plannin'."

"Planning?"

"The Christmas Festival, my dear boy."

Morgan looked around Fritz to see his uncle. He'd only met the man in the flesh once as a young boy but aside from that fact his blond hair had turned pure white, not much had changed. The man exuded an energy that touched everyone within reach. Seeing his uncle filled Morgan with the sense he had finally come home.

"Bertram!"

Morgan set the tray Fritz had brought him aside and threw his legs over the side of the bed, standing up in one swift movement. Bad idea. He closed his eyes as the blood rushed from his head and he wavered. The dishes on the tray rattled as he sat quickly back down.

When he opened his eyes again, the room had righted itself and his uncle's smiling face wavered in front of Morgan's. "Heard you took a bit of a hit to the noggin, son."

"You heard right." He returned his uncle's smile. "It's good to see you, Bertram."

"It's good to be seen. I'm pleased Mrs. Barstow had

room for you. Guess maybe she's softening a bit toward you, hmm?"

"You guessed wrong on that account. And I was the injured party, if you'll recall."

His uncle lifted a snow-white eyebrow. "You can't leave a lady waiting in the wind without word and expect she'll stay put, sonny boy. Women are mercurial creatures with their own hearts and minds. That's always a hard lesson for us men to learn and we always seem to find out the hard way."

Morgan didn't answer. He and his uncle had never quite seen eye to eye on that particular subject, but he didn't have the wherewithal to argue, especially since the truth behind Bertram's wisdom was growing clearer.

"Just what is this Christmas Festival, anyway?" Not that he was particularly interested. Christmas was a time for families and friends and had always served as a stark reminder he had neither of those things. Would that change now that he'd finally reached Salvation Falls and found the one family member he had left?

And the one woman he'd always dreamed of making a family with?

The story Willa had relayed of her journey to Salvation Falls had left an impression and a niggling pressure against his conscience, which was only emphasized by Bertram's claims Morgan shouldn't have left Willa alone for as long as he had. That it had been his actions that had led her to marry someone else. Was he right? Maybe his own role in the events that had shaped their lives deserved closer scrutiny. The thought of sharing the blame didn't sit well, but neither did losing any chance to put things right between them.

Perhaps it was time he sat down with her to see if they couldn't come to some kind of understanding. "Guess I should head over to the church."

"Guess I'll be following along behind ya," Fritz mimicked.

Morgan glared at the giant. "I don't require an escort."

"Don't care what you think you require. I ain't gonna be

the one ta explain ta the little lady why she found you face-down in the snow, frozen ta death."

Bertram chuckled. "You might want to listen to Fritz, here, son. I need to meet with a client. You and I will talk later, hmm?"

"Yes, sir," Morgan answered, though the thought of arriving at the church with a chaperone was as appealing as stripping down and running the length of Main Street in the altogether.

He glanced up at Fritz once more. "Be ready by half past the hour."

# Chapter Four

Spotting Lettie Potter in a group of women was not a difficult task. No matter how many flounces the other ladies' dresses had, Lettie's would always have more. The fripperies of bows and such would always be more extravagant, the colors or patterns more flamboyant. Everything about Willa's older sister shouted that she was someone not to be ignored.

None of which was news to Morgan. He'd witnessed Lettie's constant need for male attention from the first day he'd been hired at Stanford Timber. Not that she had ever done anything improper, but the regular barrage of flirtatious behavior quickly grew exhausting and soon Morgan grew tired of pretending he was impressed by anything she said, did, wore or knew. Because, truth be told, Lettie never said anything of interest, never did anything of consequence, never wore anything that enticed him and didn't know anything of import. She reminded him of a window dressing.

Willa, on the other hand…well, Willa was the view beyond the window. She was the lush green grass and the wildflowers. She was cloudless skies and fresh air. It had amazed him she hadn't had a line of suitors, but for reasons he could never fathom, most men of his acquaintance gravitated toward Lettie. That suited him just fine, because he'd never been sure he deserved someone as wonderful as Willa and had there been more competition, maybe she would have realized that a lot sooner than she had.

Morgan stood just inside the church and surveyed the front of the room where the women were busy planning. Well, most of the women. It appeared Lettie was more inter-

ested in sitting in a pew fanning herself despite the fact the
cavernous room was anything but warm. His gaze skimmed
over her to find Willa. Wearing a navy dress, her hair somewhat subdued in a loose knot and a warm rose coloring the
apples of her cheeks, she was about the most beautiful thing
he'd ever seen. For a moment, he simply stood there, drinking her in. He still couldn't believe she was here. A part of
him was convinced he'd discover she was nothing more than
a mirage conjured up by wishful thinking.

"Do my eyes deceive me, or is that Morgan Trent? Willa
said you'd arrived in town but I thought for sure she was
pulling my leg."

Morgan's left eye twitched and he forced a smile. Lettie
had always reminded him of a viper poised to strike; you
just never knew when she was coming. "Mrs. Potter. How
are you?"

She glided toward him, her hips swaying to and fro beneath ample layers of petticoats, puffed out to enhance her
tiny waist. "Well, I suppose I'm a far sight better than you.
I heard you were laid out flat in the dining hall during the
ruckus those rowdies kicked up."

Deep breath. Unclench teeth. Speak. "You heard about
that, huh?" Was there anyone in town who hadn't?

"Hmm." Lettie gifted him with a smile that reminded
him of the proverbial cat who had cornered the canary, then
circled around him. The narrow space caused her skirts to
brush against his legs. Once she arrived back in front of him,
she tapped him on the chest with her closed fan. "I would say
traveling agrees with you, Mr. Trent. Do you plan on con-
tinuing on from here anytime soon?"

"No offense, Mrs. Potter, but I came here to speak to your
sister, so if you don't mind—"

"I think you'll discover I mind a fair bit." Lettie gifted him
with a sharp smile and her gaze hardened. "What exactly are
your intentions with respect to my sister?"

Morgan's gaze narrowed. When had Lettie designated
herself Willa's protector? The Lettie he knew barely gave

her younger sister the time of day, and when she did, it was usually veiled with some criticism or complaint.

"Said he needed to talk to 'er," Fritz offered from where he sat in the back pew.

Lettie's blonde eyebrows lifted. "Is that right?"

"Yes." Morgan gritted his teeth. Was it necessary for his every move to be dissected by everyone with an opinion?

"I'm afraid my sister is a bit busy right now what with the Christmas Festival just around the corner. I doubt she has the time to—"

"It's fine, Lettie," Willa said, making her way down the aisle. Morgan's heart pounded louder as he watched her approach. The way she carried herself, that newfound confidence, proved a strong aphrodisiac he was powerless against. "I can spare Mr. Trent a few minutes."

A few minutes. He'd take what he could get.

Lettie let out a put-upon sigh. "Suit yourself, then. If you'll excuse me, Mr. Trent. I must get back to the women. It's as if none of them have ever planned a large event before. Quite frankly, they should be happy I've arrived to keep this festival from becoming mired in mediocrity."

Ah, there was the Lettie he knew. He waited for her to head over to the rest of the women before turning his attention to Willa.

"Is there somewhere we can speak in private?" He didn't care for an audience of onlookers.

"There really isn't any place we—"

"There's the little room jus' off the way," Fritz said. Morgan glanced over his shoulder at the cook who was pointing to his right. He hadn't expected assistance from that quarter but he wasn't about to look a gift horse in the mouth.

Willa shook her head. "It's rather small. More of a coatroom than anything. I don't—"

"That'll work fine," Morgan said before she could talk her way out of it.

Her lips pursed, drawing his attention with a jolt of desire. "Fine. But only for a few minutes."

"That's all I need."

Fritz waved them off. "I'll wait right here for ya, Trent."

Willa led the way and Morgan worked furiously to not focus on the sway of her hips as he followed behind. He failed miserably—but what was a man to do?

"Where is Fritz from exactly?" Morgan asked as they stepped into the room. Willa had been right. It was small, containing four chairs that appeared to have been shoved into the room as an afterthought.

"It's hard to say," Willa said as Morgan pushed two chairs away to make room for them to sit. "His story changes every time I ask. Like a lot of the people here, I suspect maybe Fritz comes from all over. Then they reach Salvation Falls with nowhere else to go and realize this is the place they'd been looking for all along."

When had she become so wise? Had she always been this way and he simply hadn't looked deep enough to notice? And if so, what else had he missed?

He motioned Willa toward one of the chairs. "I see your sister hasn't changed much."

She smiled at him, the first unguarded smile he'd seen since he'd arrived. It transported him back to a time when he'd received such gifts on a regular basis and hadn't appreciated them nearly enough.

"She puts on a good show, but I think Ernest leaving her as he did has had more of an impact than she lets on. It's the first time she's had to look at the world from a different perspective and she's still finding her way. Don't judge her too harshly."

He nodded and looked down at his boots. He had to. The closer he looked at Red, the more things rushed through him that he didn't yet have the ability to deal with. Regrets and needs and wishes and disappointments. He shook them off. He needed to concentrate. To pick his words carefully.

"You've really made a place for yourself here, haven't you? Makes me think maybe nobody gave you enough credit early on, myself included. We all treated you like you were made of glass." He glanced back at her, the truth of what he was about to say muddled in confusion. "Turns out you were forged of iron."

Something crossed her expression, but it happened so swiftly he didn't have time to make head nor tail of it. "I did what I had to. It wasn't anything more than that."

"That's more than most of us managed." Seeing her, what she'd been through, what she'd lost, what she'd built in its place…well, it made him feel ashamed that he hadn't done the same. Instead, he'd let the loss of her and the life he'd dreamed of buckle him. He cleared his throat. "So what is this Christmas Festival you're preparing for?"

"Oh, just a small celebration we started a couple of years ago. Meredith Donovan—" She moved her hand in an arc over her belly, indicating the pretty blonde lady with a pronounced bump that suggested a baby would be coming in the near future. "She's the sheriff's wife and chief organizer of the event this year. She's managing the festivities for the dance. The lady with her, Rachel Beckett—you met her husband, Caleb, yesterday. They own the Circle S Ranch. She thought we should make a day out of it, so she is planning the outdoor events. Sledding and snowshoe races and the like."

Morgan listened as Willa described the other ladies helping out, giving a little detail as to who they were and something deep inside tugged and pulled until a deep ache opened up in his chest. She had overcome whatever life had thrown at her and built a life in Salvation Falls that was good and solid. Would his being here ruin that for her?

He took a deep breath and let it out slowly, choosing his words carefully. "Red, Bertram's the only family I've got. I plan on staying in Salvation Falls. Putting down some roots."

Willa stilled and her fingers knotted together in her lap. "I figured."

He waited for her to expand on that, but she fell silent. "Do you have any objections?"

She didn't say anything for the longest time and it wasn't

until his lungs began to burn that Morgan realized he'd been holding his breath, waiting for her answer.

"It's your prerogative to settle wherever you wish. My feelings on the matter are of no importance."

"They are to me."

"You do what you need to do and I'll adjust accordingly." Willa's jaw tightened and her shoulders set back a little. "Isn't that what I've always done where you were concerned?"

Her words, though spoken softly, hit him hard in the chest as if Fritz had planted one of his meaty fists in his sternum, knocking the wind out of him. "What's that supposed to mean?"

Willa's eyes widened and she looked him straight in the eye. Her genuine surprise at his question threw him off-kilter. What was he missing?

"Tell me, Morgan, when you decided to leave me to build your law practice and make yourself a success, how long did you expect that to take?"

Morgan shrugged. "Six months, give or take." He wasn't sure he liked the direction this conversation was heading. He'd planned on focusing on the positives of their past relationship and steering clear of the negatives.

"Six months." A bitter smile twitched at the corners of Willa's mouth. Oh, how he wanted to kiss that mouth. It seemed a far better option than digging up the remnants of a broken and battered past. "Well, I waited six months. And then even after your letters stopped coming, like a fool, I waited six more."

There was that guilt again jabbing at his conscience. He shoved it away and grasped at the reasoning he'd clung to since the day he'd learned she was marrying someone else. "I didn't have time to write, Red. I was busy trying to make a life for us!" Morgan took a deep breath to curb his emotions. "I was doing it for us."

She nodded and settled her features into an unreadable mask. "I'm curious how long you expected me to keep waiting with no word on when—or if—you were coming back?

Another six months? Another year? Two? How long, Morgan, was I to suffer the pitying looks of everyone around me who already knew you had no intention of returning? How long was I to fight off Father's insistence that I marry Clancy?"

He blinked and looked away. The last gasp of sunlight burst through the window behind them and spilled across the polished wooden floors. He didn't know how to answer her. Or rather, he didn't have a good answer to give. That she would be ridiculed or pitied by others had never crossed his mind. That Lyle would make demands Morgan had conveniently neglected to ruminate upon. In fact, if he were being truthful, he'd been too busy thinking about what he was going through to ponder much on how she was doing.

It was a shameful admission for a man to make.

"I guess I didn't consider it, Red."

"No. That much is clear." She shifted her gaze down to where her hands rested on her lap. Just as well. The dawning realization of what a self-centered idiot he'd been was not something he wanted her to see. "Well, I did think about it. Especially after your letters stopped coming. I made excuses at first, but they wore thin as the months went on."

Her eyes shone with a gleam of tears but she blinked them away and kept talking. "Finally, Father had had enough. He demanded I marry Clancy. I refused at first, but..." She shrugged.

"But Clancy Barstow, Red? What were you thinking?" She had never liked the man—why would she agree to marry him?

She looked up and her eyes flashed with anger but her voice remained calm. Controlled. The muscle near her jaw quivered slightly, indicating the strength that took. "I wasn't thinking. I wasn't feeling. I wasn't anything but an empty husk. The man I had loved and built my future hopes on had abandoned me and the hurt cut so deep I could barely breathe. I didn't marry Clancy because I cared about him. I married Clancy because Father threatened to throw me out into the streets with nothing if I didn't."

The pain and accusation in her eyes cut through him like a thousand jagged blades. His head hurt and his heart ached and his conscience raged, letting loose all the things he'd tried to deny and avoid since the day he'd returned, too late, to convince her not to marry Clancy.

For years, he'd tried to outrun the truth, outrun his own culpability. He'd laid it all at her door. But no matter how far he rode, the truth continued to dog him, nipping at his heels until he'd found himself standing at her doorstep where it had finally caught up with him. Now the truth stared at him through those soft hazel eyes he'd fallen in love with so many years ago.

Losing her had been his fault.

He opened his mouth to say he was sorry. So horribly, incredibly sorry, but the words locked in his throat. It was far too little and once again, he was far too late.

"Red…"

She shook her head and stood, her hands unclasping to press against her skirts. A briskness filled her voice, pushing him away. "Anyway, it's all in the past. You have your life now and I have mine. Surely this town is big enough that we can both live our lives without tripping over each other on a daily basis. I'm certain your uncle will be happy to have family around. Bertram's a good man and I would never take that away from him."

"What if I don't want that?"

Her hands stilled. "Excuse me?"

He took a deep breath and wished he'd had more time to formulate what he wanted to say, the best words to use. "What if I don't want to leave us in the past? What if I think there's still something between us worth saving?"

"I…I—" She shook her head, but other than those stammered sounds, she said nothing. She hadn't refused him. It was as good a sign as any.

He stepped forward and reached for one of her hands. It was so small in comparison to his and the need to protect her, and the anger at not having done so all those years when she'd toiled alone, surged through him. He wouldn't let that happen again.

"Just hear me out, Red." He lifted her hand to rest against his chest, wishing he could rid himself of the sheepskin coat that created a barrier between them. "We had something special once, didn't we?"

She wouldn't meet his gaze, but she didn't deny it, so he forged on.

"Don't you think it's crazy that we'd both end up here? Crazier still, not to take advantage of this second chance? I know I did a lot of things wrong the first time around. I see that now. I should have replied to your letters. I shouldn't have just assumed you'd wait however long it took. And I sure should have come back for you the minute I received your letter saying you were marrying Clancy."

He let go of her hand and slipped his arms around the curve of her waist. A small tear slipped down over her cheekbone and it cut him to the quick. He hadn't convinced her yet. He could feel it. And he was running out of words. And time.

Morgan lifted her chin up to meet his gaze and in hers saw the reflection of the hope he carried in his heart. He leaned down and kissed the single tear she'd allowed to fall, tasting its saltiness on his lips.

"I'm not the same man I was back then, Red. Losing you nearly killed me. I tried to convince myself it was your fault, but deep down inside, I knew better. I knew if I'd been a better man things would have turned out different."

"It's water under the bridge," she whispered, dropping her gaze again. "I don't blame you. Maybe I should have waited longer. Maybe I should have jumped on the first stagecoach, landed in your office and demanded you make me your wife then and there. But I didn't. I let Father dictate my life just as always. Just as I allowed you to do and then Clancy. But no more. We have new lives now and I'm perfectly content with my lot."

"Content? I don't want us to be content. I want us to be happy. Don't you?"

She said nothing but he saw her lower lip quiver. That was all it took for his resolve to crumble. He lowered his mouth to hers and captured her trembling lips with his and kissed her as if his life, their future and every hope he'd ever held of having a family counted on his convincing her of his sincerity. And he was sincere. He *did* want that dream of forever with her. He always had.

Hope soared inside him the second she leaned into him, giving herself over to the kiss the way she had done all those years ago beneath the mistletoe when he'd told her he was leaving. He'd been an idiot. A true and bona fide fool to have left her that night. He wouldn't make that mistake again. Morgan poured everything in his heart into that kiss, tasting and teasing her, pulling her close so that she melded to him as if they were one. He needed to convince her. Needed to—

She pulled away, breaking the kiss and stumbling away from him until her back pressed against the wall. When she looked at him, what he saw rocked him back on his heels. Fear. Of what? Him?

"Red—"

She gave her head a quick shake and the emotions settled back behind a veil until the only thing left in her eyes was resolve. "I need to go."

"That's it?" He couldn't keep the incredulous tone from his voice. He'd just poured his heart out to her! She couldn't throw him even a small bone? Some indication of what was in her head? Her heart?

"I can't do this with you right now. I need...time. Or space or...something. I just need to think. It's too much. You can't ride into town and expect me to throw myself into your arms like the past six years hadn't happened. I'm not the same person I used to be."

That much was clear. Problem was, she was even better than she used to be.

"Fine," he said, trying not to sound as deflated as he felt. "Fair enough. I'll give you time."

She cleared her throat. "I need to get back to the others."

The message was clear. Their conversation was at an end. At least for now.

He nodded and watched as she slipped from the room and started back up the aisle to the front of the church. She didn't look back. It was as if she'd already washed her hands of him. Of their past. His hopes for a reconciliation dimmed considerably.

What if she didn't give them a second chance? What if she didn't want to patch up the tattered remains of their relationship? Morgan tried to swallow the possibility but it proved unpalatable. Much as life without her would be.

She was everything he had dreamed of for so long. She was home and family and future. How could fate dangle her in front of him like this and then snatch her away? And what was he going to do to make sure that didn't happen?

Because one thing was for sure—he wasn't going to lose her a second time.

# Chapter Five

"Is he the reason you came to Salvation Falls, Willa? Did you think Morgan would be here to rescue you?" Lettie moved about Willa's sitting room that doubled as her office, touching the spotless surface of the bureau before lifting her fingers to inspect for dust.

Willa gripped the fountain pen in her hand and held it above the ledgers where she worked. It would not do to splotch the paper where she'd written next week's orders. She considered denying the claim, but what was the point?

"I suppose I was hoping to see a familiar face. He had spoken so often of Salvation Falls I thought maybe he'd come eventually. It wasn't as if you had opened your arms and welcomed me home."

Lettie stopped moving for a moment and avoided Willa's gaze. "You know I regret that. But Ernest…" Her voice drifted off and Willa was left with the impression that there was far more to the story of what happened in Lettie's marriage than what her sister let on.

"Anyway," Willa said, pushing away the past. "The last thing I need is to humiliate myself all over again in that regard."

The hypocrisy of her statement lingered in the air. Had she not already done that? Why, she had practically swooned in his arms the moment his lips had touched hers. It had taken every last ounce of strength to walk away from him that day. She'd wanted nothing more than to believe in everything he'd said. But he'd made promises before and sealed them with a kiss and look where it had got her. She couldn't afford to be so foolish a second time. There was too much at stake now.

Lettie turned and leaned against the narrow table behind her, a knowing smile playing about her bow lips. "I know how much you loved him, Willa. How brightly that torch still burns where he's concerned."

"I am not burning any torch." The lie ground out of her and even she didn't believe it.

"Then why have you not remarried? I'm guessing any number of gentlemen in this town would be happy to call you wife."

The uncommon compliment surprised Willa, but this was not a conversation she wished to have. "I have been married, Lettie. It was a less than desirable union, if you'll recall. I prefer to be on my own, thank you."

"You can't judge every man based on the one Father chose for you. Clancy Barstow was a snake oil salesman in a fancy suit. I don't know what the devil Father was thinking having you marry that man. Even Ernest was a better choice than Clancy, though that's hardly high praise for either of them."

Her sister walked toward Willa, her satin dress swishing back and forth filling the silence in the room. Lettie's fingers tapped the writing desk. "How are you going to feel when Morgan chooses a bride? Because he will. It's just the natural way of things. And he's a fine-looking man with good prospects. Heavens, if the thought of taking your castoffs wasn't so appalling, even I would consider him."

The idea of Morgan with anyone, especially Lettie, burned like acid in her stomach, but she maintained her lie. It was all she had left to cling to. "I wish Morgan every happiness."

Lettie made a scoffing sound. "You're a horrible liar, Willa. You may want to keep that in mind when you have to come face-to-face with him and offer those good wishes."

Her sister spun on her slippered heel and headed for the door. "Now, if you'll excuse me, I'm going to stop by Mrs. Donovan's dress shop. I swear, if not for that woman's designs and dresses there would be no hope for the women in this town. Have you given any thought as to what you might wear to the festival? Please tell me you are not going to embarrass yourself and show up at the dance wearing one of your *serviceable* dresses. The idea is positively mortifying. Though if you were trying to dissuade any man from showing an interest in you, I suppose that would be the way to go."

Willa set her pen down and sat back in her chair. "I have not yet decided whether I will be attending the dance. I have a lot of work to do." And she had a certain individual to avoid.

Lettie hesitated, then gave Willa a pointed look. "One of these days, sister dear, you are going to learn that second chances are a rare thing indeed. Not everybody gets one. Don't be a fool and throw this one away."

"Who said a second chance was even a possibility?"

"For heaven's sake, Willa. Morgan didn't come to the church the other day to volunteer for the Christmas Festival. He came to see you. And I can think of only one reason why he'd do that. He wants you back. And you want him."

Willa clenched her jaw. Was she so transparent? Yes, she wanted Morgan. She had always wanted Morgan. But she also wanted to preserve her pride and dignity and wasn't about to fall into his arms because he said a few pretty words. She had her own life and granted, maybe she wasn't deliriously happy in the way she'd dreamed of being, but there was nothing wrong with content. Content was good. Content was solid and steady.

"I'm perfectly happy with my life the way it is." Willa dropped her gaze back to the ledger. It was true, or at least it had been before Morgan had arrived on her doorstep and something shifted inside her. Something that made the notion of second chances echo in the quiet of the room, resonating deep within her. Was she being a fool to deny herself a second chance at love?

Or would she be even more of a fool to set herself up for a second heartbreak?

\* \* \*

"Should probably get yourself a haircut." Caleb Beck-ett pointed a finger at Morgan's head from where he sat, stretched out in one of the straight-backed chairs in front of Bertram's large oak desk that had survived the fire with only a little scarring. Morgan patted the back of his head. Granted, his hair had grown a bit scruffy but surely he didn't look that bad.

Sheriff Hunter Donovan, who had accompanied Beckett to Bertram's temporary offices, sat on the corner of the desk. He grunted his agreement before adding his own two cents worth. "And a suit. People will take you more seriously if you're wearin' a suit."

Morgan wondered what the protocol was for throwing these two out of the office, given it was located above the dress shop owned by the sheriff's wife. Morgan was in a surly mood after his conversation with Willa. It had been two days since they'd kissed and she'd been avoiding him. Not an easy thing to do given they were living under the same roof.

"Thank you for your input, gentlemen, but isn't there somewhere you both need to be?"

Beckett and Donovan looked at each other and shrugged.

"Don't think so. Hunter?"

"Nope. Pretty quiet today."

Morgan scowled. "Fantastic." He motioned to the papers on the desk. "You know, I have done this lawyering thing before. I had a fairly successful practice too."

The sheriff picked up a paperweight and gave it a close examination. "You don't say? What happened?"

"What do you mean?"

"I mean if you had a successful law practice *once*, why don't you still?"

The two men stared at him and Morgan shifted in his chair, hesitating as he attempted to find the right words to explain the short-lived nature of his practice. "I had a change of circumstances."

"Uh-huh."

"Hmm." Beckett rubbed his jaw. "A woman, then."

"Definitely a woman." Sheriff Donovan nodded.

Morgan banged his hand on the desk. "It was not a—"

"Mrs. Barstow would be my guess." Beckett kicked his feet up onto the corner of the desk next to the sheriff, a clear indication that neither of them intended on leaving anytime soon. "Heard you have a prior acquaintance with the lady."

"Did you?"

"Ayup. Also heard you had a private conversation a couple days past at the church."

The sheriff crossed his arms over his chest. "Got witnesses that'll verify to that."

Morgan had the sinking feeling he was about to be outlawyered by a lawman and a rancher. Problem was, he couldn't even mount a proper defense given that their facts were both true and accurate. At least no one knew what had happened during said conversation.

Morgan settled back in his chair and crossed his arms. "Willa and I were engaged to be married several years back."

The sheriff's dark eyes crinkled at the corners. He looked more amused than surprised. "That so?"

Morgan had the sinking sensation a good portion of the town was well aware of their past association. Apparently news traveled in Salvation Falls faster than the fire that had wrecked Bertram's former office. Wonderful. "Yes. That's so. Unfortunately, it ended for reasons I do not care to get into—"

Beckett interrupted. "She married Barstow instead of him."

"No! That is not—" Hell's bells. He let out a frustrated breath. "Fine. Yes. She married someone else, but there was more to it than that."

Morgan rubbed at the ache in his chest whenever he thought of speaking with Willa in the church. Ha! Speaking. He couldn't even remember what he'd said. All he remembered was that dang kiss filled with passion and fueling more desire than a body had a right to contain. He was pretty sure he'd apologized though—for the past, not the kiss. He wasn't a bit sorry about that. And he was pretty sure he'd said he wanted to make amends, to shuck off this specter of guilt that clung to him like a shadow and to be given a second chance. But nothing said or done had convinced her. She wanted time. That likely wouldn't end well for him if she started thinking about all the things he'd done wrong in the past and decided he wasn't worth a second go.

Donovan nodded, a knowing look in his eye. "Made a mistake, huh?"

"What?" Morgan shook his head, realizing Donovan was speaking about the distant past, not the recent one. "Yeah, something like that."

"Guess you're wanting to rectify that mistake, then," Beckett observed.

Morgan rubbed a hand down his face. The chair beneath him creaked. "I'm not sure I can rectify it." Neither the past nor the present.

"But you want to nonetheless," Donovan said.

"Wanting and getting is not the same thing," he pointed out. He'd learned the reality of that the hard way.

Beckett's feet dropped to the ground and he stood. Though a quiet man by nature, he had a presence that made him impossible to ignore. Beckett might be a rancher now, but Morgan guessed that hadn't always been the case. There was a dangerous edge to him, even when he appeared at ease.

"Wanting," Beckett said, glancing over his shoulder, "is the groundwork for getting. What you need is a plan."

"Oh, no, no, no, no." Morgan cut his arms through the air as he stood up. This was getting out of hand. "I do not need any interference—"

Donovan cut him off. "Yeah, you do. Look, here's the thing about women—if you want to get back in their good graces, you can't be pussyfooting around it. You need to be honest. Straightforward. Maybe make a grand gesture or something."

Beckett turned and leaned against the windowsill. "Sounds like solid advice to me."

"No, it isn't. Look, neither of you know Red the way I do. She isn't—"

"Red?" The two other men said in tandem.

Morgan cleared his throat. "It… It was a nickname I gave her."

"Hmm," Donovan said while Beckett simply stood and looked at him with that piercing gaze that cut straight through a man. "Interesting."

"Go get yourself that haircut and buy a suit from the haberdashery," Beckett said as he headed for the door, Donovan following behind.

"Why?"

The sheriff stopped, the light from the window catching his badge and glinting off the shiny star. "You'll need it for the wedding."

"What wedding?"

"Yours, Trent," Donovan said as he left the office.

Beckett poked his head back around the door. "And try to show up for this one, huh?"

The two men's footsteps echoed down the stairwell, leaving Morgan standing at his desk and staring at the closed door, wondering what on earth had just happened.

## Chapter Six

Willa crossed the street, holding her skirts aloft to avoid the mixture of snow and muck that covered the ground. Life had resumed its regular pace now that the storm had passed and for that she was thankful. It helped keep her mind off the kiss she and Morgan had shared earlier in the week, though only with varying degrees of success. The evenings were the worst—having him within reach, wanting to be with him, yet afraid of risking her heart again. She'd lost countless hours of sleep tossing and turning, mulling over the pros and cons of giving their relationship a second chance. She still hadn't reached a conclusion.

Her heart jumped at the possibility, inundating her with images of the life she'd once dreamed of having as a loving wife to Morgan and mother to their children. But her head ordered caution. That dream belonged to a woman who had yet to experience the world with its harsh realities and infinite possibilities. She hadn't really thought much about what her dreams were nowadays, but she wasn't sure they were the same ones she'd had all those years ago.

In a sense, Morgan's abandonment had been a bit of a godsend. Yes, it had caused immeasurable hurt and led her down a dark path with respect to marrying Clancy. But she had survived and become a stronger person for having been through it. She'd learned more about herself through her hardships than she would have had her life sailed along on calm seas. And she liked the new woman she'd discovered along the way.

Could she really turn her back on that? Did Morgan expect her to? She feared the answer might be yes. He'd referenced their old dreams when he'd spoken of a second chance. Had he considered that maybe hers had changed? That the old ones didn't quite fit the same way as they had before? She doubted it.

Willa stepped up onto the planked sidewalk and stomped the snow from her boots and shook the hem of her dress.

"Good day, Mr. Carstock," she said as the butcher approached her.

The tall man tipped his cap to her and smiled. "To you as well, Mrs. Barstow. You tell Fritz I'll have those cuts of beef to him within the hour."

"I will."

Willa hugged the envelope she carried close to her chest as she pushed through the door of Connolly Designs & Dresses. She had come to deliver the documents Lettie had signed with respect to the dissolution of her marriage. It was a stark reminder of how things could go when a marriage didn't work out as planned.

"Good morning, Meredith," Willa called as she walked into the dress shop and waved to her friend behind the counter, where she was helping a customer, likely doing finishing touches on a dress for the Christmas dance. Meredith Donovan had opened her business a year ago and she and Willa had bonded over their shared experiences as two of the few preeminent businesswomen in Salvation Falls. "I'm here to see Bertram."

Meredith waved back. "Go on upstairs. When you're done with business, come back down and we'll have a chat. I have a ready-made that I think you'll love. I haven't given up on getting you decked out for this dance."

"I'll stop by," she called over her shoulder, though she hoped Meredith would be too busy to speak by the time she returned. The woman was painfully stubborn when she got an idea in her head. Willa reached the second floor and knocked on the door before entering.

"Oh."

Morgan looked up from the desk and her breath caught in her throat. She noticed immediately that he'd cut his hair, trimming up the shaggier edges. How was it that a haircut could make his eyes even bluer? Or was that the brilliant winter sunshine pouring in from the windows filling the room with light? Not that it mattered. The effect was the same. And it left her breathless.

"Red? I didn't know you were stopping by." He stood. His denims and flannel shirt were gone, replaced by a pair of black wool trousers and a white shirt. He'd rolled up the sleeves to reveal sinewy forearms and unbuttoned it at the neck just enough to make her imagination wander where it had no business going. She looked quickly away and cleared her throat, trying to get the muscles there working. "You look different."

He had worn suits when he'd worked for her father, but the effect had never been this potent. Time had filled him out, removing the lankiness of youth and replacing it with the hard breadth of a grown man.

His mouth quirked to one side. "I was told I needed to buy a suit."

"By Bertram?"

"No. I was judged by a jury of two men who like to stick their noses in other people's business." His answer made no sense to her but he came out from behind the desk and motioned to a chair across from it before she could ask for clarification. "Sit down."

Willa hesitated. She had expected to deal with Bertram on this matter. "I have some paperwork for Bertram. It's the divorce petition Ernest sent Lettie."

Morgan tilted his head to one side. "Ah. And she sent you over with it?"

"She doesn't particularly want to deal with it."

"That so?"

"Yes. I suppose." Though she was beginning to have her doubts. Had Lettie known Morgan would be here? Was that why she'd claimed a headache and refused to deliver the signed papers on her own? "Regardless, here they are. So—"

"Red—"

"Please stop calling me that." The plea rushed out of her before she could stop it.

"Why?"

Because she couldn't think straight when he did, that's why. But she bit her tongue, holding the words inside. This was why she needed to avoid Morgan Trent. They couldn't have a simple conversation like the one she'd had with Mr. Carstock on the sidewalk only moments before. Everything she and Morgan said to each other came weighted down by their past. Each conversation pregnant with expectation yet littered with the debris of what might have been. She didn't know how to navigate them properly. They didn't make maps for these kinds of things.

"I'm not *Red* to you anymore. I am just…Mrs. Barstow." She threw the name out like a shield across her heart.

"You will never be Mrs. Barstow to me." His words were hard and clipped and the skin across his cheekbones tightened.

"It's my name."

"It isn't who you are."

Fire burned through her at his words, incinerating any hope she had of staying calm and collected.

"How would you know who I am? You thought me a meek, pampered girl who would wait around like a faithful hound while you tried to build the life you thought I wanted. If you had known me, you would have realized none of that mattered a fig to me. I didn't want *things*, Morgan. I wanted you!"

Oh, no. What had she just done? Her hands flew to her cheeks, the heat of embarrassment burning into her skin. She needed to leave. To get away from him before she said something even more foolish. Like admitting that she loved him. That despite everything that had happened, despite every effort she'd made, she couldn't stop loving him. She didn't know how to stop. But that she couldn't promise him anything beyond that. Not yet. Maybe not ever.

"I have to go." She turned and hurried to the door.

"Hold up a minute," Morgan called out, his footsteps echoing behind her.

Willa grabbed the door handle. She hadn't meant to lay her feelings bare. She needed time to figure them out, dissect them. Determine how best to deal with them. That was how she'd survived these past six years, using her head, not her heart, and the method had served her well. It gave her strength. But her feelings for Morgan threatened all of that, because in the end, what she really wanted was to turn around, throw herself into his arms and let him kiss her the way he had at the church. And that, in a nutshell, was a recipe for disaster. Because she had thrown caution to the wind once before and it had cost her dearly.

Before she could wrench the door open Morgan's hand came down and stilled hers.

"You said you needed time, Red. Well, I've given you time. It's been almost a week since we spoke…since we kissed." A shiver wound its way down her spine. "Turn around."

She didn't. Her brain worked furiously to find a way out of this predicament, to escape the conversation she wasn't ready to have. It didn't help matters that it was exceptionally difficult to concentrate when Morgan's hand continued to rest upon hers and the heat of his body warmed her back through the wool cloak she'd worn. If she turned around, she'd be mere inches from his face. From those horribly distracting blue eyes. From his mouth, so sinfully tempting. So, no, she was definitely not going to turn around.

"Red, we need to talk," he murmured in her ear.

She closed her eyes. Heavens, was there nothing about this man that didn't make her insides feel like liquid fire?

When it became clear he was not going to budge, she complied and turned around, pressing her back against the door. "What do you want me to say? You want to talk about a future, but I can't forget the past. What happened between us wasn't exactly a pleasant memory."

"Parts of our past were pleasant, weren't they?" He leaned closer and her breath caught as he gave her that cocky grin that held the ability to render her stupid. "I remember a particular kiss that was most pleasant. And another, more recent one, that was even more so."

Willa's heart jerked in her chest. Everything in his expression spoke of sincerity, deep and imploring. She let out a small sigh. There had been a time when she could have stood there and stared at him all day. The years apart had not diminished that in the least. If anything, that need had only increased, as now there was so much more to see. Stories written in the thin lines that fanned out from the corners of his eyes. A history that unfolded deep within his gaze. She wanted desperately to hear those stories, to know the history of what had happened after he'd failed to come back for her.

"I admit I behaved abominably in the past, Red. I should have recognized that fact years ago but I was just too—"

"Pigheaded?" Maybe if she remembered the hurt, she could clear her head. Think straight.

He scowled at her. "Thank you. And yes, I suppose pigheaded would be one way of describing it."

"And self-absorbed?"

The scowl deepened. "And that."

"Mired in your own—"

"Can we stop now?" His mouth twisted and something deep inside of her keened with longing.

"But I was just getting started."

"I'm sure you were. And I'm sure we could spend all day listing my faults and shortcomings." He reached up to tuck a recalcitrant curl behind her ear, letting the tip of his finger linger upon the sensitive skin. "I'm not a perfect man. I've made mistakes that I deeply regret. But I want to be better. To do better."

Her heart picked up speed. "That's very admirable. I wish

you all the best in that regard. I hold in great esteem the idea
that everyone can improve themselves."

She was babbling like a fool! Was that what awaited her if
they continued living in the same town? A lifetime of staring
into the face of regret whenever she passed him on the street
as they continued on with their separate lives?

Her heart wrenched, shrunk back. Curled in on itself.

"Thanks," he said, though his voice carried a note of sarcasm. "I think you're missing my point."

"I need to go," she whispered, the only truth she'd spoken
in the past few minutes.

"You need to stay. You haven't answered my question yet."

"What question?"

He looked at her as if she'd gone daft. His assessment
wasn't far from the truth. "About giving us a second chance."

"Oh, that."

The intensity of his gaze deepened. "Yes, *that*. I've been
thinking on it and I want you to marry me, Red. Marry me
like we should have all those years ago. You can give up the
boardinghouse and we'll find a nice little place and finally
get our happily-ever-after. You know how much I've always
wanted that, to have a family of my own. And there's no one
else I want to do that with but you."

His proposal lifted her up then let her fall. Like an idiot,
for a second she was a heartbeat away from saying yes, to
giving in to the dream they'd shared once upon a time. His
nearness pushed through the miasma of hurt and blinded her
with wanting. His sincerity wrapped around her heart and
squeezed until it was painful. It was almost enough.

Almost.

I *want you to marry me.* You *can give up the boardinghouse.* I've *always wanted that.*

The words pummeled the hope that had slowly built inside her since their kiss, forcing her back to reality and the
fears she'd wrestled with.

She shoved hard against Morgan's chest until he stepped
back and gave her room to breathe. To think.

"*You* want me to marry you and give up the boarding-house?" Her voice was shrill with the disappointment of having such a perfect moment snatched away.

Morgan's brows knitted together. "Yes. Why? What's wrong with that? You love me, I know you do. You wouldn't have kissed me like that the other day if you didn't still have feelings. Nothing has changed, Red. We were meant to be together."

She shook her head. Because that was the thing. Something had changed. *She* had changed. She had lost everything that meant anything to her and then she'd rebuilt herself, her life. He couldn't just ride into town and expect to pick up where they'd left off. Expect her to turn her back on everything she'd accomplished and marry him so that he could have his happily-ever-after? What about *her* happily-ever-after? What about what she wanted?

Had Morgan stopped to consider that she no longer fit the mold of the submissive, dutiful wife? Maybe that had fit her idea of perfection six years ago, but she'd lived a different life in the time since and she'd learned a thing or two about herself. About what made her happy. What she wanted.

And what she didn't.

And what she didn't want was to be married to someone who expected her to be a version of herself that no longer existed. Someone who wanted her to give up her life for the sake of his.

"Red, what is the matter? I thought we—"

"Exactly," she said, cutting him off. "*You* thought. And *you* want. And from what I can tell you expected me to just fall in line with all of that. Well, tell me, Morgan, what do you think I want? Do you think I've been sitting here for the past six years waiting for you to arrive and sweep me away from all of this? Because I haven't. I like my life. I'm proud of what I've accomplished."

"I understand that, Red. But—"

"There is no *but*, Morgan. I have no intentions of giving that up. And I have a sneaking suspicion you don't want a wife whose life doesn't revolve around yours. Do you?"

Morgan didn't answer her. He didn't have to. His silence and the stunned expression on his handsome face gave her the answer she needed, even if it wasn't the answer she wanted.

"I can't marry you, Morgan."

Anger registered in the tightness of his mouth and the sudden clenching of his fists. "Can't?"

"Won't," she clarified. "I won't marry you. I won't go back to the kind of life that's ruled by someone else. I won't deny I love you. I always have. But I won't consign myself to a life that no longer fits the person I've become. Until you can understand that, I don't see any future for us beyond friendship."

Silence lay heavy in the air around them and for the longest time neither of them spoke. Willa straightened her shoulders and took a deep breath. Her refusal had surprised him, annoyed him even, confirming her worst fears. That he thought he could march back into her life and have things the way he wanted without taking her needs into consideration.

"Good day, Morgan. I hope you find whatever it is you're looking for."

She turned and groped through the tears that blinded her until she found the door handle and pulled it open. She forced her legs to move. To hurry down the stairs, out of the dress shop and as far away from Morgan as she could get.

If only she could outrun the pain and disappointment taking over her heart just as easily.

# Chapter Seven

*I hope you find whatever it is you're looking for.*

Willa's refusal rebounded around the room long after she'd left and he'd returned to sit at Bertram's fire-scarred desk. What had just happened? He'd been so sure of everything. The kiss they'd shared at the church had clearly told him nothing had changed between them. The love, the attraction, all of that was still there, alive and well and stronger than ever. She'd even admitted that she loved him. So what the heck had gone so wrong?

And why in tarnation did the idea of being his wife and mother to his children, creating a loving home, suddenly seem tantamount to death?

"You keep scowlin' like that, boy, and your face is gonna stick that way."

Morgan glanced up to see his uncle standing inside the office leaning on his cane, a smile brightening his blue eyes. The cane was mostly an affectation Morgan had discovered, as Bertram's step still remained spry for a man in his sixties. Between the bushy white beard and snow-white hair, his uncle reminded Morgan of a rendering he'd seen as a child of St. Nicholas.

"What do you know about women, Uncle Bertram?"

His uncle laughed, the sound big and hearty. "No more than you, I'm afraid. As I've said before, mercurial creatures with far more going on inside their heads and hearts than we mere men will ever fully understand." He walked over to the window and looked out. "Ah. Might've known. I take it you and Willa had a bit of a run-in, did you? Figured you two would have a bit of a rocky road trying to fit things back together."

"That a fact?"

"Sure enough. Take it you mucked it up?"

His uncle's assumption grated against him. "No, I asked her to marry me."

Bertram chuckled. "What kind of a fool are you?"

Morgan didn't appreciate the question—especially given he had no defense against it. Likely he was every kind of fool that existed, because for the life of him, he couldn't understand her rejection. "A very large one it seems, because she turned me down flat. Turns out despite the fact she loves me, she has no interest in being my wife."

"That so?"

"Apparently."

"Hmm."

Morgan glanced down at his uncle. "Hmm? That's all you've got?"

Bertram nodded and chuckled. "Pretty much. Don't suppose it ever crossed your mind, son, that you can't just blow into town with the storm and expect her to jump at the chance to give up everything she's become to shrink back down into the woman you expect her to be?"

Morgan turned and glared at his uncle. "I don't expect her to be anyone other than who she is."

"You happen to mention that when you proposed?"

Morgan cleared his throat and looked back out the window to the boardinghouse beyond. "I might have left that part out. It was a little hard to get a word in edgewise." Not to mention the fact he'd been shocked into silence at her blunt refusal.

"Here's the thing, son," Bertram said, pointing out the window in the direction of the boardinghouse. "Willa Barstow is a good woman, a strong woman. She's made her way in this world and done a fine job of it. She doesn't need you—"

"Is this supposed to be helping?"

Bertram turned the finger in Morgan's direction and

poked his arm. "She doesn't *need* to marry you, so you're going to have to make her *want* to."

"And how am I supposed to do that?"

"By giving her what *she* needs. She loves you, no doubt, but she needs to know you love her enough to let her be who she is. She spent her life ruled by men who did nothing but muck up her life. You need to show her you aren't going to do that. You need to show her that marriage to you isn't a cage, but a freedom. The freedom to be what she needs to be in a way she needs to be it. And she needs to know that you'll love her because of it, not in spite of it. You think you can do that?"

Morgan rubbed a hand over his eyes and heaved a frustrated breath. What his uncle said made sense, much as he hated to admit it. Fact was, he hadn't taken what she wanted into consideration. He'd just assumed they were on the same page because it was the page he wanted to be on. Six years ago, she'd been so cowed by life with her father, she never had the chance to determine what she wanted. But now she had the freedom to choose. And the idea that he expected her to give up everything had sent her running.

How could he have been so obtuse as to not see that? How had he forgotten to tell her that this new version of the woman he fell in love with six years ago amazed him. Made him proud. While he had faltered in the past six years, she'd pulled herself up by her bootstraps and flourished. He didn't love her less because of it, he loved her more. Then he'd opened his big mouth and everything but that had poured out.

He'd made such a mess of this. No wonder she'd turned him down.

"I think I may have dug myself a hole I can't get out of. It's going to take something special to make this right."

His uncle smiled and winked. "Don't need fairy dust, my boy. It's Christmas. The season is ripe for all kinds of miracles. But miracles don't always happen on their own, you know. Might be you have to coax them along a bit. I'm pretty sure you can enlist some help in that regard."

"Help?"

"To keep you from mucking it up again." Bertram walked over to the peg where he'd hung his coat and shrugged into it. "Ain't no shame in asking for help and I'm sure anyone in town would be more than happy to lend a hand."

"You think?"

"Sure enough." Bertram stopped at the door. "Except Fritz. Don't think he's warmed up to you quite yet. Good luck, son!"

Morgan stared after his uncle and shook his head in disbelief. One minute he'd been mooning over Willa's rejection and now he was supposed to enlist the town to help him change her mind?

This day had just gone from miserable to downright strange.

"What do you mean you're not attending the festivities," Meredith Donovan said, holding the dress she'd specially designed for Willa close to her growing belly.

"I just…." She drifted off. What could she say? Meredith had outdone herself with the forest-green dress with a red-and-green-plaid overskirt.

Meredith took a seat on the bench that rested against the wall of the dressing room and gave Willa a concerned look. "Does this have anything to do with Mr. Trent?"

"No! Of course not."

"Which means yes, of course it does. I watched you avoid him when you left the boardinghouse, skirting behind the post office and coming out through the alley."

Willa's mouth dropped open to deny it, then clamped shut. Meredith was far too astute at judging people for Willa to bother arguing. "He asked me to marry him," she admitted, sinking down onto the platform where Meredith's customers stood for fittings.

Meredith clasped her hands beneath her chin. "Oh, that is wonderful!"

"No, it's awful! His proposal mostly consisted of telling

me how wonderful our being married would be for him. He never once considered that maybe it wouldn't be so wonderful for me!"

Meredith arched one golden eyebrow. "How so? Mr. Trent seems like a fine man."

Willa shook her head and stared down at her hands. "He is. And I love him, but…"

She let out a long breath. In the two days since Morgan's proposal, she had gone back and forth between being firm in her belief that she couldn't marry him to wishing she had said yes. The problem was, her feelings in the present were too tangled up with everything that had happened in the past.

"But what?"

"I don't know. Part of me thinks I should say yes and hope for the best, but the other part fears if I do, it will end in misery. The last time I agreed to marry Morgan Trent, he broke my heart. I don't know if I can survive that kind of hurt a second time, especially if I were to have a hand in bringing it about."

Meredith's smile softened. "Well, then, I think there's only one thing you can do."

"Leave town?"

"Hardly."

"Convince him to leave town?"

Meredith laughed and shook her head. "No. You simply need to tell him exactly what it is you want. Sometimes men can be horribly obtuse in this area. And if it turns out he's not willing to give you what you need, well then you have your answer. But you can't tell him that if you're avoiding him as if he's carrying the plague."

Willa dropped her face into her hands and groaned. Avoiding Morgan was so much easier than facing him. If she told him she had no intentions of turning her back on the life she'd built for herself, a life she was proud of, and he decided that wasn't the kind of wife he wanted—what then?

"I don't know if I can withstand losing him all over again," she admitted.

Meredith leaned over and patted Willa's knee. "Have a little faith. You said he's a good man and he obviously still loves you. That's not such a bad foundation to start with, is it? Give him a chance to prove he'll do right by you. I think maybe you'll be surprised. Now, stand up and let's try on this dress. When Mr. Trent sees you at the dance tomorrow night, I want you looking so beautiful it will knock his boots off."

## Chapter Eight

The day of the festivities arrived and though the morning had started off a bit gray, by afternoon the sunshine had muscled its way over the mountains and chased away the clouds, leaving its brilliance shining down upon the pristine snow that had fallen again overnight. There wasn't too much snow, but enough to cover the landscape and take your breath away every time you looked at it.

It was a sight Willa never tired of and each time she stood on the porch of her boardinghouse and gazed upon the mountains, open sky and rolling hills, she whispered a silent thank-you for the chain of events that had brought her here. Caleb Beckett had declared Salvation Falls and the land surrounding it as God's Country and Willa was of a mind to agree.

Would that change if Morgan decided the woman she had become was not the one he wanted to call his wife? And if it did, what then?

Despite her claim that they could live peaceably in the same town, she knew better. She had never gotten over Morgan Trent. She'd tried. Lord knew, she had tried. She'd buried her feelings for him in a dusty corner of her heart and piled as much as she could over them. Marriage to Clancy, starting a new life, her own business, her independence. And in the time it took Morgan to ride into town, all of that had blown away with the storm, exposing the truth for what it was.

She loved him. Still. Despite the broken dreams, the rejection, the heartache. She didn't want to, but there it was. Irrefutable. The fact that it was Christmastime didn't help matters. She watched other happy couples and families filled with excitement over the season, purchasing tokens of affection to place beneath their trees, humming carols as they passed on the street, shopkeepers decorating their windows with bows of pine and fir laced with cranberries.

And mistletoe. She swore she could not turn a corner without finding it hanging somewhere. It was as if it had sprung up overnight and now hung from every rafter in town! She couldn't look at it without the constant reminder of the night Morgan had left and the promises he'd made to her echoing in the brittle air.

Why, just yesterday she'd caught Caleb Beckett of all people nailing a bunch of the accursed weed in the doorway of her boardinghouse's entrance hall and another clump in the archway that led to the dining area. When she asked him what he was doing, he looked down from the chair he stood on, smiled that enigmatic grin of his and said, "Decorating."

If her guests hadn't been so busy oohing and ahhing over it like they'd never seen it before, she would have torn the offending plant down.

"Good heavens, Willa, what are you doing standing out in this frigid air? You'll catch your death," Lettie scolded, coming out to stand next to her. Her sister's small frame was lost in the folds of a wool shawl pulled over a wool coat.

"I don't think a little fresh air and sunshine will be detrimental to my well-being, Lettie."

"Then why are you not partaking in the activities this afternoon?"

Willa glanced over at her sister. She had planned on going. Truly she had. But when the time had come, fear and uncertainty had all but glued her feet to the floor. Not even the coaxing of Fritz and Huck or the emptiness of the entire boardinghouse as its guests left for the church to take part had convinced her. And that made her a first-rate coward.

Not something she was about to admit to her sister.

Willa's gaze traveled down to where a burst of frothy pale blue frills poked out from the edge of Lettie's wool coat. The

frock looked completely unsuitable to the cold temperatures.
"Is that what you're wearing?"

Lettie arched one eyebrow and her gaze drifted over Willa
from head to toe. "Should I not be the one to ask that question? Where is the dress Mrs. Donovan made you? You're
never going to win Morgan over to doing things your way
with this marriage business if you look like that."

Willa knew she should never have told Lettie about Morgan's proposal, or her hope of convincing him that in order
to be happy she had to have her independence. It had been a
definite mistake. Her sister had been harping on it ever since.

"I hardly think a dress is going to be the deciding fac-
tor. Besides, I'm not sure I'm going to go through with it."

"What kind of nonsense is that? Willa Barstow, are you
telling me you're turning chicken? After everything you've
overcome in the past six years, you're going to let something as simple as a little conversation cause you to turn
tail and run?"

Willa spun on her heel and glared at her sister. "It is hardly
a *little* conversation. I am asking him to paint an entirely different picture of our life together than the one he's always
dreamed of. How do I do that? And what if he doesn't care
for the picture? Where would that leave me?"

If her outburst had any effect on Lettie, Willa could see
no signs of it. "I believe it will leave you alone, so you best
be convincing. Unless you want to die an old woman with no
children or grandchildren to send you off to your final rest.
No one to care that you were ever here on this earth to begin
with. And don't give me this nonsense that your business will
keep you warm at night because that is just a load of crap!"

"Lettie!" Willa's mouth hung open. She'd never heard her
sister use such language nor get so fired up over anything
that didn't directly involve herself.

"Don't *Lettie* me. And don't look so surprised. If you're
able to change, so am I. And so is Morgan."

"But what if—"

"Stop being a scared little mouse, Willa. It doesn't become you. The time to act is now. Morgan Trent is not going to wait around forever." Lettie took a step forward turning her pert nose up at a haughty angle. Willa had always marveled at how Lettie could look down her nose at someone while glancing upward. It was a skill she'd never mastered.

"I never asked him to wait. He is free to do as he pleases."

"Is that so? And how do think you'll feel when he proposes to someone else? Or when you see their children running about, knowing the whole time they could have been your children?" Lettie reached out and placed a hand on Willa's arm, in an uncommon show of affection. "That you should have said yes when you had the chance."

Unwelcome tears filled Willa's eyes. She blinked the offending wetness away and swallowed past the lump in her throat.

"I don't know."

Lettie's expression softened. "Willa, I know I haven't always been the best of sisters. I spent far too many years blaming you for Mama's passing and I was wrong to do so. I know that. I just thought…"

"Thought what?"

Lettie pressed her lips together briefly before continuing. "I thought maybe if Mama had lived, Father's control over our lives would have been tempered. That maybe we would have had a better chance at happiness. And when we didn't, I was angry and disappointed and I took it out on you. I'm sorry."

Her sister's apology left Willa stunned into silence. She had been aware of the roots for Lettie's animosity, but not the underlying reason. Lettie had always seemed to thrive in society, making herself the belle of every ball their father had insisted they attend. It had never occurred to Willa that maybe the reason for that had been her sister's own attempt to escape from under Father's thumb, much as marrying Morgan would have given Willa the escape she'd longed for.

Lettie sighed and took Willa's hand and led her over to the bench, sitting them both down. A squeal escaped her sister as the cold quickly worked its way through the layers of her coat and dress. "Please tell me this town warms up come summer!"

Willa smiled. "Somewhat."

Lettie moved closer, likely for warmth, but she continued to hold Willa's hand. "The truth of it is, Willa, you're a strong woman, stronger than any of us ever gave you credit for. The things you've accomplished leave me speechless. But I can look in your eyes, sister dear, and see the loneliness that lives there. And I see it in Morgan's eyes too. The two of you deserve to at least try to make a go of it. Maybe it will work, maybe it won't, but if you don't at least try you will be dogged with regret until the day you die, mark my words."

Lettie's words held the resonance of truth and much as Willa tried to dodge and weave around it, she couldn't. She *would* regret it. But would the regret hurt more or less than taking a chance and having it fail miserably?

Willa let out a long sigh and leaned against the wooden bench. There was only one way to find out.

"Good," Lettie said, pulling her off the bench and toward the entrance to the boardinghouse. "Now, let's get you ready for your showdown, shall we?"

# Chapter Nine

"Leaving town is an asinine idea. Drifting is a young man's game. You're best off being done with it."

Caleb Beckett stood next to Morgan, his arms folded over his chest as he stared straight ahead to where some of the townsfolk were ice-skating. His wife, Rachel, was out on the frozen pond with a blond-haired boy Beckett had referred to as Evan.

"I'm not that old." Heck, he hadn't even hit thirty yet.

"You ain't that young anymore either. And there's nothin' wrong with a man puttin' down some roots. Can't grow if you've got no roots. Know what happens if you don't grow?"

"Enlighten me." It appeared the man had every intention of doing so regardless of his answer.

Beckett's mouth quirked to one side. "You die. Simple as that. Problem is, you die on the inside, and that's a far sight worse than dying on the outside."

"Sounds like you're speaking from experience."

"Might be that I am." Beckett threw back the last of the coffee in the tin mug he'd carried out with him from the sheriff's office and winced. "Hunter makes a fine cup of coffee."

Morgan gave Beckett a dubious look. He'd tasted Sheriff Donovan's coffee. It had the consistency of sludge and tasted even worse.

"I don't think I can stay here, seeing her every day and not being a part of her life," Morgan admitted.

He'd given the matter a lot of thought and decided on the plan to speak to her at the Christmas dance. He'd seen no sign of Willa in the meantime. All her efforts appeared to have gone into avoiding him at all costs. He'd come up with the bright idea of hanging mistletoe about the boardinghouse thinking maybe it would remind her of their past, before everything had fallen apart. A time when they had loved each other completely, told each other their long-held secrets, talked of their hopes and dreams. He'd mistakenly mentioned the idea to Beckett, however, and true to Bertram's word, by the next day the entire town had been decked out. Now you couldn't walk more than ten feet without running into a ball of mistletoe hanging in a window or over a door.

But if it had had any effect on Willa, he'd seen no hint of it. He was running out of options. The festival had been his last chance to convince her that they could be happy. That the changes in them both had come at a price, yes, but they would ultimately make them stronger. But now the festival was coming to a close and there had been no sign of her.

"You giving up that easy?"

"Easy? She didn't even come to the Christmas Festival," Morgan pointed out. If her absence wasn't a glaring declaration of her lack of interest in a future with him, he didn't know what was. "And what do you know about it, anyway?"

Beckett gave him a long look. "I fought my own uphill battle on that account with more charges stacked against me than you can count. And I'll tell you this—it's worth the fight, even when it feels like it isn't. You think you can give up and walk away and not have that haunt you for the rest of your days?"

Morgan shifted his feet. Beckett was right. He knew it. Even now, he regretted not telling Willa the whole story, explaining what her absence in his life had done to him. What it would continue to do if he had to watch his last chance slip through his fingers and what he was willing to do to ensure that didn't happen.

"The sun is going down and my feet are freezing," he muttered, glaring down at the snow-covered ground. He'd waited all day for Willa to make an appearance.

"That'll make it harder to run off."

"I didn't say I was running off. I just said I—" He stopped and let out a growl. He didn't know what he was saying. Or thinking. Or doing. His life since she'd struck down his proposal had been a jumble of determination mixed with frustration and desperation. And failure.

"Ain't like you didn't run off before. Left Mrs. Barstow not three days before your wedding and never came back, I heard. Can't say doing that again would put you in a good kind of light with the folks around town. People here are mighty fond of Mrs. Barstow. She's a good woman and there's not a one of us that will take kindly if someone were to cause her any hurt. You understand my meaning?"

Morgan scowled at the rancher. "Your meaning was a little hard to miss."

Beckett smiled and the corners of his eyes creased. "Then we shouldn't have a problem."

"Good day, gentlemen."

Morgan turned as Lettie came up the snow-beaten path and quickly tried to school his features to hide the surprise. Her usually overdone appearance was…subdued. Extensively. Her blond hair was pulled back into a simple twist, her long wool coat a plain, unadorned navy. The dress that peeked out from beneath the coat's hem a deep burgundy. Morgan had to blink several times to ensure he was seeing things properly.

"Afternoon, Mrs. Potter," Beckett said with a nod before turning back to watch his wife, leaving Morgan to carry on the conversation.

"Try not to look so shocked, Morgan. I do know how to play the demure matron. What do you think? Success?" Lettie waved a hand at her chosen ensemble and smiled, but it wavered at the edges and it quickly registered with Morgan that the normally confident belle was unsure of herself. That was a new development.

"You look fine."

"Fine?" Lettie scowled at him and planted a hand on her hip. "Heavens, Morgan. If you're going to win my sister over you are going to have to improve your ability to hand out a proper compliment."

Her words shocked him even more than her dressed-down appearance. She'd be the last person he'd expect to be on his side when it came to convincing Red to give him a second chance. "I'll work on that. Where is she?"

Lettie nodded toward the boardinghouse. "She's getting ready, but I thought maybe the conversation the two of you needed to have would be better done in private. If you hurry, you can catch her before she leaves. And Morgan—please don't mess this up."

"Thank you for your incredible words of encouragement," Morgan said, with as much sarcasm as he could muster in his nervousness. Beside him Beckett chuckled, a low rumbling sound as if he was trying to hold in his amusement with little success.

"Don't get me wrong—I want you to succeed, I really do. But mark my words, Morgan Trent—if you hurt my sister again, I will hang your hide from the nearest flagpole. Do we understand each other?"

At this rate, between Beckett and Lettie, Morgan would be lucky to see sunset. "I have no intentions of hurting her."

"Humph." Lettie looked him up and down with a critical eye. "Well, then, get on with it."

Morgan nodded and gave Lettie a long look. Something had changed in the woman. A brand-new sense of selflessness that she struggled to make peace with. But she was trying, he would give her that. Guess maybe time had a way of changing everyone if they'd let it.

The question was, had he changed enough to win Red's forgiveness? To be the man she needed?

He took a deep breath and turned in the direction of the boardinghouse. He was about to find out.

Willa plucked her coat from the hook on the wall. She had tarried long enough until there was nothing left for her to dawdle over. Lettie had tamed her hair as best she could, pulling the mass of curls to the nape of her neck and pinning them there. The dress Meredith had made her showed off her figure to such a degree she almost didn't recognize herself.

Her time was up. She had no more excuses. Time to face her fears and speak to Morgan. She took a deep breath and opened the door to her upstairs rooms, stopping short before running face-first into a huge ball of mistletoe.

Then the mistletoe drifted downward revealing the face of the man she'd dreamed about for more years than she could count. A long breath escaped her. Would she ever tire of seeing it? Likely not. And the idea that she may not get the chance to wake up every morning and see it sliced through her.

Morgan leaned against the doorframe, a shining example of masculinity that made her knees go weak. He offered her a small, tentative smile. "Hi, Red."

"Hi." Willa's greeting whispered out of her. She wasn't sure what else to say. The words she'd planned to say suddenly deserted her. Even if she had remembered, it wouldn't have mattered. The sight of him, decked out in his sheepskin jacket and denims robbed her of breath. She still hadn't grown accustomed to this new, rugged version of the man she'd once known. But she liked it. She really liked it.

"Thought I might have a word with you before you left for the dance, if that's okay."

She pointed at the mistletoe. "Was all of this your doing?"

He gave her a sheepish grin and swept the hat from his head. "I was trying to get your attention."

"I see." Her heart pounded against her ribs. "And why was that?"

Morgan dropped the bundle of leaves and berries to the floor and pushed away from the doorframe, stepping closer. She backed up but he followed, tossing his hat onto the small table by the door. Willa swallowed but her throat had turned dry as dirt.

"Because I made you a promise once and I sealed it with a kiss beneath the mistletoe." He continued moving forward, undoing the buttons of his coat as if whatever he had to say was going to take more than a few minutes.

"Yes, I recall that."

"And I failed miserably at that promise."

She nodded. "Yes, I suppose you did."

"So this time, I thought I'd do better. That I'd come over here and make you a promise I have every intention of keeping." Morgan erased the space remaining between them, slowly and with purpose.

Willa's toes tingled and the sensation drifted up to her knees, then her thighs. Higher. She wanted to sit down, before her legs gave out completely, but she was afraid to move. Afraid this was a dream and if she said or did the wrong thing it would disappear, or worse, turn into a nightmare.

"What kind of promise?"

Morgan stopped in front of her and took her hands. His hands were cold yet still they warmed her from the inside out. She let out a breath she hadn't realized she'd been holding.

He smiled, staring into her eyes until nothing else existed but this man she loved so deeply it made her ache. A shaky laugh escaped him and he shook his head. "I had a whole speech figured out but just one look at you and I've forgotten every word. Shame too. It was a brilliant argument."

He was nervous. Just like her. The fact hit Willa hard and knocked the air out of her lungs all over again. She nodded, unable to form words until her breath returned.

"The fact is, Red, I don't blame you for turning me down the other day. You were right. I made the whole thing about me. I had this idea of what happiness looked like based on what I'd experienced growing up with Ma and Pa. I missed that so much after they were gone that all I could think of was finding the woman I loved and somehow getting that kind of life back." He squeezed her hands and she met his gaze, seeing the sincerity in his blue eyes. She returned the squeeze, letting him know that she'd heard. That her heart understood.

"I wanted it so badly," he continued. "And then I met you. But I let my vision get twisted by your father's demands of the kind of lifestyle his daughters deserved. I became determined to prove I could give you that. Any setback in my business was a failure. That was why I didn't write. I wanted you only to see my success. Turns out, I let that consume me until I lost sight of what was really important."

He lifted her hands to his lips and planted a kiss against her knuckles. Her breath came in shallow gasps and her heart grew wings and battered them against her ribs. This was what she had waited for. This was what she needed him to understand. "I didn't need any of that."

He lowered her hands again but placed one of his over the spot he'd kissed as if to hold it there. "I know that now. But then I was such a pigheaded fool. When I got your letter telling me you were marrying Clancy, I near lost my mind. It seemed I'd lost everything I'd been working for. I spent a full week drinking myself stupid and feeling sorry for myself. Then I came to my senses, realized what an idiot I'd been and rode hell-bent-for-leather to stop you."

"You did?" Her heartbeat accelerated as she tried to make sense of his words. Her whole hope in sending the letter was that he would do just that. Ride back into town like the hero she believed he could be and save her from the misery of marrying Clancy Barstow. But it hadn't happened and as she'd said her vows to a man she did not love, her heart had broken a little more.

Morgan nodded and looked at her, his expression stark, every plane and angle a study in pain and regret. "I was too late. The wedding had already taken place a few days before. If I had only headed out the day I got that letter, instead of wallowing in self-pity, everything could have been different, Red. This whole damn mess is my fault. I spent years trying to avoid that fact, blaming it on you, your father, everyone but me. But I can't outrun the truth. I failed you back then and I failed you again when I rode into town and expected you to give up everything you'd become to make me happy."

Willa took a deep breath, absorbing his admission. "I didn't know you came back."

"How could you? Wasn't like I bothered sticking around to tell you." He smiled again, but his expression held a sadness that rocked her to the core. He hadn't been the only one to place blame. She had thought he'd merely forgotten her. That he'd left her behind for sunnier skies and a better life and hadn't even had the decency to tell her.

Willa shook her head and stepped closer. He let go of her hands and wrapped his arms around her, bringing her to rest against him. She let out a deep breath. Being wrapped in his arms felt so much like home that any idea she had of not doing everything possible to keep it slipped away. How could she not fight for this? How could she justify not risking her heart and giving everything she had to make things right?

"I missed you horribly," she said, breathing in his scent. "Every minute you were gone, my heart ached a little more. When I turned around and saw you standing on the steps of my boardinghouse, I thought I'd finally lost my mind. That the loss had me seeing things. But it scared me too. Because in that minute, staring down at you, I knew nothing had changed when it came to my feelings for you. I wanted you every bit as much as I had the night you rode away from me. And the idea of losing you again had me retreating as fast as my legs could carry me." She lifted her head and gazed up at him. "Everyone keeps saying what a strong woman I am, but in that moment I never felt more weak. It scared me."

"You don't ever have to be scared of my feelings for you, Red. They've never changed. I love you. Now. Then. Always."

She shook her head. "But I'm not the woman you fell in love with," she said, voicing the fear that lived in her heart. Twice now, he had proposed to a biddable young woman willing to give up everything for him. She wasn't that woman any longer.

"Yeah, you are," he said, reaching up a hand to trace the line of her jaw. He smiled until the corners of his eyes crinkled. "I fell in love with your beautiful mind, your ideas and your warmth and your heart. None of that has changed. It's just been improved by time. Flourished in the face of adversity and made you even more amazing. I couldn't love you more if I tried, Red. But I expect with each day that goes by, I'm going to prove that statement wrong. I'm just hoping you'll give me the chance to do so."

"You don't mind if I keep my boardinghouse?"

He laughed and shook his head, dropping a quick kiss on her lips that nearly took her knees out from under her. "Red, you can run for mayor of Salvation Falls for all I care, just so long as at the end of the day you come home to me and I get to show you how much I love you. How proud I am of you. Will you let me do that? Will you let me spend the rest of our lives making you the happiest woman in Salvation Falls?"

Willa bit the inside of her cheek, certain this was all a dream she'd wake up from at any moment. "That's a tall order, Morgan Trent. There are a lot of happy women in this town."

He shook his head and laughed. "Then let's put them all to shame."

Willa took a deep breath, everything inside her shouting the answer. She smiled and for the first time in a long time, she felt true happiness deep in her heart. "Yes, let's do that."

"Really, Red?"

She nodded and Morgan grabbed her around the waist and spun her around.

"She said yes!" Through her own laughter, Willa recognized Lettie's voice and the loud whooping let out by Sheriff Donovan as a cheer rang out from downstairs where apparently half the town had congregated.

Willa didn't care. The whole world should know!

Morgan let her go and walked to the door leading out to the hallway and bent to pick up the mistletoe from the floor. He shook his head as he looked down into the main hall below, then turned and kicked the door shut.

"Come here," Morgan said, holding out his free hand. She stepped forward and took it and he lifted the mistletoe above their heads. "I made you a promise once that I would come back for you. I did, but it was too little, too late. This time, I'm going to make you a different kind of promise. I'm going to promise to love you, every day of our lives. I promise to be the kind of man you need in every way. To be worthy of the amazing woman you've become."

Willa reached up and touched Morgan's face, letting her fingertips trace the line of his strong jaw to land on his lips, which were so soft in comparison. "And I promise to keep my heart open, to rejoice each and every day in the wonderful man that you are. I love you, Morgan Trent. I truly do, with all my heart."

"That's all I've ever wanted," he said, lowering his head to capture her mouth with his. Their kiss sealed the promises made beneath the mistletoe. It built a bridge between the past and future and the wondrous life that awaited them now they had opened their hearts and minds and allowed each other in once again.

"Merry Christmas, Morgan Trent," Willa whispered against his mouth.

"Merry Christmas, Red. I've got a feeling this is about to become my favorite time of the year so long as I get to celebrate it with you."

He kissed her again, then tossed the mistletoe onto a nearby chair. "My arm's gettin' tired and I like it better wrapped around you."

Willa laughed as Morgan held her close. As his mouth descended on hers once more, she decided she didn't need a promise under the mistletoe. She already had a promise from the heart. Given by the man who had loved the girl she had once been and also the woman she'd become.

And she could think of no better future than one that brought them both the happiness they deserved and the sense of home and family they had both always longed for.

\* \* \* \* \*

*If you enjoyed this story, you won't want to miss these great full-length Historical reads from Kelly Boyce*

SALVATION IN THE RANCHER'S ARMS
SALVATION IN THE SHERIFF'S KISS

# THE SHERIFF'S
# CHRISTMAS
# PROPOSAL

## CAROL ARENS

For my grandchildren,
Caitlyn, Lauren, Brielle, Avery, Wade, Brandon and
Claire...you are the Merry in my Christmas.

Dear Reader,

I wish you a very joyful holiday. I lift my glass of
Christmas toddy in a toast that you will be blessed
with all things wonderful—delicious food, cherished
gifts both given and received, the magic of children's
laughter, carols of glad tidings and, most of all, that
you will make precious memories surrounded by
those you love.

Cheers to you!

*Carol Arens*

# Chapter One

*December 1884, aboard the train to*
*Pinoakmont, Colorado*

"Papa, I need to pee."

Roy Garner frowned as he gazed into his daughter's wide brown eyes, judging the urgency of the situation.

At only three years old, she was still fairly new to this business of going at will, and she was sitting on his lap.

"Can you wait five minutes?"

"She can't wait, Papa. I can't either," announced Lorraine, who was four and not at as great a risk for an accident.

Now with two children in need he'd have to make his way to the questionable facilities. Again. It didn't matter that the train station was only moments away.

Lifting Delanie off his lap, he set her on the floor then shot a glare at seven-year-old Robbie, then at six-year-old Jack.

Jack seemed subdued, gazing out the window with a frown at the trees flashing past. Caught up in misery, he wasn't likely to cause trouble.

But Robbie was staring at the feather decorating the hat of the woman sitting on the bench in front of him.

"Son," he said to Robbie. "I'm taking your sisters to the water chamber. If you touch that feather, I'll nail your pants to the seat."

"And Santa will bring you coal," Lorraine added helpfully.

"Ain't no such—"

"Jack, keep an eye on your brother."

Jack looked away from the scene speeding by the window. "Is too such thing as Santa."

Lorraine's chin trembled. She sniffled, dragged her sleeve across her nose.

"You're just scared you won't get anything because we're moving into the new house and you're always naughty."

Not always, Roy thought. Only since the boy's mother died a year ago.

Santa had not come that year. Colette had passed of an infection turned putrid the week before Christmas.

When he'd gotten word that she was sick, he rode across Texas hell bent for leather. Even so, he hadn't made it home until the day before the New Year.

He'd tried to salvage belief in the jolly old man by making up some story about him being delayed by a powerful windstorm. Robbie must have noticed that the wind hadn't kept Santa from coming to anyone else's house.

But damn it, Santa's absence had been the least of his problems. His wife had died. He hadn't been there.

Roy carried that shame every day. It didn't matter much that his absence could not have been helped.

As a US marshal, his job required him to be gone from home most of the time.

Colette had been the one in charge of everything. Until a year ago, he had been all but a visitor to his own home.

"Well," Delanie declared, her small brow furrowed. "I've never seen him."

"You can't see the wind either, darlin'," he explained, hoping the doubters would be convinced. "Doesn't mean it won't blow you over."

The woman with the feather stuck in her hat turned, arched a brow at Robbie. "I've seen him."

She then shot a glare at Roy as though she blamed the boy's disbelief on him.

She wasn't far off in her accusation. Had he been home,

he would have seen Colette's wound festering and got her what help could be had.

Had he been a better husband, his wife and Santa might still be alive and well.

As soon as Marshal Garner herded his children off the train, Belle Key leapt up from her seat.

"Hurry, Grannie Em," she said while attempting to lift her grandmother from the bench. "He's going to get away!"

"Not with that brood to slow him down." Grannie chuckled.

Grannie was slower getting to her feet these days, but once she was up she was as agile as a woman ten years younger. Much swifter than any other eighty-year-old Belle had met.

"Do you suppose he has our treasure in his pocket, Belle Annie?"

"He's more cunning than that, I think."

With her hand under Grannie Em's elbow, Belle helped her to the stairs that led from the passenger car to the platform.

Climbing up hadn't been too difficult, but going down? It seemed a mite steeper than it had before.

If Grannie Em were injured in a fall, she might never get her treasure back.

That would be an unqualified tragedy. Equal in its way to losing Granddaddy.

If they managed to get the wedding ring back, maybe it would help ease the pain of loss. Even after a year and a half, remembering his smile, the pleasure reflected in his blue eyes when he told a story, brought her to tears. They would come on suddenly, leave her heart spent. But at the end of it, she always felt a kiss on her forehead and his love surrounding her.

No wonder, after fifty years of marriage, her grandmother's grief had been so deep.

"Just look at him, running in circles after those children of his," Grannie murmured.

From the top step Belle gripped her grandmother's arm, watching while the marshal tried to corral his flock.

It didn't appear to be an easy task, since he was also trying to get the attention of a baggage porter.

If it weren't for the fact that the marshal was a thief, she might pity him.

When she and Grannie Em had begun their pursuit, she hadn't realized that he was the father of four. It was hard to know if this made the task of recovering the treasure easier—or harder.

The fellow deserved to be thrown in jail for his crime. But if that happened, what would become of the little ones?

Creating fatherless babies was not what she and Grannie had set out to do. Justice was all they wanted; that and the return of Grannie's precious ring.

"Come along, Belle." Grannie moved her foot impatiently, reaching her toe for the lower step. "We can't let him gain ground on us."

That did not appear likely. The trunks had been unloaded and the marshal had set a child on top of each one.

The boys fidgeted, the older girl spread her skirt daintily across a trunk lid, while the youngest girl sobbed pitifully.

Delanie—yes, that was her name—pulled on her father's coat, but he was busy speaking to someone about renting a wagon.

Drat, Belle was also going to need a wagon. Even though the town of Pinoakmont was small, the walk to the boardinghouse would be too much for Grannie Em.

They hadn't even stepped off the train, and already Grannie was beginning to shiver. Low clouds, heavy and dark, were a clear promise that snow would soon be falling.

The thief had better not be taking the only rental wagon right out from under them.

"All right, Grannie, one step at a time."

All of a sudden nothing else seemed quite as important as getting Grannie down these steep stairs. Recovering the treasured gem meant nothing if her grandmother was not here to rejoice in it.

Belle backed down the steps, watching carefully as her grandmother lowered her foot.

"Please, let me give you a hand" came her adversary's agreeable-sounding voice from behind her.

If this descent were not so critical, she'd turn and kick him in the shin—search his pockets.

Of course she could do nothing of the kind without giving their cause away.

"Thank you ever so much," she said, wondering if her smile reflected her true feelings: anger, resentment and especially annoyance that after riding in front of them for a full day, she found that she rather liked those children and felt some sympathy for Marshal Garner's plight.

Which she knew something about because she and Grannie Em had taken the time to learn a few things about him before they began this pursuit.

They knew that he was a widower. That he had retired from being a US marshal and taken the job of sheriff in Pinoakmont, where he'd purchased a large home.

Somehow they had failed to discover that he had children. Now the move to this small town made sense. No doubt he wanted to raise his brood in a safe place.

One could hardly fault him for that. But the thing that she struggled to keep in mind was that while she had some compassion for this "highly respected upholder of the law," she could not let it sway her from doing what was right. The thing to bear in mind was that pity for one's prey would not do.

She needed to keep Grannie's well-being first in whatever she did.

It was a piece of good luck that she had been able to rent rooms in the boardinghouse across the road from the house the new sheriff had purchased.

Keeping up with his doings and finding a way to take back what belonged to Grannie was going to be ever so much easier with him close by.

The distressing truth was, unless Grannie Em recovered her wedding ring by Christmas Day, she was not going to live to see the New Year.

At least that was what Grannie believed, and Belle was convinced that what one believed was often what came to pass. Even if it made no sense.

With Grannie Em safely on the ground, Belle turned about to dismiss the marshal.

But, my word! She hadn't paid attention to how handsome he was. Until she stood looking up into his eyes, she hadn't noticed what a warm shade of brown they were. How they seemed to look out at the world with a mixture of humor and mistrust.

She understood that look of wariness, because she was shooting it back at him.

All of a sudden, she smiled, hoping that he hadn't noticed her lapse in manners and begun to wonder if she was up to something. A man of his former occupation would no doubt be perceptive.

"Grannie," she said with the slightest squeeze to her grandmother's waist. "Thank this kind man for his help."

"I would—" Grannie squinted her eyes at Sheriff Garner "—if I didn't have to pee so bad."

Grannie hurried toward the station house.

Belle rushed after her but glanced back. For pity's sake, she had lavatory urgency in common with Marshal Garner. That would not do.

Of all things, Marshal Roy Garner was watching them, grinning.

And of all the foolish things she could do, she grinned back.

## Chapter Two

By the time Roy got the children and the trunks aboard the wagon, it had begun to snow. Not a picturesque patter, but a real blower that promised to be a powerful storm.

Getting the family to the shelter of the new home became suddenly urgent.

He clicked to the team but then pulled them up short.

The pretty woman from the train and her grandmother were just coming out of the station house. A pair of snow-splattered trunks remained on the platform.

He'd been told by the liveryman that he was lucky to have rented the only wagon available.

Hell's business, he doubted either of the women could drive a team even if there had been one to let.

"Can I take you somewhere?" he called, hoping the ladies' destination was not far away. Already, the children were shivering and complaining.

Distance be damned. He, as a man and the new sheriff, could hardly leave them to freeze.

"We're staying at Mrs. Farley's Room and Board," the young woman said. She looked relieved at his offer, but wary, too. "It's not far—only at the edge of town."

While he helped them into the wagon and loaded their belongings, he wondered if something had happened in the young woman's past to make her mistrustful. Had someone treated her wrong?

While her past was none of his business, in his line of work he tended to wonder about everyone he met.

"I'm so-o-o-o cold, Papa," Delanie complained.

"Her lips look blue," Robbie pointed out.

"Come here to me, child." The elderly woman, sitting beside him on the bench, turned and reached her arms toward Delanie. "Nothing quite as good as the bosoms of an old grannie to keep a little one warm."

"Arms, don't you mean, Grannie Em?" the granddaughter asked. She sat on the other side of him and he wondered what the heat of her blush would feel like if he touched her cheek.

The thought instantly shamed him. Until this moment he'd never imagined touching a woman other than his wife.

"Not arms—no, bosoms are much warmer—softer, too. Children sink right in." The old woman snuggled his youngest against her chest. "Isn't that right, princess?"

"Her teeth ain't clattering no more," Jack observed, peering over the seat and looking like he wished there was more room on Grannie Em's lap.

"You all new to Pinoakmont?" he asked, trying to sound friendly and not nosy. This natural urge in him to know all about a person was something he needed to learn to control.

This was a new town, a quiet place full of friendly, obliging folks. He wasn't chasing criminals any longer.

"Yes," the younger one answered. "Are you?"

"My pa's the new sheriff," Robbie answered for him. "We came here 'cause no criminals are likely to come."

"One never knows about that," Grannie Em stated, arching her brows.

"It seems a peaceful place so far," Roy answered.

"So far," the young woman agreed, but the tone of her answer seemed odd.

"Look, Papa, there's your new jail," Lorraine said, wagging her finger at the sheriff's office.

It was a solid-looking place in the middle of the block. Shutters were nailed shut over the windows, indicating the building had not been used in some time. He was relieved to see that there were not any wanted posters tacked to the door. From what he understood, the position of sheriff had gone vacant for nearly a year before he'd accepted it.

To the left of the office was a charming bakery with lamp

glow brightening the windows. Inside, folks gathered at tables, sipping warm drinks that he imagined might be coffee—good, hot, black coffee.

To the right there was a lending library. A woman came out escorting a pair of young boys.

She noticed them, smiled and waved as though she knew who he was, or who the women with him were. But no one in this wagon had been here before.

Pinoakmont must be friendly to strangers. He hoped the town turned out to be as agreeable as it seemed so far.

At the end of the next block, the road split. The right fork passed by a church whose tall white steeple became obscured, then invisible while he gazed at the snow swirling about it.

The left fork skirted a park. The tree-studded spot looked as pleasing as the rest of the town. The pond in the center of the park would be good for skating, then come summer, for swimming.

His children would come to be happy here.

He steered the wagon by way of the west fork. The roads became one again just beyond the church and the park.

From head to toe the business area of town was four blocks long, two blocks before the fork and two blocks after.

If one went simply by appearance, one would wonder if crime had ever blighted this picturesque place. He couldn't help but think the folks of Pinoakmont had wasted their money when they hired him.

He expected to have plenty of spare time. Time to watch his children grow, to make up some of what he had lost with them while he was out chasing criminals.

"There's Mrs. Farley's," the young woman, whose name he had been wondering about for a full twenty minutes, pointed out. She indicated the building coming up on the right with a daintily gloved finger.

The wooden sign hanging over the porch, painted with the words *Mrs. Farley's Room and Board*, creaked in the wind.

"As luck would have it, I believe that is my house right across the road."

"Isn't that a surprise?" the nameless beauty remarked.

"And so very convenient," added her grandmother.

Years of being a US marshal, and natural inclination, had taught him to read personality at a glance. There had been times when lives depended upon a quick assessment.

That wasn't the case now. He hoped that here in this little town his skill would be a useless one.

But these women had a secret. He felt it to his bones and saw it in the knowing glances they shot each other in odd moments, like this one.

His experience told him that something about them was not what it seemed.

If they had something illegal in mind, he'd know it soon enough—if they didn't it was none of his business.

It was time to quit seeing everyone through the cynical eyes that he used to have. This new life in Pinoakmont would not pit him against criminals every day. That's why he had chosen to raise his children here.

"Since we are to be neighbors, I reckon we should call each other by name." Dropping the reins, he extended his hand to the younger lady. "I'm Roy Garner."

"My name is Belle, Belle Key."

Belle Key gave his hand a curt, firm shake, then quickly withdrew her fingers.

He turned his handshake to the older woman. Delanie had all but disappeared into the folds of her coat.

"It's a pleasure to meet you, ma'am."

"My name is Emily Key. But you, my young neighbor, may call me Grannie Em, as may the children."

The children stared at her, wide-eyed in amazement. They'd never had a living grandparent.

He sure hoped the Key ladies were not up to anything illicit. The last thing he wanted was for his children to form attachments, only to have them broken.

The children seemed enamored of Grannie Em. And there was something about Belle Key that made him feel unsettled, but in a pleasant way.

Helping her down from the wagon, with his hands at her

fine little waist, something stirred inside him—something
he thought had died when he'd buried Colette.

Roy gazed out the parlor window of his new house thinking that Colette would not have approved of it. She would
have complained that it was too big. Too hard to keep on top
of what mischief the children were getting into.

Life would have been easier for her had she married a
banker or a butcher. A man like that would have been home
more often, done his part around the house.

"Papa!" Lorraine screeched from upstairs. "Robbie's trying to take my bedroom!"

"There's five bedrooms up there," he called, but figured
the problem would not be resolved until he went up to settle it.

The ruckus came from the room he had picked for himself.

Coming in, he grabbed Robbie's hand half a second before
it curled around Lorraine's braid, but not before his sweet
little girl landed a blow to her brother's shin.

"Pa-a-a!" his son wailed. Not, Roy figured, because of the
pain inflicted, but because of the injustice of it all.

Clearly, the kick deserved a yank of braid.

"You," he said to Robbie, then he pointed to Jack. "And
you, will take the room next to this one.

"Ain't fair, Pa. I got here first."

The beginnings of a triumphant smile tugged at Lorraine's
cute little mouth. Sure did look like her mother's smile.

"You and you." He pointed at his girls. "Take the room
on the other side of this one. This one's mine."

"Can you hear me in the night if I get scared?" Delanie
wrapped her arms around his knee, blinking up at him with
eyes the color of melted caramel.

He touched her curls, felt the silky texture of them. "I'll
hear you, darlin'."

"Six times?"

Heaven help him. "Seven times."

"But there's extra rooms," Jack complained. "I want one
of my own."

"It's good to share." Especially for Jack, who had never

fully accepted his mother's passing. Being alone would only make his grief worse. "It'll teach you boys to get along."

Three unhappy faces stared up at him. Only Delanie seemed content with the sleeping arrangements.

"All of you, go downstairs and bring up firewood. It'll be cold tonight."

He followed them down. Gazing about the big parlor, he felt satisfied. This would be a fine house to raise his family in. It was cozy in spite of its size.

The furniture he'd purchased, and some from the old house that he had shipped, had been delivered last week. The stranger he'd hired to set it up arranged it in a way that he would have done himself.

Taking his time getting here, planning ahead, had been the right choice. Bringing the children to an empty house with nothing that was familiar would have been hard on them. Facing another Christmas without their mother was going to be heartache enough as it was.

It would not be like last year, though. This year Santa would come and bring double the gifts. Stockings would be hung on the great hearth in the parlor. The Christmas tree would touch the ceiling.

Every night he would read them a story.

Roy reckoned he would enjoy it as much as they would. Christmas had always been a special time, but last year's tragedy had doused the joy.

By making the holiday bright for his babies, maybe he would get a bit of the Christmas spirit back.

Maybe he'd invite guests for the holiday.

That would brighten things. The children would like being around Grannie Em and he wouldn't mind singing a Christmas carol with Miss Belle Key.

At least he hoped she was Miss. He didn't know for sure. The fact that she and her grandmother shared the same name didn't necessarily mean anything.

He filled his arms with logs, surprised that it struck him as so all-fired important to find out what Belle's marital condition was.

He shouldn't care at all, not when he suspected she was keeping a secret. But in his reading of her, he sensed something else, as well. The woman had a kind heart.

She'd defended Santa, after all. She was caring for her grandmother. Whatever she, or they, were hiding, he doubted there was any ill intent with it.

Besides, everyone had secrets. He carried one of his own. Lately, the urge to move on with his life pressed upon him. Hope for the future washed over him at odd moments. So did guilt.

Grief and hope were hard emotions to balance.

"Papa, I'm hungry." Delanie dropped the piece of kindling she had lugged up the stairs.

"Me, too," Jack agreed.

"I'm about to gnaw on this here log." Robbie put his teeth on the bark to illustrate his plight.

For all that someone had done to get the house ready, they had neglected to lay in food.

The cupboards held dishes, but nothing to get them dirty with.

The only thing to do was go out in the storm, see if the general store was still open. Leaving the children alone was risky business, though.

A bold knock rapped on the front door.

He opened to find a full-bodied woman, her eyelashes spangled with snow, smiling broadly at him.

"You're early," she announced. "I was expecting you tomorrow. There'd have been food tomorrow."

"Pleased to meet you, ma'am," he greeted the stranger at his door. "I'm Roy Garner."

"Of course you are." She extended her hand and shook his with vigor. "I'm the widow Farley. You'll come to dinner of course, Sheriff. You and the children."

"I'm obliged, ma'am."

More than obliged. If the rest of folks in Pinoakmont were like his neighbor, he had no regrets about settling here.

## Chapter Three

Belle settled her grandmother into a chair at a dining table that was highly polished and set for ten. Pine cones and red ribbons decorated the center.

From where she sat, she had a view of the fire snapping brightly in the parlor hearth. She was beyond grateful for the blush of warmth coming from the flames.

Not all boardinghouses were as cozy as this one. She and Grannie had stayed in some ugly, drafty places. Mentally, she cursed her step-uncle, who had made them all but paupers after Granddaddy's passing.

Although she hated to, she silently thanked Roy Garner for picking a lovely little town to settle in.

She also thanked him, reluctantly, for delivering them to the boardinghouse. Snow blew past the dining room window; ice crystals formed on the glass.

If it weren't for him they would be waiting out the storm at the train station.

The handsome sheriff might be a thief, and she his huntress, but that did not mean she was not obliged to recognize the service he had done them.

"I'm anxious to meet our fellow boarders," Belle commented in order to purge the image of his face from her mind. To shake off the odd warmth she felt when remembering the strength of his arms, the heat of his hands banding her waist when he'd lifted her from the wagon.

"I hope they aren't a dull lot. At my age, Belle Annie, there's no time to waste on dull folks."

"The same could be said of any age, Grannie."

"Our young hero is interesting."

"He's not our hero, Grannie Em. He's our thief."

"That's what makes him so fascinating." Grannie grinned. "He's a thief, but he didn't let us freeze to death. I feel the man is not beyond redemption."

"Don't forget what he's done to you."

"I haven't—but there are those children of his. He's dedicated to them. That speaks of character."

"Even rats are dedicated to their young."

"You don't see a rat when you look at him." Grannie winked. "You see a virile man."

"I do not!"

"An old woman sees what an old woman sees. I suspect when this is all over Roy Garner will want to woo you."

"That's absurd, Grannie Em. Once we've ruined his reputation, he won't want to woo me."

"You have the most lovely breasts, dear, and don't think he hasn't noticed. He'll overlook a lot to be able to put his hands on them."

"Hush, Grannie! What kind of a thing is that to say?"

"A true thing. I've been on this planet long enough to know. Why, your grandfather—"

Belle covered her ears. "No more, Grannie! Look, here come the other boarders."

"If I were you I'd think of something bland, get rid of that blush. Folks are going to wonder."

As if the blush was not Grannie's fault. Just when she'd managed to get Roy Garner's face out of her mind, there popped the picture of him with his hands upon her charms.

Thanks to her grandmother, the blush was going to last all night. Clearly, she was going to have some trouble forgetting the image.

Three people entered the dining room at the same time.

"Good evening, ladies. I'm Jim Flynn," said a middle-aged gentleman who was tall, slim and just beginning to go gray at the temples. "Such a pleasure to meet you."

"And you," Grannie answered with a polite nod—thank the good Lord.

It was hard to predict what her grandmother was going to say. It seemed the older she got the more she bluntly spoke what was on her mind.

Mary Farley entered the dining room carrying a platter piled high with something that smelled wonderful.

"Miss and Mrs. Key." She nodded at them, then at the women standing on each side of Mr. Flynn. "Meet Beulah Banks, our librarian and a single lady. And Hilda Bee, my sister."

"Mary, why must you always point out that I'm unmarried?" Beulah complained.

"It's a pleasure to meet all of you," Grannie said.

"And you," Jim Flynn answered with a nod and a smile.

"Are there more guests coming?" Beulah Banks asked. "I see extra places set."

Perhaps it was Belle's imagination that the eager look on the librarian's face meant she hoped a single man was coming.

If so, she would swoon the first time she saw her new neighbor and sheriff.

An odd, unpleasant feeling soured Belle's stomach.

All of a sudden she wanted to run outside and fall face-first into the snow. How could she feel jealous over a man she had met one time—a man who was her adversary?

Well, she knew why! Plainly, it was because he'd been busy with his hands round her waist.

Blast! Blast! Blast! Just because Grannie had spent many years blissfully satisfied did not mean that fate awaited everyone.

Not the spinster librarian and certainly not Belle.

There had been a time when she had hoped for more, but life had turned on a dime and now all her focus was on keeping Grannie fed and sheltered.

If there was a man out there to make her heart swoon, Cupid was going to have to place him smack in her path.

A rap at the front door interrupted her emotional edginess.

"Here they are now," Mary Farley announced, then opened the door to let her guests in.

Roy Garner stepped inside, Delanie hugging his leg. Robbie and Jack sniffed the air, clearly smelling dinner. With sweet charm, Lorraine smiled at everyone.

"Everybody, this is our new sheriff, Roy Garner, and these are his children. I'll let you all get acquainted while I bring out the rest of dinner."

Beulah lifted her chin, blinked and stared. She smiled broadly, clearly setting her cap for the handsome guest.

"Our young man certainly makes beautiful babies," Grannie whispered in her ear.

"He's not our young man!" she hissed back. "He's our objective."

Their quarry! Their prey! Their criminal!

But, in spite of that, her nipples twisted against the lace of her camisole.

Blast! Blast! Blast!

Roy brushed snow from the brim of Delanie's hat, then the shoulders of her coat. He hung the garments on the hall tree beside the front door. Conveniently, Mrs. Farley had set a mop beside the door so he could wipe the moisture up.

He did the same with all the children, then sat them down at the table.

Delanie, sitting beside Grannie Em, smiled up at the elderly woman.

"Isn't she the sweetest thing?" Grannie Em asked.

"Quite adorable," Belle Key stated.

Oddly, and for no reason he could imagine, she glared at him. A bright blush stained her cheeks.

"I love children," a tall woman, slightly gaunt in the face, said. Not a single strand of hair escaped her no-nonsense bun. "Yours look as obedient as little soldiers."

Belle Key cast her a quizzical glance. She would know better, having traveled in front of his children for hours on the train.

Delicate-looking brown curls defied Miss Key's bun. Any man would notice how softly they framed her face and neck.

"No one wants little soldiers, Beulah," the other woman

declared, then swung her attention to him. "I'm Hilda Bee. It's a pleasure to have you here defending our little town."

"And I'm the town librarian, Beulah Banks. I agree that it's a pleasure. Truly. I'll sleep better in my bed at night just knowing you are close by."

He couldn't help but wonder what kind of crime the lady expected him to deliver her from.

Miss Key probably wondered, too, because she raised her brows at Beulah.

Grannie Em grinned and placed a kiss on Delanie's head.

Belle looked away from the librarian to shoot a frown at him, her arms anchored firmly across her chest.

He must have offended her in some way, but he was damned if he knew how.

"I'll do my best to keep law and order, ma'am."

"Is it true you were a genuine US marshal?" Miss Banks asked, her breath sounding raspy.

Robbie looked at her with squinted eyes. "Why does your—"

Voice sound like a frog? He knew without a doubt that was the question his son was about to ask. Luckily the boot-swipe he gave the boy silenced him.

It helped that their hostess picked that moment to carry in a big bowl of mashed potatoes.

"Pinoakmont seems a peaceful place," he commented quickly because Robbie had just noticed how large Miss Banks's front teeth were.

"Might be if the town had a decent name," the other man at the table declared.

"You, Jim Flynn, are part the reason it does not," Hilda Bee said. She arched her brows at Roy. "Can you imagine wanting to name the town Mountslide? Makes it sound like we're going over a cliff."

"Better than Oak Rot."

"It wasn't Oak Rot and you know it. It was Pretty Oak." Mrs. Bee glared at Mr. Flynn. "It was a lovely suggestion."

"It was fine," Miss Banks said. "But not nearly so exquisite as Pine Leaf."

"No such thing as a pine leaf, Beulah," Jim Flynn replied. "It would have needed to be called Pine Needle."

"We argued over the name for a month." Mrs. Farley sat down at the head of the table. "We nearly came to violence. In the end, we called it Pinoakmont."

With that discussion put to rest, they ate in silence.

At long last, Hilda Bee went upstairs. Next went the spinster, snatching up a dime novel from a side table before she made her way up.

"Mountslide," Jim Flynn muttered, screeching his chair across the floor as he stood.

"Good night, Jim," Mrs. Farley called after him.

Jim waved his hand without looking back.

"Believe it or not, all three of them are decent people. This is a good town, Sheriff—we just have a problem agreeing on certain things."

"I assume you've hired Mr. Garner to protect you from each other?" Belle Key asked. A pair of pretty dimples winked at the corners of her mouth.

He'd been hired as a babysitter? For a second, his gut twisted, seeing the way his career had disintegrated. But a peaceful place was what he wanted. It was the reason he'd moved his family here.

A safe place to raise his children, to be able to be with them instead of traipsing over hill and dale, never knowing what was going on at home, was what he needed.

He welcomed this change in his life. Until last Christmas he'd never understood what he was missing. It was a sorry thing that he'd never fully appreciated his wife, all she did, until it was too late to tell her so.

Glancing across the table at his daughters, he saw a bond forming with the elderly woman. He hoped the ladies Key were making Pinoakmont their permanent home.

He glanced at Belle. The thought of having them as neighbors was intriguing.

Just now she was watching her grandmother nuzzle the children. Her face did not have the wary look it normally did. Far from it; her eyes glowed softly, her smile sweetly indulgent.

Grannie Em was a lucky woman to be so loved.

But the Key ladies did confuse him. They were not, he suspected, who they seemed—not completely, at least. The only thing he knew for sure about them was that they loved one another deeply.

"Yes, keeping peace between us is the biggest reason we hired you, Sheriff Garner," Mrs. Farley explained. "There's not much risk of a genuine criminal taking an interest in our little town."

"But there's another reason you hired me? One that's not as important as keeping you from doing each other in?"

"It is related, of course. Like I said, mostly we are a companionable town. But when there are decisions involved, everyone wants their own way. Some folks want things one way and some another. So they form alliances, three against four, ten against fifteen—Mr. Flynn against everyone. Poor man. He only became contentious after his wife passed."

Roy nodded, feeling compassion for the fellow. He might have become bitter, too, if it weren't for the children.

He was in many ways the luckiest man in the world.

"Well, what's the other reason you hired him?" Grannie Em asked.

"To organize the Christmas pageant. It's the only way to keep the holiday peaceful." Mrs. Farley shrugged. "Amazingly, we all did agree on having you do it. With the sheriff in charge, we won't argue. If anyone makes a fuss, you can lock them up overnight."

"I'm the Pinoakmont social director?"

"That's what it sounds like to me, Sheriff." Belle grinned at him, her eyes and dimples flashing.

"Do I have a job after Christmas when you all get along like peas in a pod?"

"Of course! After Christmas is the Valentine's Ball, the Easter Parade then the Summer Social. After that it's the Fall Fair."

# Chapter Four

Grannie sat down on the edge of her bed and yawned. She bounced a couple of times, apparently judging its comfort.

"These old springs squeak. The whole house will know whenever I turn over." Grannie grew quiet for a moment, probably remembering years gone by, as she sometimes did. A slow smile curved her lips. "I remember my honeymoon—the bed was squeaky then, too. As I recall, your grandfather and I kept the entire floor of our hotel awake all night long."

At bedtime, Grannie's thoughts always turned to Granddaddy.

Belle knew all about their courtship. Sometimes more than she thought she ought to know.

Granddaddy had been married before and came to Grannie with his late wife's young son in tow. He was a grateful man to have found love again. A lustful one, too, according to Grannie.

For Grannie had found love and marriage after she had given up hope of it. During their fifty-two-year marriage, they had been everything to each other.

In Grannie's eyes, the missing ring was her link to him—the physical evidence that their love had existed. The theft had left her broken for a time. It was not until they began the mission to recover it that she'd become herself again.

Belle only wished that Grannie had not imposed Christmas as the day she would either live or die. Of course, this was not something that Belle believed—at least, she didn't think that she did.

But the fact remained that the mind could have a powerful influence over a person. Thrive or die—it did have something to do with attitude.

Even without truly believing Grannie's life was at stake, Belle would have undertaken this hunt for the ring, if only to give her grandmother purpose. The older woman had grieved deeply for her husband.

"I wonder what your parents are doing…" Grannie lay down on the bed and pulled the covers to her chin. "Still mining silver in Nevada I suppose."

Still putting everything before her.

Her parents had been adventurers, always looking for an easy fortune. Her grandparents were the ones who had raised her, and she had taken their surname when she went to live with them. From the time she was an infant, her grandparents had not put a single thing above her well-being.

"Sweet dreams, Grannie." She kissed the top of her grandmother's soft white hair, then stood up. "I've already got a sewing job. Miss Beulah wants me to refashion one of her gowns for the Christmas pageant."

"She wants to look good for the new sheriff. Better watch out that she doesn't steal your man."

"I don't have a man! And if you are speaking of Roy Garner, I've barely said boo to him."

"With your voice—but like I always say, an old woman sees what an old woman sees."

"In this case she sees the impossible. I think it's you who have gone soft on him."

"Not soft, but I see possibilities. A thief can be redeemed—forgiven. Whereas people like your parents who desert their children lack moral character. There is a difference. Even given his crime, the sheriff is devoted to his babies. In that, he is a better man than some. I wonder what your life would have been if your parents were more like him."

"Grannie, my life with you and Granddaddy was wonderful. I was a happy child. But, as far as Roy Garner goes, you aren't saying that you want to quit what we have set out to do?"

Grannie sighed. The blanket rose under her chest. "Not at all. He has my ring and I do need it. I only wonder…"

"What?"

"What would happen if my enchanted ring circled your finger?" Grannie's impish blue eyes twinkled in the lamplight.

"Nothing enchanting. The ring is nothing more than a symbol of lasting love. It doesn't make Roy Garner any less of a criminal."

"Belle Annie, love is enchanting."

"For you, maybe." Belle turned down the lamp beside the bed.

*Enchanted ring, my foot.* Just because Granddaddy had purchased it from a gypsy did not make it enchanted.

"I'm going downstairs. Ring the bell beside the bed if you need me."

Grannie had never jingled the bell. This was for Belle's peace of mind.

Granddaddy had passed away suddenly, alone in an upstairs bedroom while everyone else was below chatting by the fireside.

As much as she tried to remind herself that Grannie was in good health, Granddaddy had also appeared to be well.

Where her grandmother was concerned, she was a bit overcautious, but better to be careful than not.

"Good night, my dear. I love you, too."

This was something that Grannie said every night before she fell asleep. Belle knew the comment was not addressed to her.

Downstairs, she passed by Jim Flynn, who sat beside the fireplace in a big stuffed chair, blowing rings into the air with the smoke of his cigar.

"Good evening, Jim," she said, then sat down in a chair that was placed beside the large and inviting bay window.

"Same to you, Miss Key." He smiled and saluted her with the glowing stub.

With her sewing project on her lap, she started to thread

her needle but became distracted by the beauty of the night beyond the window.

The storm had moved on, leaving a blanket of pristine white on the ground. The full moon glittered off it while the icy wind whistled under the eaves of the house.

A movement caught her eye—a flash of pink darting across an upper window of the sheriff's house.

She watched for it again.

A few seconds later she saw Delanie sitting upon her father's shoulders while he galloped about the bedroom like a human pony. Even from here she could tell that the little girl was laughing.

He swiped the child down from her perch on his shoulder, then tossed her in the air and caught her with a tickle to her ribs.

After a moment, Roy Garner did the same to Lorraine, who wore a pale blue nightgown.

The man certainly was a puzzle. Apparently Grannie Em had no trouble in figuring him out—a decent man who had done a wrong thing. Evidently, once the wrong thing was resolved, she would be happy to forgive him.

For Belle, Roy Garner was more complicated than that. She did not understand him in the least.

How could a man who had a heart black enough to steal a widow's wedding ring be so loving toward his children? He certainly did keep that nefarious heart well hidden.

But it was only fair to remember, she thought, watching him kiss Lorraine on the forehead, that Roy Garner was not the first person to steal the ring.

Her step-uncle, Gaston Lemar, had been the first. A month after Granddaddy's death, he'd snatched it from Grannie's finger and run out the door. That had been only the first of many thefts Grannie's stepson had committed.

She and Grannie had come to find out that US marshal Roy Garner had taken the ring into custody when he arrested Gaston and then greedily kept it for himself.

Had the marshal done the morally correct thing and

handed it over to someone in authority, lives would be different.

Grannie would not have given her mortality a deadline and Belle would not have spent valuable time chasing a criminal.

It would save effort if she simply asked Roy Garner for the ring. But no, he would only deny the theft. What thief would not? Then, once he knew they were looking for the treasure, they would have no hope of finding it.

She and Grannie needed to keep the element of surprise on their side.

While she watched the bedroom window, not feeling a bit guilty for spying under the circumstances, the lamp dimmed. She saw the sheriff's dark silhouette walk to the bedroom door, turn and blow kisses, three to each little girl.

She tried to remember her own father doing the same. If he had, it was done from several states away.

More confused than ever, she glanced over at Jim, hoping to have a conversation with him while she sewed.

No such luck. He'd fallen asleep with the cigar dangling from his fingers, the smoldering tobacco only inches from the rug.

With a sigh, she stood, crossed the room and plucked it out of his hand.

"Good night, Jim," she whispered, then stuffed the cigar out on the brass plate beside his chair.

She returned to her sewing and tried to concentrate on the stitches and not the puzzling man who was probably now tucking his sons into bed.


"It's December fifteenth," Roy muttered, walking carefully along the icy road. "Only nine days until the cursed pageant."

"Just as well it's only nine days," Belle Key said, walking beside him. "They'll have less time to form their alliances."

"It was good of you to come along, Miss Key. I appreciate your help."

"Oh, I don't know that I'm coming to help so much as this

meeting ought to be too interesting to miss. And I do so love everything Christmas."

"Remind me to stop at the bakery and bring home a treat for your grandmother. It was a generous thing, offering to come over and watch the children. Being alone with that crew can try anyone's patience."

"I'm sure she will find something to do to keep her busy."

With a flashing dimple, she grinned at him. Black fur edged the hood of her coat, framed her face. Her cheeks and nose bore the pink blush of cold weather.

All of a sudden she lowered her lashes and glanced away. "To keep the children busy is what I meant, of course."

"They're always busy, mostly with mischief. But I swear, I'd rather be home with them than running this meeting. No help for it now, though, since this seems to be my job."

"Would you have taken it had you known you'd be the town arbitrator?"

"Sure would have given the offer a second thought, but in the end, it's the children's welfare that's important. So yes, I'd still be here."

A gust of wind billowed Miss Key's skirt. She pressed her hands to the front to flatten it.

"But you must miss the excitement of hunting outlaws. Making sure thieves and other wicked folks face the justice they deserve?" Her brows arched, accenting her question.

He had a notion that she was asking one thing but meaning another.

"I don't miss weeks and months away from home." He shook his head. "But at least I was good at what I did. I sure don't know anything about organizing a Christmas pageant. I had a nightmare last night involving Valentine's Day."

Belle Key laughed. The sound tinkled past the closed door of a hat shop.

What would she think if he were bold enough to call her Belle—or Belle Annie? He liked the sound of Belle Annie. Belle Annie Key. The way the names flowed together made him want to smile.

The walk from home to church was short, but slippery.

He offered Belle his arm for support. After a hesitation, she placed her hand in the crook of his elbow.

It had been a long time since he'd strolled like this with a woman. The delicate pressure of her fingers on his arm felt natural, comfortable.

As much as he'd loved Colette, she had always been a bit reserved with him. He always figured it was because each time he came home after a long absence, it was like they had to get acquainted all over again. Sometimes he felt like an awkward left foot disturbing the order of her well-run home.

"If you don't know what to do, just make something up and stick with it." Suddenly, she became quiet, apparently deliberating something in her mind. "I reckon I can help you."

"I could kiss you, Miss Key—you'll be my ally?"

"Your ally?" she sputtered, clearly distressed.

Maybe he hadn't expressed his gratitude in the most polite of ways.

"I'm sorry, I shouldn't have said I'd kiss you—that was forward. But I do thank you, and I'd like to call you Belle."

"If we are to be, um…allies…in this Christmas pageant, that would be acceptable."

"I can't tell you how grateful I am for your help."

Looking at her pretty, slightly dubious frown, he decided that, actually, he would take great joy in kissing her, and not simply out of gratitude.

He wanted to feel good about that, but somehow, kissing a woman seemed disloyal. How long, he wondered, would Colette have waited to get on with her life had it been he who died?

Given his line of work, this wasn't the first time he'd thought about it.

"Here's the church. I reckon it's time to put my head in the mouth of the lion."

Her smile burst to life again, her dimples winking and her eyebrows arching over clear green eyes. "I suppose it is."

# *Chapter Five*

Stepping inside the social room, Belle felt light-headed. What had she done? Had she lost all sense of reason?

She had agreed to become her adversary's ally. There had been talk of a kiss and still, she had done it.

Worse, she could not deny that the thought of kissing Roy Garner had influenced the unwise choice.

Or, was it unwise?

Perhaps the wise thing would be to stick close by him, discover what she could about the ring.

She had learned a few things at her scholarly grandfather's knee. Such as successful warfare being based upon deception.

Of course, she had never expected that particular wisdom to be of value in her life.

It could be that befriending Roy Garner was the right thing to do.

Belle would support the sheriff—until she did not.

When that day came, she would hand Grannie her ring, and her future. Then she would expose the sheriff for the faithless public servant he was.

Upon entering the meeting room, Belle heard the drone of conversation, but when folks spotted Roy, they fell silent. Every eye stared at him—and her.

She was uncomfortable under the scrutiny but he simply shot the stares back. For as much as they judged him, he clearly assessed them, taking their measure.

No doubt, this ability to gauge people was what had made

him a successful marshal. She just hoped he didn't see what was behind her own smile.

The only thing to do in this moment was to earn his trust before he delved too deeply.

Roy sat down. Belle took a seat beside him.

"I think the nativity decorations need to be pink and blue this year," announced a woman sashaying her wide hips into the room, carrying a platter of what smelled like cinnamon cookies. "It's time for something new."

"I say traditional red or nothing at all," Jim Flynn disagreed. "If you're going to go and change things, Flora, we might as well skip the pageant altogether."

"That's a narrow-minded thing to say, you old coot!" A slim woman stood, wagging a finger. "Nothing could be better for a sweet new baby than pink."

"Except that the baby was a boy!" a male voice added.

"There must be some way to use both?" Roy suggested.

In silence, the group appeared to be sizing him up, no doubt determining what they might or might not get away with.

"Both?" Mrs. Farley seemed aghast. "I hardly think it would look harmonious."

"Who cares about the colors of the decorations? The problem is that we have no baby for the manger. Seems a crime to me that none of you young women felt the need to think of this nine months ago."

"Only an unmarried fool would say such a ridiculous thing. I'm quite certain that if any of us had produced this 'prop,' we would not expose it to the cold."

The young woman who was speaking looked indignant and with good reason, in Belle's opinion.

"I'll let my lamb play a part," a middle-aged fellow volunteered.

He scooted his chair slightly to the right so that he sat beside the man who favored shivering infants. So did another man.

This could only be the beginning of the infamous forming of alliances.

Roy stood up. So did Belle. She stepped close to the sheriff, flanking him the way an ally, false or genuine, ought to.

She couldn't help but notice the way his posture suddenly straightened, his scowl narrowed on the men.

"The next person who suggests endangering infants will regret it."

"My word," Belle said with a great smile all around. She made sure to engage the eye of everyone in the social room. "I can't recall when I've been a part of a group with so many good ideas."

Folks looked at each other, clearly skeptical of her opinion as well as each other's.

"All we need to do is to knit them together, weave all the ideas like a prettily colored blanket."

"Who are you?" a frowning man asked.

"My assistant." Roy cast a scowl over the crowd. "I don't know hell's business about pageants. Miss Key does. You'll listen to her or I'll do what I do know how to do."

Murmurs of confusion and looks of askance spread about.

"Put you in jail, he means." Belle shrugged, smiled.

"Until you cool off and see the wisdom of working together and not against each other." Roy slid half a step closer to her.

A frizzle of sexual awareness arched between them.

Oh, my! This was the very last thing she wanted.

Judging by the half-confused glance he gave her, he noticed it, too.

When it appeared that tempers might be heating, Belle volunteered to sew a baby doll for the manger.

After some argument it was settled that the baby would be wrapped in blue with a pink blanket.

"And lots of green boughs," Beulah Banks suggested, her gaze settling appreciatively on Roy.

Not that it mattered to Belle—no, not a whit. Beulah Banks could walk up and take the kiss the sheriff wanted to give away and Belle would cheer.

Indeed, she would—heartily.

"Lovely!" Mrs. Farley declared, nodding. "We've got a start, and not a bloodied nose among us."

"Do you think the peace will hold?" Belle asked, walking up the icy steps of Roy's big house.

She didn't worry about slipping as she might have, because his big hands supported her, one under her arm and the other about her waist. My word, but the man was uncommonly strong and sure-footed.

"If it doesn't, the jail has two cells. We'll put everyone of one opinion in the first and everyone opposed in the other."

It made an interesting and funny picture in her mind. "Yes, we can plan as we like and let them out when it's time to attend."

"I like the way you think. You are a woman after my heart."

That, she was not! Not by a stone's throw. She was after justice and her grandmother's ring. The last thing she would be swayed by was his rumbling laugh, how it made her want to giggle along with him.

Which she did, but for appearance's sake. Too bad it felt good—and disturbingly natural.

"I hope the children haven't worn your grandmother out," Roy said, opening the front door.

"I hope she hasn't led them in naughty behavior."

"Pa!" Jack bounded across the long parlor and hugged his father about the legs. "I missed you, Pa."

Roy ruffled the boy's hair. "I'll always be close by, son. Never farther than you can run to me."

"Promise?"

"On my honor. Now, what have you done with Grannie Em?"

"Nothin', Pa," Robbie said. "She's just upstairs searching through your things."

Belle's heart sank. She wasn't sure if she was flushed or pale—probably both. All she wanted was for the floor to open up and the earth to suck her in.

The hunt had barely begun and they were going to be found out.

"I can't imagine what got into Grannie," she stammered. "She's—just—" What? Sneaky, daring, foolish. "Old."

"I found it!" Grannie's voice trilled from an upstairs bedroom.

A few seconds later Grannie Em hustled onto the landing with her fist folded about something.

It was unbelievable. She had found the ring. This game was over. She could now expose Roy Garner—leave Pinoakmont and never see him again.

She waited, anticipating the thrill of victory to rush through her. She and Grannie had bested the thief.

Curiously, it was not satisfaction that washed through her.

Gazing into Roy's puzzled expression all she felt was regret.

Which was ridiculous.

"What have you found, Grannie?"

Pinched between her fingers she held it up, triumph flushing her cheeks with pleasure.

"The lucky penny!" She started down the steps. Roy rushed up to guide her down. "I looked for nearly half an hour. You children did a good job hiding it."

"A lucky penny?" Belle gasped. "You were playing a game?"

"A game that I won!"

"Took me an hour to find the bedeviled coin last time I played." Roy shook his head, delivering Grannie safely to the ground floor. "The children are even better at hiding the penny than they are at finding it."

"They are quite accomplished," Grannie agreed.

"You turned Mr. Garner's things inside out and just to find a penny?"

"Not just to find a penny, Belle Annie." Grannie arched a thin gray brow. "To win the game. Next time you ought to play with us."

"I'm sorry, Roy. No doubt your room is a shambles."

"Only because the penny was tied up in the toe of a sock."

"What's her prize, Pa?" Jack asked, grinning.

The little boy had a sweet smile. She didn't recall having seen it before.

"What would you like, Grannie Em?" Roy asked.

"I'd like to keep this lucky penny and be invited to stay for dinner." She glanced at Belle, shrugged. "It's more fun over here. That Jim fellow fills the house with nasty cigar fumes, and the spinster is always fussing over the dress that you're sewing for her. Poor thing thinks she is going sweep you off your feet at the social, Roy."

Roy didn't express an opinion on how he felt about Beulah Banks's attention.

Belle had an opinion about it, which she would never express. But the truth was, the more time she spent with her adversary and ally, the more it irked her that Beulah doted so upon him.

She pressed her middle, trying to rub the pestering emotion away.

"Thank you for dinner, Roy. Grannie Em is right about the nasty smoke. We could both use an evening without it."

A small hand caught her fingers. "Can I sit next to you?"

Looking down into Delanie's soft brown eyes, another sensation filled her middle. But this one was sweet, tender and welcome.

She was glad Grannie had not found the ring. There would be time for that—just not tonight.

## Chapter Six

Roy yanked his tie loose, then unbuttoned his collar. Standing beside his bedroom window, he gazed across the road.

At midnight the full moon rose above the horizon, casting diamonds and deep blue shadows on the snow.

Sparkle and shadow—they reminded him of the Key ladies. They were a mystery he was having trouble figuring out.

Grannie Em was a sweet old lady—everything a grandmother should be. But there was more to her than that. At times, she cast him odd looks, apparently thinking he didn't notice.

Belle did the same thing. They even cast odd looks at each other.

Could be a strange family trait. Or it could be that they were sending silent messages.

Whatever they were about didn't concern him.

Except that it did.

Not as sheriff. He didn't have the sense that they were up to anything illegal.

But as a father, that was another thing.

It was his job to make sure that the people his children became attached to didn't come into their lives for a season and then move on. Their hearts were still grieving and too fragile for bonds that didn't last.

Not that he thought the Key ladies would intentionally do anything to hurt his children. To the contrary, they seemed to dote upon his babies. But if the children formed bonds with the women, and then had to say goodbye—they would be hurt.

Delanie and Lorraine were quickly becoming attached to Grannie Em. It was clear as a ringing bell that Grannie Em returned their affection.

The boys had both taken a shine to Belle.

They would, of course. He reckoned they were looking for their mother. Trying to fill the void she had left.

Perhaps he ought to discourage the bond with his neighbors, given the fact that he had no idea how long the Keys planned on staying in Pinoakmont.

The trouble was, tonight Jack had begun to smile again. Robbie had gotten into half his normal mischief and the girls looked as happy as floating bubbles.

And Roy felt a lightness of heart that had been missing for some time.

The evening had passed with them all sitting about the fireplace, telling stories of Santa and singing Christmas carols.

Anticipation of the holiday lightened everyone's spirits—especially his. This was going to be the best Christmas he could make it. Hearts would be merry and bright.

No one was ready for the evening to end. Especially not Grannie Em, who seemed to grow decades younger while she told stories of the blessed years spent with her husband—of how Christmas had been their special time. In fact, it had been the day they fell in love.

This year Christmas would be a special time for his children, too. They would lack for nothing, be it Santa's visit, sweet treats or good company.

Wise or not, he could not sever the budding relationship with the Keys because no matter what else happened, his little ones would not face heartache again this year.

All of a sudden he needed a breath of air, rich with the scent of pine. Nothing quite brought the holiday home like the scent of cold pine.

He opened the window, cherished the kiss of icy air on his face, then breathed in a lungful of—

Smoke!

The last thing he'd done before retiring was to bank the flames in the fireplace.

Hell's business! He ran out of the bedroom. Not taking the time to maneuver the stairs, he slid down the banister.

Belle coughed. She heard screaming. Oddly the sound was muffled.

She tried to sit up, wanting to discover the source of the trouble, but her body was heavy, her thoughts sluggish.

It seemed that she was awake but must not be. Perhaps this was one of those odd dreams that felt real but only until one woke to reality.

This had to be true since Grannie Em slept soundly in the bed beside hers.

Oddly, for a dream, the coughing was quite painful. She ought to try and rouse herself—push up, sit upright.

With an effort, she inhaled then gagged.

Smoke. Not a dream but smoke and fire!

Rolling off the bed and onto the floor, she crawled toward Grannie.

Mrs. Farley's screaming grew more urgent. The panic in her voice made it clear that the emergency was dire and not simply the hearth producing too much smoke.

"Grannie!" Her shout was no more than a croak.

She shook her grandmother's shoulder. She patted her cheeks and got no response.

"We've got to go!"

In a matter of seconds she became nearly blinded. Her eyes burned, her lungs ached. The room had so filled with smoke that she couldn't see the bedroom door.

Grasping her grandmother's shoulders, she tried to lift her. Impossible.

Belle felt weak—breathable air was running out.

"Going for help." She kissed Grannie's cheek, because— just in case. "I love you."

Down near the floor, the air was a bit easier to breathe. She crawled on her belly, feeling along the walls, around the bureau, past the hall tree until her fingers found the doorway.

The stairway, she knew, was to the right. She crept that way, saw crimson flames doing a hellish dance, heard the roar and crackle as they devoured wood.

To her horror, she realized that the stairs were on fire. Even near the floor the air was becoming too harsh to breathe.

*Don't die! Inhale even if it hurts. Do not die—get help!*

But she couldn't inhale. The effort ended in a fit of coughing and gagging.

*Keep on,* her mind screamed. Don't die! If she did, so would Grannie.

With her cheek on the rug, she watched, oddly detached while fingers of fire nibbled the fringe on the far edge of the hallway runner. Pretty blue flowers morphed into greedy blue flames.

"Belle!" A bodiless voice pierced the gray vapor. It came from many directions at one time. "Belle!"

She lifted her hand, coughed.

A strong fist closed upon hers. She recognized the size, the rough skin of palm and knuckle.

Roy lifted her—ran with her. Cold air brushed her arms, chilled her feet. Clear air filled her lungs.

With great care, Roy set her down. She felt his hand touch her hair, the chill when snow dampened her nightgown.

"Grannie!" She coughed, gagged, then glanced up.

But Roy was no longer there. Mrs. Farley slid down beside her. She patted Belle's hand, quietly weeping.

"Where's Mr. Garner? He carried me out."

"Yes—praise the good Lord." She sniffled, wiped her eyes with her arm. "He's gone to bring out your grandmother."

Glancing around, Belle spotted Jim in his nightclothes, his arm at Beulah's waist, supporting her.

"But the stairway—it's gone." What had Roy done?

"There's another one, off the kitchen, but—"

The whole house was aflame. There was no reason to believe that the back stairs would provide an escape.

Belle glanced across the road toward Roy's house. The wind was not blowing. Flames and sparks shot straight into the air. Roy's house would be safe.

Through an upper window she saw four frightened faces pressed against the glass.

"I should go to them."

"You can't, dear, not yet." Mrs. Farley rested her head on top of Belle's, watching while her home burned down. "The church bell is ringing. Folks will be here soon. Someone will go to the children."

Townsfolk would be well-meaning, but they were strangers. She, at least, was acquainted with the children. If there was unspeakable news to be delivered, it would be from her.

"Help me up."

"I don't think—"

Belle got to her feet in spite of Mrs. Farley's protest.

Pressing her aching head between her hands, she stumbled across the road, entered the house and climbed the stairs to Roy's bedroom.

At first, the children didn't hear her enter. Then one by one their tear-streaked faces turned toward her.

"Everything will be all right," she assured them against all reason.

Standing behind, she gathered them all in her arms.

Silently, she prayed, *Please don't let them be orphans*.

The children's breath fogged the window, blurring the view of what was happening below.

This was for the best. What they would see was bound to be devastating.

Belle wiped the window in front of her nose, though, because devastating or not, she must face it.

From a block away, she saw torches bobbing up the road. Faces, cast orange by the light, looked twisted—horrified.

The crowd surged forward with cries of dismay.

*Grannie? Roy? Please, God.*

Two men sprinted toward the burning house. She watched them vanish into the haze.

Staring into the smoke she spotted three shadows.

Praise everything good! Four figures emerged from the ugly cloud.

The men from town flanked Roy, escorting him, offering support as he carried Grannie in his arms.

By some miracle, she was conscious.

Belle studied her grandmother, who sat in a chair beside the fireplace in Roy's cozy parlor. Contrary to the way Belle felt, Grannie looked content.

"We almost died, Grannie. How can you look so calm about it?"

"By the time I knew I was in danger I was already safe. There's no point in fretting over what didn't happen."

Maybe it was because Grannie had lived a long life and experienced many things that she seemed so outwardly calm.

The fire didn't seem to rattle her any more than her feeling that she might not see the New Year.

"I can't believe it, Grannie." Belle sat on the arm of the chair, grateful for the warm flannel shirt that Roy had loaned her to wear over her nightgown. It was long enough to provide most of the modesty a lady required. "Your hair isn't even singed."

Roy's was. So were his eyebrows.

"Were you conscious the whole time? I was only half."

"Let me tell you, Belle Annie. When a handsome man wakes one and sweeps one into his arms, one does feel a swoon coming on. But that would have meant missing the whole adventure, so I resisted the urge."

"Adventure!" Belle leapt up, slammed her fists on her hips. Grannie simply stared up at her, grinning like a loon—like a whole flock of loons. "You could have been killed. Roy, too! His children might have been left orphans!"

"No one did die, though. And while it is a downright shame about Mrs. Farley's place, what has happened has happened. No one died, no one was even blistered. Best take what good we can out of the situation."

"Which is?" Belle sat back down on the arm of the chair. "We have nothing—only these nightclothes. Not to mention we stink. It'll take hours of soaking to get the smoke out of our skin and hair."

"We do have something—an invitation to live here for the time being." Grannie grew quiet for a moment, watching the flames. "Isn't life odd when one's adversary is also one's hero? I've lived a long time and never seen the like. It's hard to set things right in your mind."

Belle touched her grandmother's head, ran her fingers through the soft strands of white hair.

Voices drifted down from upstairs. Roy was tucking all four children into his own bed while reassuring them that all would be well, that he would take special care to make sure their house did not burn.

The reassurance in his voice heartened her.

Grannie was right. This whole situation was confusing. Truly, if not for the generosity of the sheriff, their situation would be bleak. If not for his heroics, they would be dead.

Did that change things? She didn't know. But it did muddy the waters.

"That is something to be grateful for," she could only agree.

"Your Mr. Garner is quite the gentleman for a thief." Grannie sighed, returning her gaze to Belle.

"He's not my Mr. Garner," she protested softly, but a picture flashed in her mind. He had suggested a kiss; the image of a shared embrace shook her.

She tried to snuff it out but it wouldn't go away. Possibly because she didn't want it to.

"Your Roy, then." Grannie took her hand, squeezed it and winked.

"He's not my anything, Grannie Em. He can't be. You know why we came here."

She had to stand up again. This conversation made her nervous.

"You know Roy Garner is not my man. Are you willing to just forgive and forget? He took what was not his—something that meant everything to you."

Grannie Em shook her head slowly, then gazed with all seriousness into Belle's eyes. "That's not true. You are everything to me. The ring, it only represents love."

"And yet you believe you will die without it?"

Grannie was quiet for a moment, as though listening to something that Belle could not hear. "Yes, your grandfather is quite sure of it."

"How do you know?"

"He just told me."

"You hear his voice?"

"As clear as I hear yours, but in the heart, not the ears."

"Grannie, I don't think I've ever been more confused in my life. Everything made so much sense when we started out. We knew what we were doing, the right and the wrong of it. All I know now is that we need that ring."

"I'm beginning to believe that you need it as much as I do."

"Of course I do! I need it for you so that you can focus on living and not dying."

"No, my little love, you need it for the love charm."

"The ring is a charm for you and you alone."

"That's not what the gypsy said. 'Given on Christmas, it has the power to bring together lovers when they would not have joined on their own.' It's just a shame that it also comes with a curse—but in the end the love is worth it."

"Twaddle, Grannie. You are far too sensible to believe that—what is the curse?"

"When one of the parties is dead, the survivor must wear the ring at Christmas or meet their loved one in the Great Beyond." Grannie pointed toward the ceiling.

"You didn't die last Christmas."

"Your grandfather convinced the gypsy to give me one more year, given that last Christmas I was all but dead inside anyway. I feel alive again this year."

"Grannie, the truth is I don't believe the ring is enchanted—or cursed."

"Christmas is coming. We'll see."

"You don't seem worried."

"That's because I'm confident we will find it and if we don't, you will simply have to ask for it."

"He'd only lie. No one wants to be caught out a thief."

"The man we set out to ruin would deny it. Now I suspect he's not that man."

"He has the ring. We do not."

"To be fair, he doesn't know we want it."

"I don't want to be fair, Grannie! I want to know that you know you are going to live. The sheriff needs to answer for his part in this mess."

"Don't sound so self-righteous, Belle. The man has saved our lives. If he confesses his crime, he deserves forgiveness."

A sneaky voice, speaking rather forcefully in her mind, pointed out that this was true.

"Christmas, Belle. Don't forget what it stands for."

"Your wedding ring becomes charmed?"

"Not just that. Christmas stands for love—things being made right."

"Let's just say we do forgive him—that I suddenly…foolishly…fall madly in love with the man. At some point he'll discover what we were up to and he will not forgive me. I do not need that heartache."

Even though she had led a wonderful life with Grannie and Granddaddy, the pain of her parents' rejection still stung. If she did fall in love with a man—with Roy—and he rejected her… Well, it would only be sensible to avoid that misery.

"There is no love without heartache, Belle Annie. But in the end, of course he will forgive you. It's not as though he has nothing to be forgiven of."

What a mess this all was. If only Gaston had not taken the ring in the first place, Roy would not have taken it in the second.

Belle would be merrily sewing her way through the holidays and Grannie would be content with her ring and memories of Granddaddy.

"Do you think he feels guilty for what he did?" she asked.

"Yes, I do. But there's more to it than that. There's something else he regrets."

"What makes you say so?"

"It's there in his eyes, a sadness especially when he looks

at his children. I don't know what it is, but I feel it. You'd see it, too, if you looked hard enough."

The sound of footsteps coming down the stairs prevented her from asking more about Roy's supposed torment.

The villain-hero walked into the parlor carrying an armful of blankets. His amber-brown eyes barely showed over the top of the load. But barely was enough to feel his gaze linger on her.

Concern for her well-being was what she read in his expression, as though rescuing her went deeper than him simply doing his job as sheriff. She sensed that he was greatly relieved to see her standing unharmed in his parlor.

"I'm taking these down to the jail for Mrs. Farley and the other ladies," he said. "The girls and I made up rooms for each of you. One upstairs for you, Belle, and another behind the kitchen for you, Mrs. Key. Make yourselves at home."

Gray ash still smudged the bridge of his nose. "Oh, and there's a hot bath in the kitchen. More water warming on the stove if you need it."

With that said, he left the warmth of the room for the dark and the cold outside.

"Your Roy is quite a man, Belle."

"He's not my—"

But what if he was and she was about to ruin him?

Then again, what if he was not, and she failed in her duty to Grannie?

## Chapter Seven

It was two in the morning before Roy finished transforming the jail into a temporary home.

He'd lit the stove, reassured the women that it was safe and made up three beds.

It felt like he'd been awake forever. If he didn't fear freezing to death, he'd fall face-first into a snowbank and sleep where he was.

Wind shoved at his back, hurrying him along. Glancing up, he watched a bank of clouds slide across the face of the full moon.

It would be snowing by sunrise. With any luck the children would sleep later than normal.

In the distance, he saw smoke rising from the burned house, the coals beneath glowing red in the dark.

He thanked his lucky stars for the coming storm since it would prevent his sons from exploring where they shouldn't.

If Colette were here, she'd be worried about the danger that the smoldering ruin presented. Even now it was simple to imagine her uneasy spirit guarding the front door, making certain the boys did not wander into mischief.

She'd have her eye on Roy, too, with a thing or two to say to him on Judgment Day if harm came to her children.

"I'm feeling the need to go on with my life, Colette," he admitted, watching the swiftly moving cloud bank cover the stars.

Saying so made him uncomfortable. Laying one's wife to rest in the ground happened quickly, but severing the marriage bond took longer. "I hope you don't mind."

She had never been one to hold a grudge. He didn't reckon she did so now, even though he should have been home when she passed.

For some reason, thinking of Colette led to thoughts of Belle.

Hell's business, that was disloyal.

*Idiot*, a small voice in his mind muttered.

Odd that he couldn't be sure if it came from his own thoughts condemning him or from Colette's heavenly voice offering a teasing approval.

He hoped it was approval, because he was ready to move on, past the guilt and the grief toward new hope.

When he thought of new hope, once again, a vision of Belle flashed into his mind.

He ought to court her. She was pretty, devoted to her grandmother, and the children liked her. Not only that but she made him feel like living again, like smiling and laughing out loud.

It was true that he didn't know her all that well, but beginning tomorrow, he was going to.

Also, come tomorrow, he was going to figure out what to do with the blamed rings.

The decision about his wife's wedding ring was easy. That would go to Lorraine.

But the other ring? It troubled him.

It was a pretty thing, old and delicate. He figured it must be important to someone.

From the beginning he'd known that person was not Gaston Lamar, or the slatternly-looking woman he had been trying to sell it to.

Two things had happened while he was arresting Lamar. The first was that the woman snatched the ring from the thief. Roy took it back and shoved it in his pocket with the intention of handing it over to a judge.

But then in the middle of her caterwauling and Lamar's vows of innocence, the second thing happened.

The town sheriff informed him that his wife was near death.

He'd turned the arrest over to the sheriff, mounted his horse and forgotten about the ring.

In dealing with the tragedy at home, he hadn't given the jewelry a thought. Not until he began to pack up the household and had come upon it in the bottom of a bureau drawer.

A couple of months ago, he'd wired the prison where Lamar was incarcerated and asked them to question him about it, find out who it belonged to.

Not to anyone's surprise, the thief continued to claim it was his.

Now Roy had a ring that didn't belong to him and a guilty conscience that did.

He needed to do something with it, but what? Sell it? Donate the money to charity?

He was too tuckered out to make that decision now, but it had to be made and soon. A charity would be able to make good use of extra funds at Christmas.

Even though her hair was clean and her skin scrubbed, Belle could not sleep.

The pair of nightgowns heaped in the corner still smelled of smoke, of fear and near death.

Standing beside the bedroom window, she looked out at the ruins of the boardinghouse. Steam curled from it like mournful ghosts. Snow had been falling for a while now. It wouldn't be long before it covered and cooled the smoldering heap.

She'd heard Roy return home just before the storm hit. It sounded like he had gone into the kitchen. When, after a time, there had been only silence, she figured he'd gone to his bedroom. To his sleeping children.

And they were sleeping. She knew because she'd checked on them while their father was out.

The first time, Jack had been restless and Delanie frightened. After she told them a story of elves and sung a song about reindeer, they settled down. When she checked on them the second time they were awake but staring about the dim room. Thankfully, the third time she checked on them they dozed as sweetly as the little angels they resembled.

Roy Garner was a lucky man.

A sudden gust of wind rattled her bedroom window. She turned away, paced in circles around the rug five times before she realized what a waste of time it was.

Since the smelly clothes in the corner were preventing her from sleeping, she gathered them up and took them downstairs.

A good washing was in order. She wasn't properly dressed to go out of the bedroom, but since the household was asleep, propriety hardly mattered.

Going into the kitchen, she realized her mistake. Someone was up, just not awake.

Roy sat on a dining chair, his head resting on the table and cradled in his arms.

His shirt was off, crumpled in his fist.

Ashes dirtied his neck, accented the curve of muscle and bone. A fine dusting of gray coated his dark, curling hair.

He looked exhausted—paying the price for saving her and Grannie Em.

What kind of man was she intending to ruin?

No one would have faulted him earlier tonight for doing the sensible thing and keeping safely away from the flames.

He should have. For the sake of his children he should have. He had come close to dying, himself.

Zebras, pandas and cattle came in black and white; apparently people did not. She was quickly learning that a man could be wicked and sainted at the same time.

How was a woman to know what to do?

Launder his shirt. She could do that, along with her own remaining wardrobe.

Carefully, she pried the fabric from his fingers. The last thing she wanted to do was wake him.

For the sake of his needing sleep, of course, but also, she wanted this chance to freely look at him.

Which was probably not wise.

It was also downright rude.

But my word! The man was something to look at.

She shouldn't wonder—but what woman would not be imagining how it would feel to touch the swell of his biceps, feel the scrape of beard shadow on his cheek, stroke the ash-dusted arch of his brow?

Perhaps it was her duty to care for him. To take a damp cloth and wipe away the smudges under his eyes—to wash away the path of sweat that tracked down his naked back—

Or to quietly step away and simply wash his shirt.

Quietly, she put a large kettle on to boil, then dumped in the clothes.

"Obliged," came Roy's deep, weary-sounding voice from behind her.

She turned, holding a wood paddle in her hand. He was sitting up, scraping his hand across his jaw.

"You're obliged?" She stirred the pot of clothes. "I'm the one who is beholden to you."

"Only doing my job, Belle."

Like earlier, his gaze upon her was almost tender, intimate. She had a feeling there was more to it than that.

"Just because you were doing your job doesn't change the fact that you risked your life to save mine and Grannie's. The least I can do is wash your shirt."

*And your face and your back and your—*

A smile lifted Roy's mouth. His teeth looked extra white against the ash covering his face.

Had he guessed her thoughts?

Not likely, but he did seem to have thoughts of his own. His gaze drifted from engaging her eyes to studying her bare calves and feet.

She removed the pot from the burner then hurried around the table and sat down, hiding her exposed parts.

Still, she held the advantage as far as exposed parts were concerned. She could hide her legs under the table while his chest remained in view.

Delightfully in view.

"Sure do hope this is a generous town," he said, still smiling. "I don't have enough shirts for all you ladies."

"I can sew—it's what I do to support me and Grannie."

"It's a shame I didn't keep my late wife's clothes. I think they would have fit."

It was a generous offer but one she would have refused. Surprisingly, she didn't want him to look at her and see his wife. She wanted him to see her.

Admittedly, not all of her. The last thing she wanted was for him to see deeply into her jumbled thoughts.

"So what brought you to Pinoakmont? It's not the kind of town most people dream of settling down in."

"A man." That was not a lie.

"Maybe I can help you find him." For just a second, she thought regret flashed across his expression. For another second, she was glad to see it.

"Not for me, for Grannie Em. It's someone she loved, but really, I don't know that we will find him."

He grinned. The warmth in his expression enveloped her. She smiled back as though there was nothing but friendship between them.

Friendship with the desire for more.

And she did want more. The realization hit her with equal parts joy and regret.

Had she met Roy Garner under different circumstances, she would be the happiest woman wearing a man's shirt with no clothing to call her own in the state.

She clenched her fingers to keep from swiping away the ash on the tip of his nose.

"Your children are delightful."

"They are a handful, but yes, a delightful one. It's all to Colette's credit that they are. My job kept me away from home most of the time."

"Your career was important to you?"

He nodded, glanced at the snow drifting past the window.

"Always figured it was an honorable thing, keeping folks safe from criminals. But, Belle, I never figured the cost would be so high."

"Putting thieves away is important." It was. She was more

than happy that US marshal Roy Garner had put Gaston behind bars where he could no longer hurt Grannie.

"So is protecting your family. My wife became ill. I found out about it right in the middle of an arrest. By the time I made it home, she was gone."

"I'm so very sorry, Roy."

She leant across the table and squeezed his hand. When she let go, ashes smeared her fingertips.

"It happened last December. My children missed so much. I wasn't there—Santa wasn't there. I failed them all."

He reached across the table, but drew back.

"You were making a living, doing what you thought was right for your family—sometimes doing right doesn't work like we want it to. It's not anyone's fault."

"I try and think that way but sometimes—well, thank you for reminding me."

"All we can do is move on, give those little ones the best Christmas ever."

"We? Is that an offer of help?"

"Naturally. Christmas is the most wonderful time of the year! I reckon we all need a bit of holiday cheer. I'd like to help make it merry and bright for the babies."

And, she had to admit, for him.

"I could kiss you." This time he did not refrain from squeezing her hand.

Suddenly the implications of what she had just volunteered to do hit her. So did the mental image of him kissing her. It bloomed in her imagination, more heated and consuming than the first time.

Also, in volunteering to promote Christmas cheer, she added another complication to her already twisted goal of justice.

If she found the blasted ring, she could not expose Roy. Not without ruining another Christmas for the children.

On the other hand, if she did not find the ring and expose him, what would happen to Grannie?

All of a sudden she felt confused, foggy in her mind. The distance between right and wrong narrowed.

The only thing she knew for certain was that, given the freedom to do what she wanted, she would sit up all night with Roy, find an hour of contentment in his good-humored gaze.

## Chapter Eight

A Christmas angel walked beside him. Belle Key was his saving grace where December twenty-fifth was concerned.

As much as he'd been determined to make this the best Christmas ever for his children, he was not sure he knew how to go about it.

There was baking to do, presents to buy and to wrap, carols to sing, and good cheer to be spread. Oh, and Santa to be watched for.

On his own, he'd have fumbled it.

Looking at her, watching her smile, admiring the holly-green sparkle in her eyes, there was nothing he wanted more than to kiss her.

Wanted to, and would.

To his way of thinking, the courting had begun. Last night he'd touched the lady's hand, and admittedly left her fair fingers dirty.

That smudging, though, was proof that he had worked up the nerve and taken the first step.

Of course he didn't know what she thought of that. For all he knew, she might not have recognized the friendly gesture as courting.

Could be she only thought he was grateful that she would help with Christmas. Which he was.

If he survived the next hour attending church with his children, then the pageant meeting afterward, and if the weather held, he would ask her to go skating at the pond tonight.

If she accepted, he would be a grateful man.

He was as nervous as a mouse without a hidey-hole.

Sitting in a middle pew, he bowed his head but kept one eye open to make sure Jack did not tug the bow tied on the braid of the little girl sitting in front of him.

What Roy had to offer was not what every woman wanted. Life in a quiet town with four young children might be some women's nightmare.

While the preacher led his flock in a prayer asking for peace and goodwill, Roy asked that Belle Annie would not see a future with him as a bad dream.

With the preaching and the prayers ended, folks came up to thank him for rescuing Miss and Mrs. Key.

It would be interesting to see what changed when, in fifteen minutes, the meeting began for the pageant.

He reckoned that he wouldn't be such a hero then.

When the service ended, the children went to play in the social room with Grannie Em their appointed guardian.

Belle stood on the far side of the sanctuary, speaking with Mrs. Farley. Hell's business if she didn't look as pretty as a snowflake in her donated dress.

He worked his way toward her, anxious to offer his arm for the walk to the store.

Suddenly a large, firm hand latched onto his arm.

"Just the big brave man I need to escort me down the steps," Beulah Banks declared. "I can't imagine why Mrs. Brown thought these shoes would be a fit for me. They are miles too big."

Too small more likely, Roy figured. Beulah's mouth was pinched and she hobbled beside him with a limp.

"I can't tell you how grateful I am that you saved my life—Roy."

"I didn't." He glanced back at Belle and Mrs. Farley, who walked behind him. "You were already in the yard when I got there," he reminded Beulah.

"Oh, yes, but the sight of you heartened me. Who is to say that I might not have dropped dead of an apoplexy had you not been there."

"You seem a sturdy sort, Miss Banks. That sad event was unlikely."

"Oh, no, I'm as delicate as a feather." Miss Banks blinked her eyes, looking like a startled owl. "I've been pining for a big strapping man to take care of me."

He heard a sound—a snort. He didn't look behind to see who expressed it, but it would have been Belle or Mrs. Farley.

"I reckon he'll come along one day," he said.

"I do believe he already—"

"Look, Beulah! Here we are in front of the store." Mrs. Farley swept up beside them, took Miss Banks by the arm. "Maybe there will be some smaller shoes for sale."

To his great relief, Mrs. Farley escorted her cellmate into the general store.

The snort came again. This time beside him. He glanced down to see Belle grinning up at him.

"Will the wedding be before Christmas? Your intended seems in a hurry."

The words *wedding* and *Christmas* coming from her mouth put a lovely vision in his head—but not of Beulah.

In his mind's eye he saw Belle in his bedroom, slowly unfastening the buttons of a satin wedding gown, her gaze on him soft with love.

"Will you go skating with me tonight? I reckon we'll need a pleasant hour after facing the pageant dragons."

"If you can convince them to sing 'Silent Night' in peaceful harmony and drink their Christmas punch without a dash of whiskey, then yes, I'll go."

"I'll give it my best." He'd give it more than that. He really did want to be alone with her tonight.

"Better get inside before your sweetheart misses you."

"Keep close, Belle—please."

Going inside the store, he spotted ice skates for sale.

His spirits lifted.

He'd give a month's pay for the skates without blinking.

At nine o'clock that night, Roy began to court Belle Annie Key in earnest.

He carried the shiny new skates over his shoulder while she walked beside him toward the frozen pond.

Even though he hadn't convinced the citizens of Pinoak-mont to drink Christmas punch without whiskey, they had agreed to a group singing of "Silent Night" and "O Holy Night."

Luckily that had been enough to make Belle agree to step out with him.

"I hope the children don't wear your grandmother out playing Find the Penny."

"I doubt it," she said, gazing into the windows of the closed shops that they passed by. She must be thinking of all she had lost and all she needed to replace.

The pretty blue bonnet she had just paused to admire would make a nice Christmas gift.

Or not.

Given the brief time he'd known her, the gift might not be appropriate.

"If anything, they are good for Grannie." She slid her gaze away from the berry-bedecked bonnet to look at him. "Her eyes seem brighter—she smiles more often these days. I'm sure it has to do with the children. She always wanted a house full of babies, but all she got was my mother and that was late in life, and then me."

He'd like to say that the same was true for him—that since he met her, he smiled for no particular reason. Emotionally, life had been dim for a very long time. Now, light was creeping in.

As much as he wanted to tell her so, he knew it was too soon for such declarations.

"Your grandmother is good for them, too." That declaration was as easy to speak out loud as it was true.

Moments later the pond came into view, its glassy surface reflecting the bright globe of the moon.

As he'd hoped, no one else had ventured out on this cold, breezy night.

Conditions were right for a kiss under the stars—he hoped.

He had a feeling—a good one—that once he tasted her lips, life would never be the same.

Roy led Belle to one of the benches surrounding the pond. Tree branches scraped against each other. At this time of night the park was isolated, the setting intimate.

He placed the lantern he carried on the ice. It cast a soft yellow glow over the glossy surface.

Sitting, he took off his boots and put on the new skates. Beside him, Belle did the same, tugging and pulling the stiff new leather over her stockings.

"Here, let me help."

He knelt in front of her, yanking the laces. His shoulder brushed her knee. She shifted away from him, but not at once.

"For a man, you're skilled at tying bows."

"I practice by candlelight. Wouldn't want my girls to be embarrassed in front of their friends who have mothers to do it." He gave a final tug on the double fancy bow he fashioned on Belle's skate, then nodded in satisfaction. "Thanks for coming out, even though I didn't get my way with the spirits."

"The truth is, it was a trying meeting—a trying week. I need this respite as much as you do. I'm beginning to wonder if we can pull this pageant off peacefully."

Her smile down at him was warm, her lips as pretty as sugarplums. He could taste the sweetness, even without an actual kiss.

"Would you like to skate now? Or just take a minute to sit here, feel the peace and quiet?"

"Isn't there something so beautiful about snow and moonlight? Let's sit awhile and breathe it all in."

He rose from his crouch then sat down beside her, closer than a casual friend would sit—but not as close as a lover.

"You are a good father, Roy."

He hadn't always been, not like some men were, but he was trying his best to change that.

"There's a lot to learn. Every day I wake up and find something I'm still doing wrong." He let out a long breath, watched the vapor curl away into the dark. "But the truth is, I love every minute with my children. I never knew I was missing out on so much."

Reaching over, he took her gloved hand in his and held it. When she didn't snatch it away, he squeezed her fingers.

Her smile at him was one of the loveliest and most welcome things he had ever seen.

"Tell me about you and your grannie. What exactly is your connection to Pinoakmont?"

For a second she glanced down and away, but her smile held.

"I'm here because of Grannie." Her fingers clenched but he wasn't sure she was aware of it.

"Does she have a connection with the town because of the man? This isn't a place folks just come to."

"No, the man is something of a dream. Pinoakmont is as far as we could go with the money I had." He felt she was telling the truth—but not completely.

A dog barked in the distance; an owl hooted.

The secret she kept moved behind her eyes. He saw it in the shadow dimming her expression.

"What is it that's troubling you, Belle? Maybe I can help."

"I'm sure you—" All of a sudden, she caught her lower lip between her teeth. "The truth is, ever since Grannie Em's stepson sold her house and ran off with her money, we don't have much. We move from one boardinghouse to another making do with what I earn by mending and sewing."

A ghost of the man he had been urged him to leap onto the nearest horse and chase the criminal down.

"I'll wire a friend. Maybe if we catch him, some of your grandmother's property can be recovered."

"He's already in prison." She gave him an odd look, one that made him think he ought to know that already. "Of course, everything is still gone so it's only a slight comfort to know he's getting his due."

"How quick are you with a needle? The girls need new dresses for the pageant." They didn't, but something pretty would make them happy and give Belle some income.

"I'll need to make the manger baby. And I was working on something for Beulah that burned up. But I'd rather sew dresses for Lorraine and Delanie."

"I'd appreciate that." Now that he thought about it, seeing his babies' eyes light up when they put on their new dresses would cheer his own heart.

"You'd appreciate it even more if you knew that the gown I was working on for Beulah was meant to turn your head. She does have her cap set on you."

As far as caps being set went—his was set on Belle. It might be unwise to feel so drawn to Belle, given that he barely knew her. But that was why he'd invited her here to-night—to change that. To see if just maybe she felt the draw for him that he felt for her.

He lifted her hand, kissed the fingertips of her glove. As kisses went, that wasn't what he'd had in mind. Just as soon as the moment felt right he would taste her star-dappled lips.

"Let's skate," he said, then stood to offer his arm.

# Chapter Nine

Belle glanced up into the invitation of Roy's whiskey-brown eyes. What would it have been like to actually feel the warmth of his lips on her fingers, flesh to flesh?

She considered the gloved hand he offered.

Conflicting emotions lined up inside of her like combatants on a battlefield.

The warriors on one side waved spears and swords, demanding justice for the wrong he'd done—but on the other side—well, her heart was all but laying itself on the ground in surrender.

Roy was ready to move on with his life—he considered doing it with her. She knew this as much as she knew her heart was beating triple time.

It was why they were here at the pond, to see if something would grow between them.

No, that was not quite right. Something *was* growing and had been since the beginning. Tonight was to see if the seed could be nurtured.

The bond that was budding between them had the possibility of developing and blooming into something beautiful.

If she would let it.

What if she forgot about the ring? What if she pretended that they had just happened to meet like a man and woman would—casually, by chance and not deceit.

A vision teased her mind. She was the happy mother of half a dozen sweet children, in a home of her own where she and Grannie were forever safe. No more moving on, wondering if the next boardinghouse would be warm or drafty. Or if it would burn down because of a careless smoker.

The problem with this vision was that her grandmother might not be there to enjoy it. Could Grannie really know she was going to die? Probably not, but a broken heart could cause loss of appetite, loss of life's joy. That would be devastating for someone her age.

"I'd like to skate," she answered after a pause.

Impossible imaginings and out-of-control emotions swirled inside her like madly flying snowflakes. Hopefully, exercise would soothe her.

She gave him her hand and was struck by his warmth. Not physical warmth, of course; two pairs of wool gloves prevented that. But from the speculation in his gaze, the masculine tug of his smile—understanding what he wanted from her—she was well aware of the heat building inside him.

Did he recognize that an answering steam was simmering within her?

If he didn't, he would in a moment. Before a blush could give her away, she snatched her hand out of his.

In the end, there was nothing she wanted more than to glide round and round on the pond, pretending that nothing existed beyond the ice scraping under her skates and the cold breeze brushing past her face.

There was absolutely nothing she wanted more in the world—except, maybe, to respond to the seductive invitation radiating from the man gliding along beside her.

There was no ring, no theft of it and no resisting where her heart was leading.

For now she would put away her suspicion of Roy and learn who he was at heart. Discover if Grannie had the right of it and perhaps he did deserve forgiveness if he asked for it.

Glancing sidelong at his profile, so handsome in the cold moonlight, she saw a man who had known grief. One who had given up the career he was devoted to for the sake of his children. He was a man doing his best to provide a life for those he loved.

In that, he was not so different than she was. He would do anything for his children just as she would do anything for her grandmother.

"This is so very peaceful," she murmured. "I could go on all night without stopping."

"Do you like me, Belle?"

"Of course." More than was wise. "You carried me and Grannie out of the fire. We are forever grateful for that."

"That's not what I mean. Any lawman would have done the same. Do you like me—as a man?"

"I like you." Blamed if she didn't feel fondness embedding its tender little roots into her heart.

Maybe she shouldn't, but she offered her hand. When he took it, the joining of their fingers felt—right. Almost as though it was fate between their palms and not wool.

What a silly, fanciful thought.

All of a sudden the pace Roy set slowed. He twirled her about, then drew her against his chest.

She felt the quick thump of his heartbeat, the warmth of his breath as it fogged between his mouth and hers.

Her inner warriors rattled their spears and swords in warning, but in the end, they tossed their weapons down.

When he kissed her, she surrendered.

Coming down the parlor stairs and seeing Belle Annie Key sitting beside his hearth, her head bent over her sewing, Roy knew two things.

She belonged there.

And he was going to marry her.

Logic told him he ought to take this romance more slowly. But logic and his heart were not telling him the same thing, and his heart was speaking louder.

The most urgent question was, did she want the same thing he did? Was she even close to feeling for him what was growing in his heart for her?

Having the woman he was courting living under his roof ought to give him some advantage. Sometimes he thought it did, but once in a while he caught her staring at him in a way that did not make him feel encouraged.

It had been more than twenty-four hours since he'd kissed her.

Hell's business, calling what happened between them a kiss was like calling a shooting star a candle flame.

Lips had met, been warm and exciting. But souls had soared as well, met someplace out of body—and bonded.

To see her going about her business today, he wondered if it had ever happened. She was cordial, attentive to the children and caring of her grandmother, but she had distanced herself from him.

Still, watching her from across the room with the fire's glow on her face and hands, the shimmer of light warming her hair where it curled over her shoulders, his dedication to this courtship remained.

Belle Annie Key was going to become Belle Annie Garner. Belle Garner—it sounded right in his mind.

Only one thing stood between them. The secret she kept.

It troubled her deeply. Until she trusted him enough to confide it, he did not believe she would give herself to him.

"Evening, Belle," he said, sitting down in the chair beside her. "Delanie is going to love that pretty little dress."

She held it up, turning it this way and that, smiling at her work.

"She'll be a Christmas angel."

"She'll look like one." His youngest truly was an angel, when she wasn't being an imp. "You sure do stitch fast. Only this morning that was a hunk of cloth."

"One learns to be fast when one needs to provide food and shelter."

"Life's dealt you a hard blow, Belle Annie, but something tells me this is not your first."

She set the dress in her lap with a thump. "Only Grannie Em calls me Belle Annie."

"I'd like to."

She tilted her head to the side, studied him for a long silent time, then smiled.

"I think that would be nice."

"Belle Annie." It felt good to be able to speak the endearment out loud. "I do admire you. Not many people would do for your grandmother what you do. I'd say you were her angel on earth. But I wonder—what is the cost of that devotion to you?"

A woman like her—smart, beautiful, full of humor and mystery—ought to already be the wife of some lucky man.

Good for him she was not, since he intended to be that lucky man.

"It's Grannie who's done everything for me."

She was silent for a moment, seeming to consider whether to speak of her past or not. If she really was his Belle Annie, she would.

The grandfather clock ticked away a full thirty seconds while wind pelted the windows, and his heart raced in apprehension.

"My mother was too young when she had me. So was my father." Roy wanted to jump up and shout, not for her sad parentage, but because she was sharing herself. "Being parents was not what they had in mind when they—well, it was adventure they wanted, not me. As soon as they could hand me over to my grandmother, they ran off to the silver fields. As far as I know, they're still there."

"Is that what troubles you about me?" He braced his elbows on his knees, let his hands dangle between them and stared into her eyes. "You think I was like them?"

"I'm not troubled." Gazing intently at her sewing, she shook her head. "You hardly took off for the silver fields. You were making a living for your family, doing good for society, not chasing a foolish dream."

She looked up. "No matter what, you are a good father."

"You know that I'm courting you?"

Her cheeks flushed a sweet shade of pink. "I know."

"Do you welcome it?"

"I—" She glanced away and then back. "I want to, but—"

"But there's something holding you back. What is it, Belle Annie?"

"We hardly know each other, for one."

"Fair enough." It was a valid point. "I'll tell you a secret about me, then you tell me one about you. Before the rooster crows, we'll know each other."

That caught her interest. Curiosity sparkled in her eyes when only a moment before, apprehension had clouded them.

"Tell me your darkest, Sheriff Garner." Her left eyebrow rose in a delicate arch.

"The first time I fell in love, I was fourteen. I was too nervous to kiss the girl so instead I gave her the lumpiest toad I could find."

Laughing, she looked down, weaving her needle in and out of the dress.

"Did she keep it?"

"She tossed the toad in a bush but kept the wart it gave her."

"That is funny. But what about something more recent? Maybe something you did as a marshal."

Christmas punch spiked with whiskey would not be as intoxicating as her smile.

"Nothing very interesting, since US marshals tend to live by the same letter of the law they enforce. As far as secrets go, my mischievous youth was better. You've heard my secret now. Out with yours."

"You might not think the same of me once I tell you."

"Nothing will change my high opinion of you."

"I'll hold you to that." She grinned, pointed the tip of her needle at him.

"When I was seven years old, there was a neighbor girl who was spoiled, snooty as a fat cat in a sunny window. Well, one Christmas Eve, she told me there was no such thing as Santa Claus. Grannie dried my tears and assured me that there was. If our neighbor thought there was not, it was because she was a nasty little thing and therefore Santa did not come to her house.

"It sounded right, but I needed proof. So after everyone was asleep, I went next door. I peeked in the window and saw her folks putting gifts under the tree. That only proved what Grannie told me to be true. Since Santa didn't bring naughty children gifts, her parents had to do it. Well, one big gift intrigued me. After her ma and pa went up to bed, I let myself in through the window, which conveniently was not latched. I unwrapped an expensive doll and cradled it for a while. Then I saw Grannie's face looking in the window. I thought I'd be in trouble, that Santa might not visit my house now. But Grannie was laughing. She told me that—"

All of a sudden Belle stopped speaking.

"What was it that she said?"

"That even good people—children, that is—make mistakes." She stuffed the needle into the small dress on her lap and stared at it. "You've got a similar problem here, Roy."

"My children are making mistakes?"

"Not that. Robbie is telling his siblings there is no Santa."

"I reckon he's of an age that he questions things."

"One should never become too old to believe in Santa. I firmly believe that."

"You still believe?"

"In the spirit of him, of course. Of magic and giving." She looked up from her work, her eyes wide and beautiful. "Don't you?"

"Teach me to believe, Belle Annie."

Sliding off his chair, he knelt before her and touched her cheek. "Show me the magic."

She dropped her sewing onto her knees, leaned forward in her seat. With a sigh, she pressed her lips to his mouth. She nipped his lower lip, then melted against him.

Her heat made him dizzy, but bold. He slipped his arm about her back, drew her out of the chair. Her knee pressed his. Thigh to thigh, hip to hip, he drew her tight. Her waist felt small under his fingertips; her hair tickled his hand as he crept up the ladder of her ribs.

If she didn't resist, poke him with her sharp little needle, he was going to touch her even more intimately.

He broke the kiss. "Belle Annie?"

She rested her forehead on his, her breathing quick and shallow.

"Um…well, what we are going to need, in order to make Christmas special for the children," she murmured, "is a Santa suit, and boots—tall black boots."

She wasn't ready for him yet—but she would be.

He smiled, nipped her lips one more time. "And a beard?"

She nodded, then glanced down, her hand lightly grazing his ribs. "And pillows."

Even though he hadn't touched her the way he wanted to, she had not poked him with the needle. In fact, in calling a halt to the amorous moment, in suggesting the costume, she had proposed something as intimate. She had said *we*.

It felt so damn good not to be alone.

The door to the future lay wide-open.

## Chapter Ten

"You've a glow about you, Belle Annie." Sitting at a table in the bakery, Grannie Em squinted at her while wiping a cookie crumb from the corner of her mouth. "You've lain with our young man!"

"I have not! Grannie—for heaven's sake, lower your voice."

"I know that glow, miss. You did at least let him enjoy your breasts?"

"Nearly." Belle swallowed a gulp of cocoa so hot it burned. "But I can't and you know it. Remember why we came here? Even if do we change our minds about that, I can hardly confess that we were going to ruin his reputation."

"Confess? I'm sure I raised you smarter than that." Grannie pursed her lips, a smile lurking at the corners. She winked. "I have a plan to get the ring and the man."

"There's no way to have both."

"Do you want him?"

More than she did yesterday—not as much as she would when she woke tomorrow and every day after that.

"More than anything, Grannie. He's not the villain we thought—I'm positive of that now." She touched her grandmother's soft, bony hand. "So, what is your plan?"

"We find the ring and take it. All he thinks is that he lost it. You are free to give yourself to him, and he'll be none the wiser."

"That's deceitful—I don't know if I could live with the guilt. Besides, he'll see it on your finger."

"Not if I keep it on a chain between my charms." She touched her chest.

"What if, after all, I do just ask him for it? Tell him that you can't live without it?"

"Then you'll have to explain everything. Even the best of men don't like being deceived."

"What if we can't find the ring? You've looked high and low already."

"There are only so many more places it can be. It'll turn up."

"It might not." Belle swirled the cocoa in her mug, watching the brown waves circle. "But, Grannie, I don't believe you will die on Christmas Day."

"Your grandfather is convinced. Another Christmas without the ring would be unheard of. There are widows up there who are surprised that the gypsy gave me last year. They all say it's unfair."

Belle set the mug on the table with a decided click. "That's nonsense."

"Not according to your grandfather." Grannie patted her hand comfortingly, which only left Belle more distressed than ever. "But not until late in the day. I won't miss the pageant. I'm glad of that, since it ought to be an interesting event. I wouldn't want to miss something interesting."

"You make it sound like dying doesn't bother you at all. And how do you know this isn't your imagination?" It had to be.

"When you get to be my age, you just know things." Grannie took another cookie from the plate, nibbled it, then said, "Like I know you don't need to worry about me. We will find the ring and Roy will never be the wiser."

"If only it was that easy." She clamped her fingers about the warm mug. Her heart felt like it weighed a hundred pounds. "Roy and I talked last night. Nearly until dawn."

"Talk is also important, dear."

"I got to know him better than I've ever known anyone—except you."

"And soon you will know him even better." Grannie's gray brows wagged.

"I can't do that—not knowing—Grannie, I could never

make a choice between him and you and that is what it might come down to if things go any further. Not that I believe you will die—but if you believe it, it might affect your health, which could lead to decline."

Grannie lifted her mug and sipped. Her eyes, peering over the rim, looked bright, as full of life as ever. "You won't have to choose. I feel it in these old bones."

Belle wished she could believe the promise in Grannie's bones, but Grannie also believed in the curse.

Coming up with a Santa costume might have been a diffi-cult thing, except that the town of Pinoakmont had one stored away. It hadn't been used last year because a week before Christmas, the sheriff had tossed it onto the floor, stomped on it, then quit his job—or been fired. The story changed from one teller to another.

Just now, Roy's role as Santa had placed him alone with Belle Annie in the storage room of the general store. There were things he'd rather be doing than trying on the musty old costume.

"Do you have enough pillows?" she called from the other side of the curtain where he changed.

He stepped around the partition. "You be the judge."

Patting his belly, she nodded. "You'll do. But the beard?"

She reached up to tweak it. He caught her hand, kissed it.

Hell's business but she had a pretty smile when she used the full force of it on him.

"What moral value do you hold dear?" she asked, con-tinuing the question-and-answer game of "getting to know you" that they had begun two days ago.

There was so much to learn about one another. Posed as a game, it seemed easier.

Not that anything was difficult about falling in love with her. It was the most natural thing he had ever done.

"Honesty, I reckon. Enforcing it is what I do for a living." He yanked on the white cuff of the sleeve, trying to pull it all the way to his wrist. "What's yours?"

"Honesty is fine, but I would say forgiveness."

"In all honesty, I want to kiss you." In all honesty he wanted to do a lot more than that.

For a second she looked uncertain, but in the end, she nodded.

"I like kissing you, so I'd forgive that boldness."

Slowly, she lifted on her toes, held his gaze. Cradled the promise of his future.

He stroked her cheek, kissed it, then inched toward a sugarplum kiss.

A woman's scream shattered the moment.

"Sheriff!" the voice wailed from the outer room.

"Beulah?" Belle's eyes widened. She shoved away from his chest.

Stifling a red-hot curse, he rushed into the front room. Running past the counter, he saw the spinster standing in the open doorway.

He rushed by her, felt her hand brush his sleeve, then her screech became a dad-gummed sigh.

Jim and a farmer rolled about in the dirt, scrapping and throwing punches that could only have missed on purpose.

It was a lucky thing that there were no children about. It wouldn't do to have them see Santa holding the miscreants apart by the scruffs of their necks.

"It's my goat that's going to be in the nativity stable!" the farmer demanded.

"It'll be Pete's newborn lamb or nothing," Jim shot back.

Roy glanced at the boardwalk to see Belle covering her mouth, stifling a laugh. Beulah stared at Belle, not hiding the fact that she was glaring.

She had to have followed them to the store in order to know he was within shouting range.

No doubt she'd noticed Belle come out of the storage room at the same time he did. She could not have missed the fact that the pair of them were flushed of face.

Roy yanked on the collars of the middle-aged scrappers.

"You couple of—" He shut his mouth. Calling men he was honor bound to protect "idiots" was not wise.

"Any reason we can't have a goat and a sheep in the manger scene?" he asked.

"The Good Book never mentioned a goat," Jim growled.

"Didn't mention Santa either," Roy growled back. "But he'll be there. Don't force me to make an arrest dressed in his red suit."

"I reckon there wasn't direct mention of a lamb either," Jim admitted. "Howdy, ladies. We didn't mean to distress you."

"Looks to me, if we can have Santa, who wasn't there, we can have a sheep and a goat who might or might not have been," said the goat owner. "I reckon you can let loose of us now. We'll act peaceable."

"Let's go have a drink, Horace," Jim declared.

"We ain't got a saloon."

"Pete's barn is better anyway. Bring your goat. Let it get acquainted with the lamb."

The men walked shoulder to shoulder down the road as though the confrontation had never happened. Jim glanced back at Beulah and waved.

Miss Banks rushed Roy, standing closer than was proper.

"Our sheriff certainly is a brave one," she declared, her smile wide and toothy.

"That was interesting," Belle laughed, now on the other side of him. "Which animal do you prefer—sheep or goat?"

"Sheep!" Beulah exclaimed. "Goats are smelly. Sheep are sweet and soft to the touch. Don't you think so, Sheriff?"

Clearly, by the look Beulah was casting at Belle, she was comparing herself to the sheep and Belle to the goat.

"I'd best get inside before I ruin Christmas for some curious tot."

The jolly old elf did stand for love, kindness and the magic of Christmas.

A magic that his children would have in abundance this year. Very much due to Belle Annie Key—who one day, he hoped, would become Belle Annie Garner.

Back behind the barrier of the screen, he changed into his clothes and pinned on his sheriff's badge, all the while wondering how his children would feel about having a step-mother.

As much as he wanted to marry Belle Annie, the children would have to want it, too.

From all he'd seen, they would. Their eyes sparkled when she was with them. A sparkle that was echoed in Belle's eyes.

He believed that their young souls were beginning to heal—and that Colette was smiling down in approval.

Life was lovely, if she didn't delve too deeply.

Dusted in flour up to her wrists, Belle laughed with Lorraine and Delanie while they took turns cracking eggs and dumping them into the beginnings of cookie dough.

"I'm going to cut my cookies into swords," Robbie announced, his elbows on the table and his chin propped in his palms.

"Swords don't have cats to do with Christmas," Jack argued. "Reckon I want one anyway, though."

It warmed her heart to see that Jack said this with a grin. When she'd first met him he'd been a sad little thing. Within the last few days he'd seemed to take a turn for the happier.

Roy must think so, too, because Belle saw him grinning as he sat in a chair beside Grannie at the hearth. He was acting as a yarn warrior, untangling the skein that she intended to knit into socks.

"The sword of truth!" Robbie raised his arm, hoisting an imaginary weapon.

"I want's a sword of truth," Delanie declared, her small brow wrinkled. She arrowed a glance at her oldest brother. "Nobody could tell me a lie about Santa. I'd know if he's real."

"Jacob Peabody saw Santa breaking up a fight in the street yesterday," Robbie said, slashing his invisible sword at the bowl of cookie dough. "I reckon I believe that, Delanie."

"Santa is full of wonder." Belle flicked a finger full of flour at Robbie just to see Jack smile—and Roy, too.

Roy's grin at his son was playful.

The expression in his eyes when he looked at her was

an invitation. A sultry summons to something she dare not accept.

"Why isn't he at the North Pole like he's supposed to be?" Clearly, this made no sense to Delanie even if the incident made a believer of Jack.

"He's magic." Grannie Em clicked her knitting needles together. "He pops in and out at will, making all things right. Things that seem impossible are easy for Santa."

No one but Belle would know that that last comment was directed at her as much as Delanie. She would need every bit of faith in the spirit of the jolly old man to take courage in the message.

Last night, she'd stood over Grannie's bed, watching her sleep and looking for signs of illness. In that moment she'd been more convinced than ever that an impossible choice was coming her way.

If she didn't find the ring, she would have to ask for it. Grannie believed her life hung in the balance and if she believed it…? This was not a risk Belle dared take.

"I like you, Miss Belle." Lorraine tugged on her apron. Her attention had wandered from Christmas cheer.

"I like you, too." She stroked Lorraine's cheek, leaving a white smear. "Very much."

"I need to tell you a secret." Belle bent her ear. "Papa smiles more since you came to live here. I hope you don't go away."

What was she to say to that? She didn't want to go away—not at all. Looking about at the big house, so secure and warm—so full of love, every inch of the place infused with Roy's masculine protective presence—she did not want to leave.

The thought of hauling Grannie Em to yet another boardinghouse was nearly unbearable.

This could be a home for them. Even though Roy had not proposed marriage, she knew he wanted it. The children wanted it. Grannie needed it.

"You wouldn't mind having a stepmother?" Belle whispered back.

"Not if she's you." Lorraine slashed an imaginary sword at the bowl. The swoop of her arm knocked three eggs onto the floor.

Laughter started first with Roy, then Grannie, and soon they were all swinging magical Christmas swords at the smear of eggs.

In her heart, she sent up a prayer that somehow Christmas night would come and find her still in this wonderful home, with Grannie healthy and Roy still caring for her.

It was past time to do something with the blasted ring. Having it was a constant gnaw at Roy's conscience.

Walking into the general store, he reached into his pocket and rubbed the delicate gold circle. He'd always be sorry for not returning it to the owner. At least if he sold it, the money would help the orphans' fund.

"Good day, Ben," he greeted the storekeeper.

"Howdy, Sheriff. What brings you out in the cold?"

"I've got a ring to sell, then I'm taking the children to cut down the Christmas tree." Roy slid the ring across the counter.

"Selling? I thought you might be buying." Ben grinned.

"You got any?"

"Three, besides this one I'm about to buy." Ben picked it up. He looked at it from every angle. "Interesting."

"Do you think a Christmas wedding is too soon?" Roy asked. He didn't think so but that was because he was impatient to make Belle his in every way.

"That depends. You marrying Miss Banks or Miss Key?"

Miss Banks? Why would anyone…? "Who thinks I'm interested in Miss Banks?"

"Miss Banks does." Ben reached under the counter and pulled out a box. "It's clear enough to the rest of us that it's Miss Key you're courting. Here's what I've got."

Maybe it was too soon.

But then again, life was too short.

"We can swap rings—or I'll give you thirty dollars."

"Can't swap. The money for this one is going to the orphans' fund."

"In that case, I'll give you forty dollars."

"That's kind of you, Ben. I thank you."

Ben brushed the air with his hand as though he were sweeping away the gratitude. "Here, how about this sweet ring? It's got engraved snowflakes, and a diamond."

Roy picked it up. Sensible folks would say it was much too soon to propose, but since when was love sensible?

Hell's business! He had yet to declare his love and here he was buying a ring.

## Chapter Eleven

"They're gone." Grannie turned away from the window where she had been watching Roy pull his children across the yard on a sled. "Let's find that ring!"

Belle paused in polishing the dining room table. She saw her blurry reflection on the glossy finish.

She was frowning, even though this was the moment she had been waiting for. With no one home she was free to snoop with abandon.

"Giddyup, girl." Her grandmother yanked the polishing rag from her fingers. "The woods are full of Christmas trees."

"I don't feel right about this," she said. But looking into Grannie's eager blue eyes, loving her, she conceded, "I'll search upstairs, you search down."

After spending an hour feeling guilty about going through Roy's belongings, she thumped down on his bed.

Sadly, it seemed that she was searching for something that no longer existed.

What if Roy hadn't taken the ring at all? Until this moment she hadn't considered that possibility. What if Gaston had made the story up to appear innocent?

Sitting on Roy's bed and inhaling the masculine scent that lingered in the blankets, wondering if he slept in a nightshirt or in the altogether, was not going to help her find the ring.

Opening his bureau door, she felt like the criminal she used to believe he was. She skimmed her fingertips over neatly folded long johns, wool socks—a wedding ring.

Belle lifted the delicate silver circle from its nest within a handkerchief.

Roy had told her that Colette had not been completely happy wearing it. Of course, Belle could only wonder if this was his guilt speaking and not how his late wife felt.

Any woman would be blessed to have Roy Garner as her husband.

If she were to have any chance of being that woman, she had to find the ring. Not only find it, but hide it and learn to live with the guilt of coming to Pinoakmont to ruin him, the man she loved.

Loved to her bones. There was no point in hiding from the fact.

While it was true that she hadn't loved him when she and Grannie had concocted this scheme, in the end her situation remained the same.

Folding the ring back into the handkerchief, Belle searched the next drawer where she found the badge he had worn when he was a US marshal.

While she was caught up in her imagination, seeing Roy riding to the rescue of law-abiding folks, she heard excited young voices crossing the yard.

The Christmas tree had arrived!

For the sake of the children and Grannie Em, she would put away her frown, her guilt and fear. She had come to love Robbie, Jack, Lorraine and sweet little Delanie. No personal angst would prevent her from helping Roy give them a blessed Christmas.

One by one, his children had fallen asleep, their pillow being Belle Annie.

Robbie gave up the day with his head pressed against her arm. Jack's curly-haired head lay on her lap; so did Lorraine's. Delanie had snuggled up to Belle's chest. His baby could only be dreaming of sugarplums.

"This was grand," Grannie declared. "Sugar and spice and everything nice. And now I'm headed for bed. Help me up, will you, Roy?"

"It would be my pleasure, Grannie Em."

When Grannie had her balance, she snatched his ear, tugged his face down. She kissed his cheek.

"I like you, Roy Garner—no matter what happens, I like you."

"I like you, too. Can't imagine that anything could happen to change it."

"Quite right, it is Christmastime."

Grannie blew her granddaughter a kiss. Roy's heart warmed seeing her walk down the hallway toward her room.

With any luck, the Key ladies would become his family.

He glanced back at Belle Annie. His heart tripped over, melted into a heap of holiday pudding.

She would make a wonderful mother. Not only for these children, but the ones he hoped to have with her.

"Will you walk with me? Once I've got the little ones to bed?"

"I'd like to help tuck them in."

Belle Annie did put the children to bed. But in watching her, seeing her give kisses and stroke sleepy heads, she also tucked herself in—deep into his heart.

So securely was she in there that if she refused his proposal tonight, he might not get over it.

His life, or at least his emotional well-being for the rest of it, was at stake.

Half an hour later, escorting Belle out into the moonlight, he was nervous. This was not like when he had proposed to Colette. Marriage between them had been the predictable outcome of their predictable courtship.

This time with Belle Annie, it was different. The development of their relationship had been fast—anything but predictable.

His future—and his children's—hung upon her answer.

"Brr!" Shivering, she stepped off the porch. "I hope Santa dresses warm tonight."

"Hilda Bee claims her big toe is predicting snow," he said, working up the nerve for what he really wanted to say. "So does Jim Flynn's knee."

Snow, left over from the last storm, muffled the sound of their footsteps.

"What do you prefer, Belle Annie? A full moon or the little one we have now, with all the stars so bright?"

"Full moon. What do you prefer? A snowy Christmas or a sunny one?"

"Snowy Christmas Eve, sunny Christmas Day."

"So do I." Her quiet laugh tripped across his heart.

"A kiss under the mistletoe, or one under the stars?"

She tipped her face up. Downy fur bordering the hood of her cloak rippled in the breeze. It feathered her cheeks where they were nipped pink by the icy air.

"Both."

Lifting her hand, she touched his jaw with her gloved fingertips.

He dipped his head, kissed her lips. They were not cold like her cheeks were, but hot, like the fire they had banked when they left the house.

He reached inside her cloak, drew her against his chest.

Wind whispered across the snowy ground, no doubt blowing in the predicted storm. It didn't seem so cold, though, not with the two of them pressed close.

"What do you prefer, Belle Annie? Living in my house or in a boardinghouse?"

"Your house," she said slowly.

"I love you, honey. Will you marry me—me and my babies?"

Tears pricked his eyes, clogged his throat. It was hard to believe that dumb chance had brought him this woman. Strangers bound for the same place at the same time.

It could only mean that they were meant for each other.

Tears shimmered in her eyes, as well.

Strangely, she did not hug him closer, or answer with a joyful kiss—with a yes.

She stepped out of his embrace, her back straight, stiff looking.

"I want—I've got to have my grandmother's ring."

She hugged her arms about her middle.

"If that's what you want. Whatever makes you happy, Belle Annie." He'd sell the one in his pocket, make another donation to charity. "I reckon Grannie'll be pleased to have you wear her ring."

"How can she when...? Where is it, Roy? Give me the ring that you took from Gaston Lamar when you arrested him!"

Belle wanted to double over, lose her dinner in the snow, but she stood erect, held Roy's stricken gaze.

Marry him? Become his wife? It's what she wanted more than her next breath—more than anything except possibly seeing Grannie take her last breath.

Mentally, she formed a fist and stomped her dreams into the dirt-crusted snow beneath her boot.

Now that she had cast her future away, she had to win Grannie's.

"I want the ring you stole from her."

"What are you talking about Belle Annie?"

Seconds ago, emotion welled in the corner of his eye. Now a single drop of moisture slid alongside his nose. It would not be an expression of joy.

"Is that why you came here? For a piece of jewelry?" He backed away from her. The distance seemed an icy mile. "We didn't meet by chance?"

Her throat dry, she shook her head. "It was for the ring."

"Why didn't you just ask me for it?"

Because she'd believed him to be a criminal, figured he would only lie about it. Now that she knew him—now that she loved him—she understood that he was not that person, but back then....

Silently, she stared at him, at his darkening expression.

"What makes you think I stole the ring?"

"Gaston Lamar is Grannie Em's stepson. He says you did."

"Hell's damn business, Belle," Roy muttered, his arms spread in supplication, in disbelief. "The man's a criminal— why would you believe him?"

Why indeed? She should have asked for the blasted ring

in the beginning. But, she reminded herself again, things had been different then.

And later? She'd feared facing this very moment.

"I've got to have the ring, Roy."

"Too bad you didn't ask me for it." Roy shoved his hands in his coat pockets. "I sold it yesterday."

Her head buzzed. It felt like her heart stopped beating.

"You had no right!" She rushed at him. Hammered his chest with gloved fists. "It wasn't yours to sell. You don't know what you've done!"

He held her at arm's length, staring hard into her eyes.

"All this time you thought I was a thief? You let me fall in love with you, let my children fall in love with you." His breathing came fast, harsh. "When the whole time all you wanted was a ring? You want the truth, Belle?"

No longer Belle Annie, but just Belle.

She knew the truth. He had taken property that didn't belong to him.

But there was another truth, a worse one maybe.

He was much more the wronged party than she was. She had deceived him—had let him love her, had loved him back and all the while she knew it would fall apart.

"I already know the truth," she gasped.

"If you did, you wouldn't be looking at me like I was the devil." He breathed in, let it out in a slow, white-misted hiss. "That day, I had every intention of handing the ring over to the judge, but while I was arresting Lamar, I was informed that Colette was dying. I forgot about the ring. Months later when I came across it, I had Lamar questioned in prison but he still claimed the property was his. I didn't feel right keeping it so I sold it and gave the money to charity."

If she didn't lock her knees she might slip down onto the snow and not get up again.

"I reckon that's not the truth you knew," he said, his voice cold.

She wanted to reach for him, beg his forgiveness, but what right did she have to do that?

Not only had she misjudged and hurt him, but now with the ring gone, Grannie might become ill.

"All you had to do was ask for it, Belle. I'd have gladly given it to you."

Misery was etched on Roy's pale, drawn face. And she had caused that despair.

"I'll leave as soon as I can pack our things."

"You will not." His mouth was set, a grim angry line under his narrowed eyes. "You will stay and celebrate Christmas with the children. I've allowed them to become attached to you and I won't see them face another holiday heartbroken."

"Of course."

Without a word, he spun about and walked toward his house.

When he was on the porch, beyond hearing, she murmured, "I love you. I'm desperately sorry."

For all it mattered now, she was sorry.

# Chapter Twelve

At three in the morning, Roy sat at the kitchen table drumming his fingers on the highly polished wood.

Sleep was as elusive as a wish fired at a star.

From the beginning, instinct had warned him that something about Belle was not what it seemed.

Still, he'd rushed into love, blind to everything but her pretty face, her intriguing charm.

He'd never known his gut to be so wrong about a person.

For himself, he could bear the pain—he'd lost love before.

Tonight he would grieve. But tomorrow, for the sake of his children, he would laugh, look forward to Santa's visit.

They would have a joyous day.

"Hell's damn business." Bowing his head to the table, he closed his gritty-feeling eyelids.

Fingers brushed his shoulder.

He spun about on the seat.

"What are you doing up, Grannie Em?"

She shrugged. Her donated robe was too big and hung from her shoulders.

"The older you get, the less time you have. You don't want to spend it in bed."

"I'm sorry about your ring." He watched while Grannie Em walked to the other side of the table and sat down. "Why didn't you just ask for it in the beginning?"

"We thought you were a thief. Since we had plans to ruin you, we couldn't ask."

"You planned to ruin me?"

"Only your reputation, dear." Grannie patted his hand

comfortingly. "One doesn't just let criminals go free without facing justice. The world would be a sorry place if that were the case. I'm sure you of all people understand."

"Can't say that I understand anything about this." He eased his hand out from under Grannie Em's, jabbed his fingers through his hair. "I was in love with your granddaughter."

"You still are."

She was right, of course. It would be a long, painful time before he quit loving Belle Annie Key.

"I'd best get back to my sweet girl. She's cried her eyes out six times over."

"I'm sorry." The thought of Belle in pain cut him.

"If she'd listened to my advice, you'd be celebrating your engagement."

"What advice?"

"Find the ring and keep mum about it. That way I'd have my property and you would believe you misplaced it. Belle Annie would have the love of a good man."

"She doesn't believe I'm a good man. She came here to ruin me. Don't forget that."

"You can hardly hold that against her. She just didn't have it in her to deceive you."

"It's why she came here." Had the smiles, the kisses, all been a lie? Worse, a means to an end? "Why would you advise her to be deceitful?"

"It was the one way to have us both." Grannie sighed. "Since you've sold my ring, she will lose us both."

"What? Why?"

"Without the ring, I'll die."

"Are you ill?" What the blazes did the ring have to do with it?

"Fit as a fiddle—at the moment." Roy felt as if he'd fallen into a pit, unable to judge up from down. "My husband has decreed from the Great Beyond that I will wear the ring on Christmas or meet him at the Pearly Gates."

"You believe this?"

"Of course. You don't go a lifetime with a man and not know his voice. It's because the ring is magic that I need it."

"Magic ring?" This conversation made no sense.

"Charmed more than magical. On Christmas, it brings folks together who might pass each other by on their own."

"I wonder if it would work for me and Belle."

"Oh, I don't think so. The pair of you get on quite well on your own. The only magic you need is what is already between you."

True; while Belle's betrayal had cut him, it had not killed his love for her.

"The only reason she agreed to help me rescue my ring is because she doesn't want me to die tomorrow." She covered his hand with her delicate fingers. "I know you are feeling betrayed, but understand that for Belle, it came to a choice of loving you or watching me die. I told her I think she made the wrong decision. With or without the ring, I don't have many more years. The two of you have your whole lives."

"Grannie, your life is as precious as anyone's. The length of what's left doesn't make one more important than another."

"Burtrum, did you hear that? You are making a mess of things."

Grannie cocked her head to one side, as though listening to a voice he could not hear.

"He says that if he didn't send us after the ring, Belle Annie would never have met you."

Some old folks became addled, hearing and seeing things that did not exist. Grannie Em was not addled.

"What can I do?" Not likely a single damn thing.

"Do you believe in Christmas miracles, Roy?"

"Yes, yes I do."

"I say we pray for one."

At first, Roy had been relieved that Beulah accepted his invitation for coffee at the bakery.

But now his palms were sweating, his stomach in knots. It seemed no matter how much money he offered for Grannie's ring, she refused.

"It's a pretty thing and I want it," she stated. "I purchased it fairly from Ben and I am keeping it."

"I made a mistake when I sold it. It belonged to Em Key."

There was only one way to make this miserable situation right. That was to get Beulah to sell the ring.

After speaking to Grannie last night, he'd understood why Belle had deceived him.

Putting her grandmother first, at the cost of her own happiness—it made him love her all the more.

Not that it mattered unless he got that ring back.

His family's future hung on convincing a stubborn woman to sell the ring.

"Beulah," he said—no, he begged, giving her the most beguiling smile he knew to give. "Grannie Key believes that if she doesn't have the ring, she will die—tomorrow."

"That's silly." Beulah glanced at the ring on her finger, frowning. "I don't believe it."

"Well, she believes it. She thinks there's some kind of enchantment involved."

All of a sudden Beulah gasped, shook her head and clutched the ring to her heart. "No. I purchased it and I will keep it, no matter what you offer. It is charmed. I feel it."

Looking pale, she scraped her chair back, stood and left him alone at the table.

He watched her hurry away, taking his future with her.

"Thank you," Belle said, then tucked the train tickets she had just purchased into her coat pocket.

"We're plum sorry to see you leave us so soon," the man at the ticket booth said. "Are you sure you don't want to wait until after the New Year?"

"I'm sure."

She pulled her coat tighter against the rising wind. Leaving on Christmas Day was the last thing she wanted, but that was exactly what she was going to do.

She had wrongly judged Roy and there was no way of going back from it. If remorse and tears could make it better, she would have paid for her crime a hundred times over, but regret changed nothing.

Roy's heart was broken by her own hand and there was no way to heal it other than by going away. Let time and distance do what she could not.

Besides, if Grannie Em was going to pass on as she predicted, it would not be in front of the Garner children.

So far, this morning, Belle had been able to avoid seeing Roy. If she could manage it, she would avoid seeing him forever. To look in his eyes and see the affection, the love he used to have for her, gone—well, she didn't think she could bear it, especially knowing that it was all her fault.

Coming down the stairs of the platform, she glanced at the sky. It wasn't snowing yet, but it would be by tomorrow. Christmas Day was sure to be magical, and tragic.

It would take all her power of will to make sure the children knew nothing of the situation. As soon as she got home—no, not home but to Roy's house—her smile would be bright and she would set to making them a Christmas Eve meal.

She would help the little ones string a popcorn garland for the tree. They would sing songs and tell stories about Santa.

They would not pay for her mistake.

The price she was paying for that would be buried under Christmas cheer.

The wind at her back was icy. She hurried along the boardwalk, then slowed as she passed the bakery. The scene through the front window was warm and inviting with folks gathered at tables, munching on sweets and sipping warm drinks.

Perhaps she should buy some peppermint sticks for the children to suck on while they waited for Santa.

She had her hand on the doorknob but drew it back as quickly as if it had been a hot coal.

Through the glass in the door she spotted Roy sitting at a table near the back.

He wasn't alone. Beulah Banks sat across from him. The

spinster's eyes were gazing at him softly, affectionately, but she shook her head at whatever he was saying.

Roy shot her an engaging smile. Beulah stopped shaking her head but she frowned—blushed and frowned.

It was a very good thing that Belle was leaving tomorrow, even before the pageant was finished. She could hardly begrudge Roy courting a woman who would certainly be honest in every way, but it would break her heart to witness it.

By the time she stepped into Roy's parlor, her tears were dry. Too bad her eyes were as red as holly berries.

The children, busy with convincing Delanie that Santa was indeed real, didn't seem to notice.

Grannie did. She pushed up out of her chair and came to fold her in a hug.

It took everything she had not to break down in front of the young Garners.

In the unlikely event that her grandmother did die tomorrow, how would she cope? She would have no one in the world to love and it was all her own doing.

She should have done the honest thing the moment she and Grannie stepped off the train. She ought to have demanded the ring on the spot.

But she had been set on serving justice, too. To an innocent man, as it turned out.

Now she would spend the rest of her life paying the price for that blunder.


"You really see'd Santa?" Delanie asked while sitting on Belle's lap and gazing at the Christmas tree.

"I did." In fact, she was drawing on the spirit of the jolly old man at this very moment. How else was she to make it through this horrid, wonderful evening?

"I'm gonna stay up all night so I can see him, too."

"That's not so easy as it seems, since he waits until you are asleep."

"How did you see him, then?"

"My cat woke me up. I heard an odd noise. When I crept

down the stairs, there was Santa putting the prettiest doll in the whole wide world into my stocking."

Delanie's eyes grew as round as peppermint candies. "Did he see you?"

"He turned with a wink."

"I want a cat in my stocking," Jack declared.

She glanced at the green-striped hosiery hanging on the mantel. When she did, her gaze collided with Roy's.

All day Grannie had been whispering in her ear about Christmas changing hearts, about forgiveness.

She believed that. Hadn't the whole purpose of Christmas been about forgiving a wayward world?

But if absolution was in Roy's heart, it didn't show. His gaze at her was...unreadable.

"If Santa's going to come, you children need to go upstairs and get to sleep," he announced.

"I can't sleep unless Belle tucks me in." Jack plopped down beside her on the couch. Without thinking, she stroked his curly hair, kissed the top of his head.

Roy smiled but she wondered if even the children were fooled by the gesture.

She dropped her hand from Jack's head. Acting happy for the sake of the holiday was one thing, but expressing her love for the children was another.

With her tickets purchased and her bags packed, to demonstrate affection was inexcusable. In the end it would only cause them pain.

"You all head up to bed. Miss Belle will be up in a minute."

He didn't refuse the request—she supposed it was for their sake more than hers.

"I'm going to keep my eyes open all night." Jack bounded up the stairs two at a time. "If Jacob Peabody saw Santa, I'm going to see him, too."

"Miss Belle and I will be up shortly." Roy sat down on the couch not close, exactly, but closer than she would have expected.

"The kitten will be a great surprise," she murmured.

It was a ridiculous thing to say when there was so much heartache between them, but if she didn't say something the tension would burst the room wide-open.

"We need to talk."

No—she could not. She'd been deceitful. Even in loving him, she had not seriously considered the fact that he might be an innocent man.

Why was that? Love for Grannie would explain why she had deluded him in the first place. Still, at any time after the night they had skated on the pond, she might have asked for the ring.

She was quite simply a coward—a deceitful and horrible woman.

Roy would never forgive her, of that she had no doubt.

She stood up, putting distance between them. "Grannie and I will be gone before the pageant ends."

"Hell's business," she heard him mutter as she dashed up the stairs.

# Chapter Thirteen

"Who would have believed that they had it in them to be-
have so well?" Belle said.

To her surprise, Jim and Horace, who had recently come
to blows, stood elbow to elbow toasting the season with mugs
of mulled wine. Not only did they smile at each other, but
also at the rest of the people gathered around the candlelit
Christmas tree.

Belle didn't think she was mistaken about the tree casting a magical glow over them.

"They must be afraid that Santa is going to throw them
in jail," Grannie declared.

Belle swallowed hard, trying not to dwell on the handsome sheriff—on how she would have joyfully married him
had she not been a two-faced wretch.

She looked hard at her grandmother's face, watching for
signs of distress. So far she showed no indication of with-
ering.

As soon as she knew the pageant would remain peaceful,
she would take her grandmother and board the train.

It wouldn't be long. The joy of the season was clearly
overruling recent grudges.

Arms linked, the citizens of Pinoakmont sang the two
agreed-upon Christmas carols, then three more. They prayed
together, giving thanks for the blessings of last year, then for
guidance and safety for the new.

Side by side the lamb and the goat munched hay in
quiet camaraderie. The doll in the manger looked peaceful,
wrapped in pink and blue.

Standing beside the wide church doors, breathing in the scent of cinnamon and pine, hearing the voices of neighbors chatting, laughing, the very last thing Belle wanted to do was flee.

Pinoakmont, with all its strife and cheer, might have been her home. She and Grannie would have been happy here.

Childish laughter brought her back to the reality of the here and now. A dozen children chased each other about the hall, some with cookie crumbs on their mouths, some with candy canes between their lips.

Delanie, Lorraine, Jack and Robbie would haunt her heart forever. If only she—

"Where did Santa get to? He was here a moment ago." Grannie craned her neck, glancing about. "Oh, there! He's just come back in and gone straight to Beulah Banks. Imagine that."

She didn't want to imagine that. It was further proof that he was finished with her—as well he should be.

Beulah was a woman he could trust. She was who she was. There were no secrets lurking behind Beulah's eyes.

And right now her eyes looked softly at Roy, blinking and troubled. Santa-Roy appeared to be pleading with her, his charming smile trying to win her over.

Beulah shook her head, twisted her long slender fingers together.

What could be wrong with the woman? She wanted Roy and he was now courting her.

Belle felt as if her heart had been cut in half. Had he quit loving her so quickly—so completely?

But then, he had loved the woman he thought she was, not the one she really was. He would get over her much sooner than she would him—if she ever did.

"Are you going to let that woman snatch him right out from under you, Belle Annie?"

"Yes, and I wish him the best."

"You do not! That's nonsense and you know it."

"After what I did, I owe it to him to wish him the best." Just not with Beulah, not when she had to witness the budding romance under her very nose. Not when she feared the woman would drill the Garner children like little marching soldiers. "Besides, we're boarding the train in a few minutes."

Try as she might, she could not stop staring at Roy and Beulah. She ought to be happy for the woman. The poor thing had faced a life of spinsterhood.

Now her future looked bright as a new penny. Belle did not begrudge her the life that she herself had thrown away.

Well, that was a lie! She did begrudge it. She ought to at least be honest about something.

With supreme Christmas goodwill, she forced her mind to genuinely wish Beulah the best.

It would be easier if Roy was not looking at Beulah with such intensity.

Holiday goodwill be dashed! If honesty was to be her guiding star from now on, and it was, she hated the fact that it was the spinster feeling the warmth of attention.

Beulah wiped a tear from her eye. That was odd. But no doubt it was a tear of joy.

"Come on, Grannie Em. It's time to catch the train."

"Don't be a fool, Belle Annie. Fight for your man."

"He's no longer my man."

Hell's damn business! Would Beulah Banks even refuse Santa Claus?

Yes, it was becoming evident that she would. No matter what he said, how much he offered, she was refusing him.

Out of the corner of his eye he watched Belle from across the room.

Unhappiness drew her mouth tight, and it seemed to make her shoulders hunch inward.

Even though Beulah was speaking, when Belle took Grannie's arm and led her toward the door, she lost his attention. While he watched, the two women he loved walked out of the room.

Time was running out. He doubled his efforts to convince Beulah that giving him the ring was the right thing to do.

He brought her punch, he talked about his children, about

how they had lost their mother—and about how much Grannie meant to them. He told her about the criminal stepson. About how he had sold the ring without knowing.

Suddenly, the train's whistle wailed through the walls, announcing its departure.

"Beulah," he murmured in desperation. He had hoped to spare her feelings on this, but now—he couldn't. "I know you had hopes for us and I'm sorry. You are a fine woman. Any man would be lucky to call you his own, but I love Belle."

"How are you feeling, Grannie?"

Sitting stiff as a dried board, Belle watched steam roll past the train's window, felt the rumble of the great engine as it idled.

There were no passengers on the station platform waiting to board, although there were a few sitting behind her from a previous stop.

The whistle blew. Belle's stomach heaved.

In the distance she spotted the church steeple. Try as she might, she could not help but imagine the scene inside. By now everyone would be congratulating Roy and his new lady.

She wished them well. At least the woman she wanted to be wished them well.

"No fever, Grannie Em?" She touched her grandmother's forehead. "I don't feel one."

The whistle blew again, longer this time. Didn't it sound like a cry of deep despair?

"If it happens, I'll just fall asleep. Don't you fret about it. You did what you could. I'm only sorry about what it cost you. I don't suppose what's left of this old life was worth you losing your long happy future."

"That's not true! You are everything to me. Do you feel faint? Weak?"

"Not a bit." Grannie smiled with her usual poise. "It's been a good life. For however long I have left, I will not waste it worrying."

"I don't believe you'll die." Belle put her arm about Grannie's shoulders. Leaned her head against her soft white hair.

The next town on the line was bigger than Pinoakmont. There was bound to be a physician. "We still have a long time together."

"No matter if I have an hour or a year, I'll always be with you. Love cannot be separated."

Outside the window snowflakes began to fall, coming down as gently as sifted flour.

"What in tarnation is going on out there? We should be moving by now" came a man's voice from a few rows behind. "Must be a cow on the track."

The wood frame of the window groaned when he slid it open. Icy air rushed inside. She tugged Grannie's coat tighter about her, adjusted the blanket about her legs.

"I'll be blamed! That ain't no cow—it's Santa Claus!"

Belle leapt to her feet, turned and dashed three rows back. Shoving the man aside, she stuck her head out the window.

My word! It was Santa!

He stood on the tracks, his long legs spread and one arm raised in the air. He appeared to be pinching something in his fingers.

"Belle Annie Key!" he shouted over the thrum of the engine. "I'm not stepping off the track until you agree to marry me!"

He hoisted his other arm in the air. He held something in that one, too.

Drawing her head back inside, she stared at Grannie.

"Santa wants to marry me!"

"Do it, baby." Grannie's grin crinkled her cheeks. "Go get your man. I promise not to go anywhere while you're gone."

"I think—I can't be sure—but I think he's holding rings. Two of them!"

*Dear Lord, please let him be holding rings.* She kissed Grannie's cheek in passing, then dashed for the door. Luckily a grinning porter was standing beside it so she didn't have to break a leg leaping for the ground.

"Best of luck to you, ma'am," he said, helping her down.

It wasn't luck she needed so much as a Christmas miracle. Lifting her skirts, she ran beside the track toward Santa.

He opened his arms, rushed forward to meet her. Wrapping her in a hug, he lifted her off her feet.

"Marry me, Belle Annie." His breathless whisper grazed her temple. "I love you so damn much."

"I love you so damn much, too." She drew back, seeing the truth in his eyes. Snow dusted his dark lashes and collected on his brows and fake beard. "But what about Beulah?"

"She resisted selling the ring back to me at first, but after what seemed like hours of pleading, and after offering her what felt like half my wages for the year, she gave it up."

"That's what— You sold the ring to Beulah?"

"No, I sold it to the general store. Ben sold it to her."

"But you have the ring now?" Her throat tightened; tears welled in her eyes. She could not hold them back any more than she could her sobs of relief.

Grannie did not have to fear dying tonight.

"I'm sorry, love." His arms banded tighter about her. "If I'd known, I would never have sold it. I should have tried harder to find you."

"You aren't to blame. When it happened, you were dealing with the unimaginable." She buried her face in his neck, unable to stop the tears.

"Say you'll marry me." His voice rushing past her ear made her weep harder. "I need to hear the words."

"How can I say them? You'll never be able to forget what I did—what I meant to do?"

"Forget? Belle, honey, we don't forget. We forgive. That's so much deeper, more powerful, than forgetting."

"But how can you—"

"Because I've needed forgiveness. I wasn't there when Colette died—I wasn't there when she was alive either. I reckon that took a lot of forgiving on her part, but I feel that she's done it."

He kissed the trail of tears on her face, then set her on the ground. Curious-looking faces peeked out of train windows.

"What I did to her was worse than what you did to me. You only acted out of love. You put your grandmother first, no matter the cost."

"So did you. You had to make a living."

"I didn't have to do it that way. Look, Belle—you need to forgive yourself. It's a hell of a lot harder to do than to forgive someone else."

He was right, of course. Still, how was she to know that deep inside he wouldn't always…?

Gazing intently at her he opened both of his hands. Grannie's ring was in one white, Claus-like glove. In the other was the wedding ring he was offering her.

But in his eyes, she saw what he really offered. Love—everlasting, unconditional love.

She understood now. Love forgave, it did not hold grudges. It did not turn its back in affront.

This was what the folks in the church were celebrating. The Christmas miracle—love freely given to all—given to her.

"Belle Annie?"

"Yes! Yes, I will marry you."

He'd been touched by a miracle—call it the spirit of Christmas or the spirit of love, it didn't matter. To his mind they were one and the same.

Walking back to the church with Belle on one arm and Grannie Em on the other, watching snowflakes flutter down from the sky, his heart was full, beyond blessed.

Life was perfect. Euphoria rose in his chest, made him want to—

"So how much did you have to pay to get my ring back?" Grannie grinned up at him.

"I'd have given any amount of money for you, Grannie."

"You're a good boy. You probably paid more than my husband did."

"Miss Banks did put some store by that ring. She had this notion that it would bring her true love."

"She did? My word!"

"I had the devil of a time convincing her to sell it back to me."

"It's no wonder you did. The ring's magic must have been

giving her a terrible itch." Grannie looked at her finger, at the long-lost treasure circling it. "It did me. I got no relief until I let Granddaddy scratch it."

"I don't doubt Beulah wanted you to do the scratching," Belle muttered, squeezing his arm.

"In the end, she understood that I loved you." He leaned sideways and kissed his bride-to-be.

"Poor woman." Grannie sighed, shook her head. "Everyone deserves to be loved. Especially today."

Before going inside the church, Roy shed the Santa suit and stuffed it into a box beside the door. It wouldn't do for the children to see the jolly old man kissing Miss Key, and he didn't think he could go the rest of the evening without doing it.

A buzz of happy activity greeted them when they entered. People sang and laughed.

Roy watched his intended remove her coat, then her gloves. He wished he could remove her red dress. He might not be wearing an "enchanted ring" but he sure did have an itch.

For all his joy, the sight of Beulah standing in a dim corner with a decided lack of Christmas cheer nipped at his conscience.

There wasn't anything he could have done differently, but it troubled him to be the cause of her misery.

Roy glanced about the room at all the joyful folks knowing that he was the happiest of them all.

Not only did his future promise a lifetime of love, but his first assignment as sheriff was going smoothly.

"I think we've pulled this off."

The ladies were gathered about the Christmas tree, their conversation high-pitched and lighthearted. The men circled the punch bowl, their guffaws deeper but just as amicable.

All of a sudden Jim turned from the fellow he was speaking with, as though someone had tapped him on the shoulder. He shrugged, then went back to his conversation.

The only one left out was the one standing in shadow, wringing her hands.

"She wants to be loved so badly," Grannie murmured. "The poor dear. I believe my husband and the gypsy want me to do the right thing."

"What gypsy?" Roy glanced about, concerned about an uninvited guest.

"The one who sold the ring to Belle's grandfather, of course. Explain it all to him, won't you, Belle Annie?"

While the image of a gypsy selling a ring to a besotted young man formed in his mind, Grannie turned and made her way toward Beulah in her isolated corner.

"Who's the gypsy?"

"According to Grannie, the gypsy woman sold the ring to Granddaddy, along with assurance of finding true love on Christmas Day. I never did believe it, of course. It was always just a lovely story. But for a sensible woman, Grannie has put some store in it over the years."

From across the room, they watched Grannie speaking to a downcast Beulah.

She patted the spinster's hand. She listened while the dejected one spoke.

In the end, Grannie Em gave her a hug, removed the ring from her finger and slipped it on Beulah's.

Belle sucked in a sharp breath, then hurried to the big window at the far end of the room where her grandmother had gone to stand—and grin.

After all that had gone into regaining her ring, given the value she put on it—her life, even—Gramie had just given it away.

Roy could not have been more stunned if the real Santa suddenly came down the chimney singing "Jingle Bells."

He stood behind his bride-to-be with one hand at her waist and one on her shoulder because the color had drained from her face.

"Grannie!" Belle grabbed her grandmother by her hands. "What have you done?"

"Why, I've given my ring to Miss Beulah."

"But what about you dying?"

"I'm fit as a queen, thank you very much."

"You aren't going to die?"

"Things have changed." Grannie laughed and seemed to look inside herself. At happy memories of a Christmas long past, unless he missed his guess. "Been fulfilled."

"I think you ought to sit down. You aren't making sense." Belle tried to drag her grandmother to a chair.

"Oh, it's clear enough if you look with your heart, Belle Annie. I've been blessed by the ring and now I've passed the magic on to poor Beulah. She won't be a spinster much longer."

"How do you know you won't die and Beulah won't remain a spinster?"

"Because your grandfather told me so."

"When?" Roy asked.

"As soon as you handed me the ring and I put it back on my finger."

"Are you sure you aren't imagining Granddaddy speaking with you? He's never spoken to me," Belle pointed out.

"Watch and see." Grannie Em nodded toward Beulah, who was now smiling at the ring.

And why wouldn't she be smiling? She now had the ring and a goodly-sized portion of his money.

But in exchange, the tinkling melody of Grannie's laugh filled his heart. He was coming to love this woman deeply.

"Oh, in all the excitement I nearly forgot. Next Christmas the two of you will be crooning over your three-month-old twins, a girl and a boy. That's what your grandfather says, anyway."

"I'm not sure I believe that he can just decree things and they happen—or don't happen." Belle Annie arched her brows. "Or in a gypsy with a magic ring."

But Beulah's smile was beaming. He noticed Jim staring at her.

Roy was beginning to think that, just maybe, he ought to get some sleep before the twins came.

"Not decrees, exactly. But given where he's at, he knows things." Grannie cradled Belle's cheeks in her wrinkled hands. "I won't die today, and not simply because I got a ring back. In the process of getting the ring I found new love, which is the greatest reason for living."

She nodded her head at Robbie, Jack, Lorraine and Delanie, who were arguing in a corner. Intuition, and a pile of crumbs, told him the dispute was over who could eat the most cookies without getting caught.

"You could not be more right, Grannie. Loving Belle Annie has brought me new life."

"As it will to Miss Beulah. The ring only leads the way. Just watch and see."

It was going to take some doing for Miss Beulah to find— Or maybe not.

Jim was crossing the room now, smiling broadly at Beulah and carrying two glasses of spiked punch.

Hell's business…it was hard to say whose expression held more wonder, Jim's or Beulah's.

Something magical was going on here.

Until this moment, he hadn't noticed the mistletoe hanging on the rafter over Beulah's head. It sure hadn't been there when she'd handed over the ring.

Jim and Beulah clinked the rims of their cups, smiling at each other. Then, as if bound in a spell, Jim bent his head, kissed her.

Belle gripped his hand. Her squeeze helped his insides quit spinning, but only a bit.

If the ring could unite lovers, what was to say Grannie's dead husband could not predict things?

With the twins three months old next Christmas, then that would mean…

"Belle, honey, we better meet with the preacher." He glanced about and spotted him in front of the Christmas tree, passing out peppermint sticks and wishing everyone a merry Christmas. The snow swirling past the window beyond seemed a pretty picture for reciting marriage vows. "Tonight."

"That might be wise." Belle couldn't seem to take her

gaze off Beulah and Jim, off new love blooming over spiked punch and under mistletoe.

Roy squeezed Belle Annie's fingers, then hurried her toward the preacher and a future guaranteed to be blessed by Christmas magic.

* * * * *

*If you enjoyed this story,
you won't want to miss these great full-length
Historical Romance reads from Carol Arens*

*REBEL OUTLAW
OUTLAW HUNTER
WED TO THE MONTANA COWBOY
WED TO THE TEXAS OUTLAW*